BITE BACK!

PHOENIX PHIL MORLEY

WWW.PHOENIXPHILMORLEY.COM

Written by Phoenix Phil Morley

Edited by Laura Carley-Read

Cover Art by Paramita Bhattacharjee

Get all the news and scoops here:

www.phoenixphilmorley.com

SUBSCRIBE TO MY NEWSLETTER HERE!

Any queries:

Email: phoenixphilmorley@outlook.com

I am not a vampire. My own fangs are just the product of genetics and 1980s British dentistry standards.

Second print edition 2024

ISBN: 9781068648618

*This is dedicated to the people of Sittingbourne
and the Summer of '95.*

Also special thanks to:

*My beloved Laura for all of her love and support, Mum and Dad,
Luke, Elliot, Jemma, Ivan, Owen, Anna, Astrid, Axel, Theo
Graham-Brown, Steve Mclean, Peter Richard Adams, Dom
Myers-Green, Frankie Moloney, Steve Horry, Lisa Hughes, F D
Lee, Rob Halden and Will Preston, Mike Hibbert, Jon Stuart,
Slimfit, LillyAD, Shannon Johnson, Sam T, Fluffy the Hamster*

*And anyone and everyone who read,
reviewed and supported my last book.
I hope you like this one too.*
xxx

ENTER AT YOUR OWN RISK!

It's not my intention to offend or upset anyone with the contents of this book but I feel a warning of sorts might be appropriate. Bite Back is a fantastical story about young vampiric blood-drinkers in the 1990s and as such features lewd language, dark humour, lurid encounters and acts of violence that some may find distasteful.

CHAPTER I

THERE'S NOT A SOUL
OUT THERE

TESTIMONY: BENJAMIN COOPER REGARDING THE NIGHT OF THE 5th June 1995

Benjamin Cooper:

The summer of 1995 looms, Britpop explodes around me and I'm stuck in the body of a goth. Everyone thinks I am a goth but I'm not. I'm really, truly not! I mean honestly, it's an unfair assumption, just because I have pale skin. And fangs.

If you should ever catch me looking ill and miserable walking around on my own in the rain, it isn't a lifestyle choice. Can I help it that I live in the United Kingdom where grey, damp skies and class-based compromise are by and large the default setting? Oh, and it appears I have nothing in common with anyone and, as such, no friends to walk with. I don't want to be a goth. I don't like the clothes and I don't like the music but my life is one of solitude and sadness. So, alone in the rain I must walk. Looking like a goth.

Yesterday, on a train heading to Canterbury, the ticket inspector managed a carriage-pleasing moment when he gave my unintentionally mopey face a patronising glance and muttered, 'Cheer up son, it might never happen.'

I felt like replying, 'Yeah, that's what I'm down about.'

But of course I didn't. I searched for the easiest way to get back to the seclusion and sanctuary of my earphones by apologising, feeling appalled at my lack of spirit and sinking further into my seat.

Everyone watching probably supposed, in between their hushed mockery and giggles, that I was listening to some mopey grunge music or angsty thrash metal or some nonsense involving a man sounding like Cookie Monster on horse tranquilisers dribbling on about Satan but that's not me, it really isn't. I was there moments earlier enjoying the sunny side up sounds of the Beach Boys. And no, it wasn't the tortured artist middle-period stuff. It was pure early Beach Boys. Fun, Fun, Fun indeed. I'd love to be a Beach Boy but this aint California, it's Sittingbourne, Swale, with my failing teenage experience left to rot in the Garden of England like a neglected compost heap. My tutors and family members counsel me to smile more, be more tolerant of conversational differences and acquiesce to the rules of the social playground. But I simply can't. I have to be me, no matter the cost and I will die alone and cold on that hill if I have to.

And so it's here, on the eastern edge of the 'bourne in the loneliest bedroom in Woodbury Drive, I sit night after night with only my insidious pride as company. Unlike that poem A-level types like to quote, I have plenty of time to stand and stare. Frankly, it's the only thing I do have.

I've often struggled to locate sufficient and notable short-term memories to answer the question, 'How's your day been?' but the long, lonely nights have always lingered.

Amongst the moonlit shadows and the beam from the streetlight outside my bedroom my mind is alive; uncluttered, uncompromised and alert. Often a little too alert.

Throughout my adolescence, I was the fussy baby, the night terror-afflicted pre-schooler, the 'why aren't you asleep yet?' thorn in the side of my father and stepmother's nocturnal plans. After a while, when there were no sheep left to count and no more bedtime stories to read, my step-mother gave me a tired old clock radio to help fill my hours of insomnia. It was truly on its last legs but worked hard to drag voices and music from local and oldies stations through its tired mechanics. The thought, I guess, was that it would bore me to sleep but the crackles and melodies that crawled through its one dusty speaker called out to me.

And so music became my nighttime companion. The joys of Invicta FM and Atlantic 252 had faded a little for me over time and I found myself favouring my own growing collection of tapes and CDs. My current tonic for the twilight had become ABBA Gold. A compilation of music I bought for quasi-nostalgic and ironic purposes but found held greater depth once I had listened to it through headphones. As something of "an impossible case" myself I felt seen and heard by so many of the songs. "How it hurts to see you cry and how it hurts to see you sad" indeed.

Last night, the heat and tension that had hung in the air for most of the previous week finally met its match. It was a perfect canvas of summer sky; dark blue, peppered with stars and just itching for lightning to arrive and scratch a path straight through it. I could feel the storm approaching as the seconds passed, each tick and tock from the clock pulling the moment gradually closer like weathered work-horses pulling a relief wagon through the mud to a village in need.

The sound of light, drizzling raindrops hitting my bedroom window caught my ear first, with the slightest rumble of thunder following soon after. I stood static, staring into the sky waiting for a dazzling flash of lightning and a crash of thunder but instead another sound captured my senses. Footsteps treading the dampening pavement.

I wondered who it could possibly have been; walking through a street that stands deserted and forgotten night after night in the hours surrounding midnight. I feared being seen by whoever approached – what if it was someone known to my father or sister? What if the truth about my nightly voyeurism of the void became exposed? The footsteps continued to approach, growing louder and clearer with every step taken, while clouds rolled overhead eager for the summer night to break. I simply couldn't look away.

And then she appeared, emerging from the darkest corner of the left side of the street. The staggered street lamps of Woodberry Drive would briefly capture her visage – a girl in her late teens, wearing a long black coat with a short, choppy haircut that had been left to grow out for a month or two.

I found myself fascinated – people in Sittingbourne didn't tend to look like this or carry themselves like this. Though there was something familiar about her manner. A strange mood took hold of my head and heart; I felt unsure if it was based on a memory or the fantasy of a future I could claim as my own.

Either way, I decided to turn from the window and leave this mysterious teen to her night but the moment had other plans, as her perfect pace ground to a sudden halt directly outside my home. Before I could duck out of sight, she turned her head and swung her glance towards my window and our eyes locked. She smiled mischievously and I could have sworn her eyes flashed a golden glow.

I panicked and flung myself away from the window and onto my bed, where I hid and fretted for ten minutes or more. Eventually, I rolled off my bed and made my way back to the window to either set my mind at rest or to confront my voyeuristic decision. I feared that she'd still be standing there, grinning up at me or even worse; see me at the window and head towards my front door. To my relief, she was gone and apart from the faint sound of a car parking somewhere down the road, the street was once again quiet and still.

The day had been long but the last fifteen minutes had felt longer. I knew it was time to sleep and get a night's distance away from the unsettling eye contact of earlier. With my duvet nursing my body and my pillow cradling my face, I was moments away from submitting to sleep when all of a sudden I heard some kind of terrible noise. The din shattered the silence like an animalistic air-raid siren. It was soon joined by the sound of my father thumping his fists on his bedroom window and the flash of several lights being flicked on in the house.

I staggered out of my room to see what all the fuss was about and heard my father banging on at my sister about 'bloody cats and foxes or druggy teenagers in the alley ' and about how he would be tired for his early shift in the morning. I considered suggesting to my dad that staying up hollering and moaning about it rather than just getting back into bed and going to sleep was kinda counterproductive to his predicament but I don't think his ranting was a request for advice.

I made my way back into my room and attempted to slide back into bed, but with the lights all out and the area falling silent once more my mind decided to fill the emptiness by drawing on the image of the young woman that had passed my window. And no matter how I tried to alter my thought process, her knowing smile and the yellow tint of her eyes stalked my thoughts until they were sequestered by sleep.

CHAPTER 2
THE NIGHT IS MY WORLD

TESTIMONY: CHRISTINE REGARDING THE NIGHT OF THE 5TH June 1995

Christine:

Ok, let's not bury the lead (pun only slightly intended). I am what you blood-bags would call a 'vampire'. That's a label you lot came up with, by the way. Personally, I'm not fond of the term and I'm certainly not one of those ironic, irreverent blood-drinkers who seem keen to reclaim it as a fun tag for our kind. However, I know my own worth so while it feels like a slur I've never let it hinder me. So yes, purely for your benefit, I'll use the term if only for the sake of narrative ease.

So yeah, I'm a vampire but not one *of lineage*. I'm way down the pecking order; I am what they call *of the night*. In essence, I used to be human just like you until one foolish yet fateful night back in '85 when I was spotted, hunted and turned by a sick old bastard who was born with pointy, proper fangs (or as they say *of lineage*) just like his blood-drinking mama and papa. But I don't want to talk about him right now and I pray I never have to.

I'm not going to give a full lecture on the lore of it all. The only thing more boring than vampire lore is the hard-on all the Lestat wannabes have for it. So, short and sweet: NO, it's not true that garlic hurts us, though a lot of us have a very slight allergic reaction after touching it; YES, stakes through the heart will kill us (though driving a large, sharp object through anything's heart would most likely cause it to cease, no?). Daylight? If you're *of lineage* you're fine but woe is me – being *of the night* means I'm mainly condemned to spend my daytimes hidden in shadow and shade as YES, direct sunlight would burn straight through me. Holy Water? Depends who blessed it.

And there's the fear you lot have of my kind. Am I going to kill you? Am I going to eat you? Realistically, probably not. For one thing, murder is a bit of a chore. There's the hunting, the struggling, the 'trying to find a good vein' of it all and then the escaping from the crime scene afterwards. More often than not, it's incredibly difficult, messy work and as wonderful as the tasty, heady rush of fresh blood from a kill is I'm frankly far too lazy to do that three times a day. Nah, I mainly dine out on blood nicked from donor centres and hospitals. But don't get me wrong, sometimes when the mood's right and the moon shines bright there's little in life as deliciously fulfilling as consuming sweet, rich, warm blood from a deserving victim.

Am I soulless? Perhaps. Being *of the night* I am forever frozen in time with the face and age of my last mortal moment. Eighteen forever sounds ideal to some, but to watch everyone and everything around you move on and up while rooted to a spot-of-sorts is tough. Admittedly some 'vampires' are definitely soulless – evil, insidious predators but I kinda get the feeling that these arseholes would be arseholes no matter the form they found themselves existing in. The rest of us, I think, have to become soulless because trying to share our heads and hearts with an ever-changing, always expanding cast of characters with all the laughter and pain and memories that come with them, is emotionally exhausting. There's only so much room inside and detachment keeps that side of things manageable. And Christ, I've only been in the game for ten years but I certainly feel that strain. In fact, it was one of the reasons (but not the biggest reason) I left my childhood home of Sittingbourne in the first place.

But, having spent enough time on the coast for the thrill of seaside living to diminish and following an unsuccessful yet eventful attempt to reside in France, I had decided to return to my roots. An old hippy blood-drinker I knew called Bates had decided to go travelling around the world for a few years. Following some reassurance that a certain spot of bother I'd previously found myself in wouldn't be a problem anymore, he had kindly offered up his home on the west side of town as a place for me to stay in exchange for a bit of caretaking. I was broke, hungry and without purpose; how could a girl resist?

Out of curiosity, I wondered if I could stir up the long-lost feeling of nostalgia into my cold, grey heart and I found myself walking down the street I used to live on, Woodberry Drive. There had been a lick of paint here, a fresh coating of creosote there; some of the old, rotting wooden window frames upgraded to shiny, white plastics, but aside from that, not much had changed, really. The street was still two rows of semi-detached houses in complementary yet contradictory sizes and styles. My own family moved out of the area and on with their lives years ago, which makes me sad and relieved in equal measure.

The street at night continues to be as still and deserted as my memories of the early '80s always paint it. The curtains had been drawn hours ago, shielding those inside from the night reminding them that another small town day and opportunities held within had slipped through their fingers once again. Many residents of towns like these often don't like to look beyond the day or consider the veil that separates the light from the darkness. That's why creatures of the night like myself prefer to dwell in such locations; it's easy for the inconceivable to stay hidden when no one is even considering what else might be out there.

However, as I progressed along the pavement I began to sense something. A strong, deep, relentless heartbeat. Full of hurt and fear yet strong – pumping rich, crimson blood through frustrated veins. I followed the trace like a greedy, cartoon character following an aromatic vapour trail of a freshly baked pie and it led me to a house with a curtainless window. And in that window, he stood. A young man, in his mid to late teens, illuminated only slightly by the pale blue light of his HiFi's display. His slim build contrasted with his broad shoulders, a contradiction that matched his dark black, medium length hair style framing his boyish face uncertain whether it wanted be short or long. Follicles forever locked in an existential battle trying to settle on being a curtains cut or a mullet.

Our eyes briefly met and I felt an instant connection, an uncertain need and the thrill of intrigue. Thankfully I sensed no salaciousness in his glance, if it had been some beautiful girl in the window it would have made my intentions far more complicated. I realised that there, in front of me, stood the answer to so many of my afterlife's problems. A golden opportunity: a young, starved vampire, born of lineage, possibly naïve, unaware and ripe for corruption.

To my dismay, he resisted my usually beguiling glance and fled from the window. It didn't matter – I now knew where he lived and I had plenty of free nights to return and wait. The dark, however, is less patient and in a few hours I knew it would be shuffling off to tag in the ever-hateful sunrise so I decided to continue on my journey westwards, towards Bates' pad.

No sooner had I begun to walk than I heard a car speeding down the road. As I made my way towards the lower numbers of Woodberry Drive, a once crisp, showroom-white but now tainted-by-dirt-and-rust Nissan Sunny caught me in its headlights and screeched to a stop beside me. The paintwork around the lock on the door was surrounded with long, spidery scrapes like crow's feet around an ageing eye, almost certainly from the moments before whoever was driving the vehicle managed to steal it. I decided to keep walking and cursed the sky as I heard the window of the front passenger side being frantically wound down.

'Alright luv,' a quasi-cockney-sounding voice bellowed from the opened window, 'need a lift?'

I decided to keep walking only to hear the car reversing to match my pace. I was tired and hungry and really not in the mood for this sort of thing so I stopped and spun my head to see who was deciding to dice with death tonight.

Through the passenger side window, I saw the driver leaning forward, a track-suited young man wearing a gross gurn on a face which looked like a rat had fucked a Doberman and somehow produced a human child.

'What is it?' I replied in a tone that would have made my displeasure known to any intelligent life form. However...

'I asked if you fancied a lift. And then I was going to ask if you fancied anything else?' he replied, bobbing his head up and down, the seediness of his gurn growing as he did so.

My focus became a tad distracted as I started to pick up the aroma of two separate blood types. This was especially frustrating as one of the aromas was a faint but flavoursome hit of some sweet, rare B-negative (which I would literally, and I do mean literally kill for) and also puzzling as he appeared to be the only person in the car. The stronger scent I picked up was a body's worth of common and less-than-healthy O+, which admittedly I would drink but is a bit shameful really, kinda like having a dirty chicken and chips on the way home after a night out.

While lost in my thoughts of blood drinking, the driver continued to natter on. 'Oh yeah you're a right tasty sort aint ya? A lot of people wouldn't probably say so because you're all dressed up like a grunger n' that but you're secretly fit aint ya?'

Despite the growing urge to feast on some fresh, flowing blood I decided to keep walking but as I turned to walk away his voice, now tinged with disappointment and an underlining aggressive frustration called out again, 'Don't be like that. I only wanted a chat. No need to act like a rude fucking lesbian about it.'

Right there and then I thought fuck it I'm drinking some dirty O+ tonight. I felt bad for his family and all that for a moment, but then I saw a rag beside him on the passenger seat. I leaned forward a little more and saw that the rag was concealing a knife and I realised where the B-negative scent was coming from. I could also smell that blood on his right-hand knuckles and in his fingernails. So aside from being a sex pest and possibly a car thief, he'd also spilt rare blood. I was starving – I hadn't feasted properly on fresh blood for months. Why shouldn't I treat myself?

'I'm Deano by the way, what's your name darlin'? I bet you've got one of them grunger names like Lucy or Angelica or something?' he continued to waffle on making little sense to anyone but himself. Lord knows what he had taken but he was clearly high as a kite. And who proudly calls themselves Deano? I doubt that's the name his parents gave him, unless the Dad loved the Dandy comic and the Mum loved the Beano and they couldn't decide which to name him after.

He then started to sound a little slurred and at first, I thought he was asking in one sentence my opinion on the old bride woman in Great Expectations, Jeremy Beadle and Judaism. I looked at him blankly so he tried again, 'Haver-shambeadlejews?'

He even realised the sound spilling out of his mouth was a complete mess and so relaxed his gurn and tried again much slower. 'Have yer seen Beetlejuice? Yeah, you're like that Lydia in it, aint ya? Like she tries to make herself look ugly but she can't hide the fact she's proper fit. Yeah, I like that Lydia from Beetlejuice. You're like one of them girls. A grunger but actually sexy. Like Lydia. From Beetlejuice.'

It seemed weird that he'd find it more normal to call the very famous actress Wynona Ryder by her character's name in a movie that came out half a decade ago and I felt like raising that point but then I remembered she appeared in that bloody awful Dracula movie and thought I better not pull too hard on that thread, lest it gave my own game away.

'So you wanna get fucked or not,' I snapped, keen to shut up his chatter and to get my fangs wet while the street was quietly lost in the midnight hour.

'Blimey you aint backwards in coming forwards are ya?' he cackled, opening his passenger side door and urging me to hop in.

'Nah,' I replied, 'Car seats aren't comfortable and I don't wanna wait while a drive gets in the way. If you want to get it, there's an alley just down there.' There was no way I was being driven to god-knows-where only to have to walk all the way back.

Deano wasn't keen on me declaring the terms of our encounter and decided to aggressively re-propose his original pitch of me getting in the almost-certainly stolen car he was sitting in. He was almost getting quite heated with it all (bless him) but the moment I follow the orders of a snack is the moment I need to walk out into a sunrise and end it all out of shame.

So I flashed him a smile and teased a little eye contact before slowly walking towards the alley a few doors up the road. It was a nice, unlit area familiar to me from my childhood games of Forty Forty – it led down between two of the houses and then branched off behind the back gardens of the neighbouring street. I glanced over my shoulder to check that Deano was following and found him rather hesitantly loitering a good few steps behind me. This wasn't ideal – time is of the essence when it comes to a hunt, so I slowly gave him a glimmer of my eyes and ran my hands down my hips, flicked back the sides of my coat and teased lifting my skirt. Tacky and lazy I know, but it's what he needed.

'Oh you're proper naughty aint ya?' he croaked, 'yeah you're a right naughty one.' He wasn't wrong, I mean cannibalistic murder is probably as naughty as it gets.

Eventually, he caught up with me. I guided him by his rough hand through the darkening alleyway into a secluded corner, shielded from view by homes concealed behind rows of prickly bushes, which protruded from barbed wire and tall, panelled fencing.

I slid my backpack off my shoulders and dumped it on the floor. Pulling him close to me, I laid a soft kiss on his neck, partially to distract him but mostly to gauge where a good biting point might be. One of the things I forgot to mention earlier was the incorrect representation of our fangs in modern media. Somehow it's become standard to always show vampires in films and whatnot with pointy incisors, which is mad. What do they think happens? We get bitten on the neck and suddenly our flat teeth change shape and go pointy? Oh no-no, the canine teeth become more pointy as we begin to live off a mostly blood-based diet. It's a little bit of an evolution thing and a little bit of a wear and tear thing. Like I said earlier, drinking someone's blood out of the neck is a tricky ordeal. We have to bite into the neck with our incisors at the front and then have to try and move our mouths and our dinner's neck into a position where out canines can tear through the skin and pierce a vein. It's no easy task, especially when one of the people involved is, more often than not, unwilling to help.

I knew the kill had to be quick so I pulled my lips off him, then repositioned them and closed them softly around a pulsing vein. Deano sighed in pleasure and I felt his heart pumping, it's pace escalating, beating away like the peak of a drum solo. He'd never felt so alive, which is kinda ironic considering I was seconds away from killing him. I clamped down with the incisors, locking that area of his neck while he wriggled and attempted to fight his way out of my wicked embrace. Widening my mouth I then clamped down with my canines. Usually, at this point, I'd break the victim's neck to shut them up and sit them down, but both my bite and my neck-break were off, causing Deano to scream out briefly. I quickly repositioned my hands and twisted his neck until I heard a snap. Deano fell limply into my arms and, eager to get the deed done, I clamped down fast and hard.

Unfortunately, my impatience perhaps wasn't the best approach as I'd hit that vein hard and, for better or worse, struck the mother lode. Deano's blood came gushing out, spraying out in every possible direction like a broken kitchen tap. I tried to fit the entirety of my mouth over the fountain of scarlet goodness and began downing each gobful of the stuff as it flowed in. The problem was that fresh blood from a kill is surprisingly potent, especially if you've been off the stuff for a while like I had. A rush of light-headedness and giddy freedom took over as my balance became dizzied and disorientated. It had been too much, too fast; my fangs had been bigger than my belly.

Still, it was a shame to waste it so I tried to reach back for my backpack on the floor to pull out an empty flask I keep for such moments. I attempted this with my right hand flailing about while still trying to keep hold of Deano's increasingly limp body with my left hand, my mouth open ridiculously wide and still clamped around the spurting wound on his neck. The whole thing must have looked like a cross between a weird Weekend at Bernie's porn parody and the least appealing game of Twister ever. Eventually, I lost my balance and tumbled backwards. Deano fell face first onto the alleyway floor with his neck still firing out roping arcs of scarlet which peppered the various bushes and trees of the back gardens surrounding us with berry red dots. It'd look charmingly festive if we were in December rather than June, but oh well. Without hesitation I quickly grabbed the flask from my bag and captured the remaining claret from the dearly departed Deano.

Feeling still a little buzzy from the initial consumption, I slowly screwed the lid and cup back onto my flask as I stood back and considered the right mess I'd made of the alley. This wouldn't do at all. I'd been back in town for less than half an hour and already I was making a rod for my own back. It'd have been quicker and easier (though less tasty) to have spray-painted "Christine the Vampire eats here!" across the Welcome to Sittingbourne sign as I passed it on the A2. This needed cleaning up and fast, otherwise I'd have all kinds after me; the cops, vampire hunters, certain other vampires, and Deano's inevitably sprawling and furious family. Thankfully it appeared that Old Man Ludlow still lived in the Coombe Drive house that backed onto the alley-way. His wonky fence panelling and unkempt, overgrown, full of half-completed DIY and engineering projects garden had been a real boon to me as a teen. It was the perfect place to stash booze, weed and (yes, I hold my hands up to this) copies of shoplifted porn mags from the prying eyes of my parents and was now the perfect place to hide and hopefully dispose of a dead body.

So many British Vampires I meet are very cynical and closed-minded when I mention my abilities and talents as a familiar handler. Especially as I'm not *of lineage*. But I swear I have very strong relations with many of the nocturnal beasts. Cats, badgers, hedgehogs, foxes and suchlike are as much on my side as I am on theirs. There's a bat around these parts called Igor that's one of my best ever friends. Everyone thinks I'm daft and imagining too much of a connection with these creatures' natural behaviour but I'm not, I can feel it. As such, I closed my eyes and sent my thoughts out through the long grass and sprawling weeds of Ludlow's garden. Within seconds my call was answered, as first of all one rat, then another two, then five, then finally a further dozen all came scurrying and scratching out from the garden to join me in the alleyway. I stared into the eyes of the largest of the creatures, hoping to see a flash of green. Alas, they flickered red – it couldn't understand my words then, but may sense my intention. To my relief, the rat stood on its two hind legs and squeaked out a short pattern of rhythmic screeches, dozens and dozens of its brothers and sisters began to emerge over fences and through the bushes to join us.

I quickly removed all the clothes and jewellery from Deano's lifeless carcass as the greedy rodents started to gnaw and chew at the flesh, fat and sinew that lay upon it. The younger rats, intimidated by their larger, more domi-nant relatives were content to simply lap up the puddles of blood slowly clotting on the alleyway floor. Deano's gold chain and sovereign rings would serve me well down the line so I pocketed those. The clothes, however, were covered in his blood and would need to go, so I bundled those up to dispose of later. With me pushing his bottom half and the rats biting into his shoulders and dragging the top half, we eventually got the increasingly tatty remains of Deano's body through the slot in Ludlow's fence and into the long grass and abandoned foliage so he could be feasted upon out of sight. Of course, the bones would eventually be discovered, but a good day or two's distance was all I needed. I gave a nod and a salute to the last of the rats as they disappeared into Ludlow's garden, picked up my backpack and made my way out of the alleyway.

As I stood at the foot of the alley, I decided to take a moment just to absorb the thrill of the kill and savour the feeling of my consumption from it. I pulled my 'Walkman-on-a-budget' Alba personal cassette player out of my coat pocket, lifted the headphones from around my neck and placed them on my ears. I half-heartedly attempted to wipe the leftover blood and the satisfied grin from my face with my sleeve and then hit the play button as I started to stroll on. Deano's blood flowing through my body hit hard as I left the confines of Woodberry Drive and emerged back on the main road towards the town centre with my Alba cassette player gliding Laura Branigan's 'Self Control' into my ears matching my pace and consuming the moment. Each inhalation of the night air felt like I was absorbing some form of delicious mischief into my lungs, providing counsel to my guilt that it would be an evening without consequence.

The night remained relatively quiet though a steady sequence of headlights passed me as I strutted alongside the main road eventually making it to the quieter East Street. I found a large, open bin outside D & J Smith newsagents and stuffed Deano's DNA-covered tracksuit into it. I like to be prepared for such moments and, as such, had some matches and lighter fuel in my backpack. With a blazing bin behind me, I continued up into the town centre, passing the bingo hall, cinema, St. Michael's church and the graveyard, still lost in the happy haze of being blood-drunk. High street chain stores and cafes drifted past my blurring vision and before I knew it I was sat giggling to myself by a bunch of billboard advertisements on the edge of town. The silent sky suddenly shook from the rumble of thunder, before a flash of lightning stabbed at the stars. There'd been a light drizzle earlier but it had been a sunshiny start to June and the heat in the sky seemed to fend that off, but this time the clouds burst and the rain descended upon me as I cackled my head off.

The rain lasted a good five minutes or so but left almost as quickly as it arrived. The rush from Deano's blood was starting to fade and by now, I was exhausted and nauseous. Also, my clothes were soaked through and then it dawned on me – if my clothes were sopping wet from the rain what would that mean for Deano's tracksuit? I reassured myself that surely it would have been burnt to a crisp in the time it had taken me to get from the heat of East Street to the sudden downpour in West Street. What's the worst that could happen, right? And that's when I heard the sirens wailing and saw the flashing blue lights of police vehicles speeding past me in an Easterly direction. Shit.

CHAPTER 3
AS THEY CALL YOU TO
THE EYE OF THE STORM

TESTIMONY: BENJAMIN COOPER AND CHRISTINE REGARDING THE morning of the 6th June 1995 and the three nights that followed

BENJAMIN COOPER:

Out of all the daily rituals a human must endure, I'd say waking up is the most hateful. If you're having a good dream it sucks to be yanked away from it. If you're having a bad dream it's disconcerting to be suddenly awake pondering whether it was real or not. If you didn't remember your dream? Well, then you've been torn from a sweet state of restful oblivion back to the thankless grind of the day-to-day. After you survive the shock of waking, you're stuck laying on your side with a dead arm underneath you, vision blurred, head aching, morning breath in your mouth, bedhead setting up another bad hair day, and then like a bullet to the gut, the anxiety of remembering all the things you'd rather not have to do that day. Seriously, waking up can fuck right off. I've never been suicidal but I do often feel like I can't be bothered to live. It feels like life is like a gym membership that I somehow got tricked into signing up for and even though I despise every moment I spend there it's all become too complicated and awkward to back out of so I resign myself to enduring each accursed session. I realise this entire paragraph isn't going to convince anyone that I'm not a goth.

The morning of the 6th hit harder than usual, I remembered the events of the night before and the unpleasant eye contact I made with the girl passing my window. I don't know why I found it so troubling; after all, it was just some random stranger passing by. The chances are that I'd never see her again and if I did – what's the worst that would happen? She'd say, 'Remember that time I caught you staring out of your window past midnight?' But I knew in my thumping heart and my churning stomach that there was more to it than that. Nobody walks past my house at that time of night by chance, let alone to stop and take a quick look up at my window. Then there was that cryptic smile she flashed me and the way her eyes seemed to glint in the darkness. I shuddered and tried to shake it from my mind.

In some (but very much not all) ways, I was blessed to have a full day at sixth-form college that day, if only to distract my mind. After checking they were still relatively fresh I chucked yesterday's clothes back on; Burtons' black jeans and a charcoal grey polo shirt from Sittingbourne high street's favourite Family Allowance-friendly discount clothing store, QS. Yes, I do seem to wear quite a lot of dark colours but I must reiterate I am not a goth. I can't help it that on the rare occasions I choose to buy clothes, the stuff in my price range and in my size happens to be dark. Naturally, I selected fresh pants and socks before attempting to tackle the day's affairs because I'm not a crusty either.

I made my way downstairs to the kitchen to fix myself some breakfast and found my sister Kelly looking uncharacteristically forlorn. I should probably explain that she's actually my half-sister, born two and a half years after me to my step-mum and my biological dad. I always find it amusing to call the old man who potters about (and full credit to him, pays for) the house my 'biological dad' as it makes him sound like he's made of washing powder or something.

To be fair to my biological dad it's not been easy for him. I'm not sure what the deal is with my birth mother. I've been told that she died when I was barely a toddler. I wasn't old enough to understand much of anything going on back then and then the woman who'd become my step-mum entered my dad's life.

My step-mum Janet was, to all intents and purposes, the person I think of as my mum. She was kind and funny – maybe a little forthright on occasion, but ultimately a good person who kept me healthy and safe for fifteen years and I regret not fully appreciating all she did before she died three years ago. Most of the time the days and their duties just roll over the sadness and strangeness of having lost two mothers before reaching adulthood. Sometimes I wonder if I'm cursed. Sometimes the way my dad looks at me doesn't help that.

Kelly has pretty much kept the family together since my stepmother passed. Kelly was always the poster child out of the two of us. Smarter, faster (she won a load of medals for running at 'county' level), friendlier and well, just more normal acting and looking, she seemed to be blessed with a tan since birth and didn't have fangs. She's totally un-goth like. Though she does love the band Suede. Are they a goth band? I mean, they have songs that go on for an age while a bloke in a blouse flounces around wailing on about lord knows what, that seems pretty goth to me.

Lo and behold, I found Kelly listening to a Suede song about pigs while dejectedly staring through the steam of her morning cuppa. I tried flashing her a smile and an, 'Alright?' but it came to nothing. I gave a gentle, 'excuse me' as I brushed past her to get to the milk and she seemed oblivious to my presence. Or had I pissed her off somehow? It was very unusual for her not to take the lead in conversational situations; in fact it tended to be her who would bombard me with small talk while I hid within my shell. I thought about asking her if things were ok but that's not really the way of an eighteen-year-old male, especially to a technically younger but actually more mature sister. So I thought I'd break the ice instead with a little pop culture chat.

'Kells,' I piped up, 'are you a bit of a goth?'

She looked up unimpressed. 'No. Why?' Her tone was flat and defensive.

'It's just,' I started, suddenly nervous about completing my sentence, 'you really like Suede. And they're kinda like a goth band, right?'

She looked at me like I was a moron. 'They're a Britpop band. Like Blur and Elastica.'

I was confused. 'So like an indie music band?'

'Yes, like an indie music band,' she answered in a dry tone with a small, sardonic pause between each word, before sliding a newspaper over to me. 'There you go, have this NME. I'm done with it. It's yours now. Have a read through that and find out about some current bands instead of just sitting in your room listening to the bloody Monkees or whatever.'

This was a bit harsh considering I did actually have a fair number of songs by Blur on my 'taped off the radio' cassettes and I bought a copy of the New Musical Express into our home back when she was covering her walls with New Kids On The Block posters, but maybe she did have a point. I had built a comfort zone around a handful of greatest hits albums and homemade compilations. If fashion was swinging its aesthetic a little more toward my favoured direction of tuneful song-based guitar pop then maybe I should try and show willing. Lord knows it's only going to be a matter of time before the cultural barometer swings back towards boring, booming dance music and bloody awful heavy metal nonsense again. When it comes to the choice between enjoying a melody or the chance to rub against each other half-naked to a tuneless racket, I know what the majority will go for, unfortunately. People are animals and can't help themselves.

'Actually I do quite like a bit of indie, so thanks,' I beamed, trying to raise Kelly's spirits but barely stirring an acknowledgement. 'I'm quite looking forward to diving into this whole Britpop thing.'

'Cool,' she half-shrugged. 'I tell you what, I'll make you a tape as a starting point.'

As pleased as I was with the free NME and the promise of a compilation tape of indie-flavoured British Pop music, I was still concerned by my sister's unusually withdrawn nature this morning.

Getting the awkward words out of my mouth felt unnatural and I feared the can of worms they would almost certainly open but I had to ask. 'Kells, is everything... are you... ok?'

She looked at me with an expression that was hard to read. Possibly urging me to try again, as if she did actually want to talk about it or possibly trying to tell me to 'fuck off' without using words. Maybe it was a bit of both, leaving it up to me to choose whether to stick or twist.

I'd gone this deep; I figured I might as well carry on. 'It's just, well, you seem a bit down and distant. You're normally making plans – seizing the day and all, being well adjusted.' I went for a bit of humour to end my concerned brother sales pitch, 'To be frank I'm worried you're trying to steal my role in the family.'

She continued to wear an expression that I'd label as 'definitely pissed off but not necessarily at me,' and blessed my probing with a weary sigh. 'I'm fine, I suppose. I met up with Jon Miller last night for a date of sorts.'

This was a strange and unwelcome surprise, one which caught me at such an angle that I responded in a less than tactful way. 'Jon Miller!?! What were you doing with him? He's a complete bastard.'

'Well, I know that now!' Kelly's voice was spurred out of its doldrums, eager to match my criticism. 'I didn't go to your fleabag school, did I? I didn't know who he was. All I knew was he seemed like a nice guy who gave me his number at JJs the other night.'

She was referencing JJ's Nightclub, tucked away above the as-good-as disused tiny shopping arcade opposite the Sainsbury's. A very popular nightspot for my generation, lord knows why – the one time I went it was like the last days of Rome sponsored by Argos' Elizabeth Duke jewellery range.

'JJs!?! What did you think would happen if you pick up blokes from there?'

'Well some of us want more from life than being a lonely old hermit,' her knowing eyes locked on to mine somewhat accusingly, 'shut away in a bedroom, wanking ourselves dry over the lingerie section of a Grattan catalogue.'

If she was throwing shade at how I chose to spend my evenings she was very much mistaken. It was a Littlewoods Catalogue.

The awkward silence that followed gave Kelly the opportunity to switch down gears. 'Anyhow, so yeah I met up with him and yes, you're right he was a complete dickhead. I was just in the process of telling him to get lost but then he had some friend called Deano turn up and there was some kind of situation about a stolen car and it all got a bit nasty, so I just came home. And ever since I've felt a bit weird about it all.'

'Fucking hell, they didn't hurt you or anything did they?' I asked using 'hurt you or anything' instead of 'sexually assault you' like the out-of-his-league man-child I knew I was.

'No, I'm fine. It's just some of the things they said *to* me and *about* me. And, well, let's just say it was just a shitty night. How was your evening? Who was the lucky catalogue page number last night?'

I didn't dare tell her about my evening. Considering the amount of mileage she was able to get from finding an old catalogue open at a certain section shoved under my bed, lord knows how much teasing she'd get out of a mysterious goth girl outside of my window and my decision to hide from her.

'Ah, you know me; it was pretty quiet, all in all. Anyhow, I've got to get to college.' Having made my excuses, I got myself fed and dressed before legging it to the station.

Christine:

The first thing I realised when I awoke on a surprisingly factory-fresh-smelling sofa was that I didn't remember getting back to Bates' flat the night before. I vaguely recalled finding the keys under a brick by his front door as per the instructions he'd sent me. I must have then collapsed on his sofa as that's where I woke up.

Daylight stretched its intrusive arms out and probed its fingers through the gaps in the curtains, luckily avoiding my very sensitive skin. And then it all came back to me – walking along the A2, seeing a young prospect (*of lineage* no less) staring out of his window at me, (note to self: go and integrate myself into his life later) and then, oh yeah Dirty Deano and his sweet, sweet gushing blood! This brought me to the urgent and sorry realisation that I had left a flask full of Deano's blood untended overnight. If you're collecting surplus blood for use later you really have to protect the sample with some kind of anticoagulant.

I rolled untidily off the sofa like a lackadaisical gymnast and lurched towards my backpack, pulled the flask out and unscrewed it. Hoping for the best but expecting the worst, I stuck my finger in and hit a wall of spoiled, clotted and crispy blood. Such a waste. Maybe I could pull some of it out and eat it like some kind of Jerky snack.

There was something else troubling me, a deep burning concern I couldn't immediately place, kicking around in my gut. I was safe here at Bates's so it wasn't that. Guilt about killing Deano? Unlikely. I then reached out for my rain-soaked coat and it all came back to me; the bloody-bloody clothes I left burning in a bin on East Street and the downpour that followed.

I so desperately wanted to go back to East Street and give that bin a once over. I needed a frame of reference – a clear picture of what was sat waiting to be found. How much was still there for examining, how much had floated away as embers or lay amongst the ash?

I needed to make a plan but had nothing to go on. Later, I switched on the local Meridian news, expecting and dreading Fred Dineage to break the story of a missing Sittingbourne youth called Deano, only to experience a disconcerting disappointment when he didn't.

Maybe I'd gotten away with it, maybe I hadn't. It was an uneasy and uncertain start to my hometown comeback. I decided to nurse my haemoglobin hangover and rest up while the sun shone so I could be at full strength for my return to Woodberry Drive that evening.

Benjamin Cooper:

Within forty minutes of leaving the house, I was sat on a train heading towards Canterbury. I had somehow found myself almost halfway through a two-year course studying Travel and Tourism. It wasn't going well but if I could get myself together, decode what the hell my tutors were expecting with my work and actually start getting the marks I needed I could end up with a GNVQ Advanced diploma. This would ultimately, I guess, help secure me a job in a hotel or a branch of Thomas Cook or something, I don't know. I harbour zero ambitions to work in a hotel or Thomas Cook but here I am. This is what happens when your GCSE exam results crash land into a field of D grades, I guess.

I'm almost one year in with another year to go though if my grades don't improve I have a feeling that I will be asked to leave by the head tutor, a small bouncy fellow with a thin beard who looked like Mr Claypole from Rentaghost. This will not go down well with Biological Dad who seems to harbour the expectation that after three years of post-secondary school education, I'll waltz into some kind of high-ranking civil service role or something.

But before I settled down to another day of doodling in my A4 pad while various tutors presented possibly beneficial but ultimately ignored information to my distracted senses, I had the half-hour train ride to Canterbury to enjoy. I was overjoyed to find I had a glorious cluster of four seats all to myself. I reached into my spacious backpack and pulled out the copy of the NME that Kelly had given me. It was a couple of weeks old but still felt current, at least to me. I couldn't wait for her mix tape later, to brush up on some of this stuff. She was right; I needed to bring myself back into society a bit. It's just tricky because the further I drift away from it, the more I feel my anxieties and frustrations fade. But am I content when I find myself adrift? No, I feel like something's missing. I don't know what it is I need to do but it needs to be big, something beyond what the people I meet in my life can comprehend. Lord knows what this goal is in real terms but I figured this NME was as good a place to start as any, perhaps The 60ft Dolls and Menswe@r held some deep wisdom that'd make sense of it all. It was unlikely but not a complete impossibility.

My reading was interrupted by a familiar and unwelcome cough. Two big wheezes chased by a hacking gurgle and choke back of tobacco-stained phlegm signalled the arrival of Darren King, strutting through my carriage. Incredibly tall, wearing a long, padded Manchester United FC coat that was somewhere between a trench coat and puffer jacket with a great big, more-yellow-than-blonde bowl cut with a central parting hairstyle above an ever-present, shit-eating grin that made him look like a smug mushroom. People (mostly girls) would comment on his mushroom hair and he'd roll out the line, 'I don't know about looking like a mushroom but I am a fun guy.' That's right, the fucking Fun-Guy/Fungi joke. And it would get a laugh every damn time. People (mostly girls) loved him. I hated him. He was one of my fellow students on the Travel and Tourism course and one of the most fucking annoying people I had met in my eighteen years on the planet. Somehow, my reluctance to be sucked into his cult of personality had seemed to foster a growing need within Darren King to become acquainted with me on a social level. However, whereas others enjoyed the warmth of his spotlight, I had no interest in being anywhere near him.

'Alright there, Mr Cooper,' he boomed through the last remnants of his cough. 'What's that you got there? Horses?'

Horses? I had no idea what he was on about and grunted, 'Eh?' in the coldest, least inviting manner possible.

'In that-there betting paper you've got there. You gonna put some notes on a horse?' he replied managing to stick an extra 'there' into the sentence as was his wont.

A betting paper? It clearly said NME on the front page and underneath that was a picture of Paul Weller. Did he think Paul Weller was a horse? It got me thinking; *does* Paul Weller look like a horse? It's not an opinion I'd instantly agree with but considering the photo on the front cover with his chestnut brown mane sweeping over the eyes on his long face maybe it wasn't such a wild misunderstanding. I pondered on it for too long and before I knew it, he'd swooped down like a thieving magpie and plucked the paper out of my hands.

'Ah right, I see now – indie music, yeah?' he said, giving the front cover an up and down once-over before quickly flicking through a few pages. 'You into this stuff? I don't mind a bit of it myself. Dance music's alright for dancing, but sometimes, I aint dancing.'

He served up that last sentence with punctuated pauses in a comma sandwich as if it was the most profound thing anyone had ever said on a Network SouthEast train. To be fair, it may well have been.

Certainly, his gaggle of followers would have lapped it up and, as if on cue, they arrived. A clutch of wannabe lads bundled on first. They had hitched their wagons to Darren King's star at the beginning of the year and were now condemned to squander their remaining teenage years withering in his shadow. However most of Darren King's clique were girls; a squealing, squawking, ever-chatting tsunami made up of velvet puffer jackets, home perms and the stench of Hubba Bubba gum.

The parade of young ladies made their way down the aisle, perhaps being drawn to his throat-scraping, phlegm-harvesting noises as if they were animalistic mating calls. Although despite his magnetic appeal to members of the opposite sex, it never appeared to go anywhere beyond them following him around. Admittedly there was a wild week of giggles and incessant chatter when he went on a date with Louise D'Souza, one of his platonic harem's quieter girls. The morning after however found the excitement of the date reduced to hushed, earnest conversations about how the pair of them were going to remain just friends. It was an anti-climatic result that the clique all accepted but I could tell it had caused an unspoken but noticeable discontent amongst his flock. I found it all very odd but having never gone on a date I have zero frame of reference for such trivialities so that's to be expected.

Darren King handed the NME back to me and greeted his gaggle with arms held aloft. 'Lots of seats here, ladies' he boomed before treating himself to a quick cough.

All of my precious once-empty seats began to fill with the girl's shrill voices and faffing about looking for things in their impractical, small bags. I felt the urge to tut, sigh and shake my music paper like a disgruntled bowler-hatted commuter cliché but felt some eyes on me. I peeked over the paper to see Louise D'Souza looking at me in a manner that was hard to read. It was a strange moment but thankfully it passed swiftly as her attention returned to one of her crowd pulling out some photos of one of their dreadful-sounding nights from one of the impractical bags. Between the weird situation of the girl outside my window the previous evening and the twenty minutes stuck on a train surrounded by Darren King's round table of twits, I decided to skip the first lecture that day and hide in the park dreaming of a day where everyone around me would just fuck off.

Christine:

The evening arrived sooner than I would have liked. My head was still rattled from the night before and my nerves a little frazzled from the uncertain status of the incident with Deano. I flicked on the TV and sat through some soaps until the news appeared. Once again, there was nothing about Deano's body or his bloodstained clothes, nothing about him being missing. Though it had only been sixteen hours or so and Deano didn't seem the type to keep his family abreast of his to'ing and fro'ing. I normally couldn't give a fuck about murdering fools so I wondered why this one had me on edge. I had drunk too much and been careless afterwards, I was disappointed with myself over that but the sinking feeling in my stomach was over something more. Anxiety over Deano was the symptom but not the cause. Coming back to Sittingbourne after everything I'd been caught up in years ago was always a risky move. My sources had assured me that there wasn't currently anyone *of lineage* controlling either Swale or Medway at the time and that I would be safe to re-establish my bad self in my old stomping ground.

There was, of course, Scratch. He was still a consideration. I'd never met him but I'd heard of him, even before I was *of the night*. A shadowy figure in town and heir to a small crime empire which was said to go back generations. That's how most teenagers initially hear about him, after you become part of the dark magik scene; the stories grow wilder and more frightening. Luckily for me, it's those *of lineage* who fear him the most and know to respect his rank. My one little kill wouldn't be enough to get Scratch narked. If anything, I'd heard he had certain sympathy for those like me who were *of the night* and his ire was directed at those who had turned us in the first place. Still, I wondered if word of my kill last night might reach ears less favourable – those of old enemies. I could feel a certain heavy tension in the air. Even with Scratch running a tight ship at the moment I didn't feel like I had enough contingencies in place. I really needed to secure the inherited talents and protection of that young man in the window from the night before.

Benjamin Cooper:

It had been another shitty day at college. Deciding to skip the first lecture of the day had been a mistake as it turned out the Mr Claypole-lookalike had turned up to have a quick catch-up with me and he wasn't best pleased when he discovered I wasn't there. He handed me a letter requesting a meeting with my Dad to talk about my lack of attainment, which I felt was a bit rich seeing as how I'd just turned eighteen and was no longer a child. I said I'd see when he was available even though I had no intention of mentioning it to him.

My anxiety continued to bubble up at home. All evening and long into the night my un-curtained window nagged and taunted me, urging me to take a look for myself, to satisfy my curiosity. Eventually, I caved in, slowly rising from my bed, my heart thumping but certain that the street outside would be empty and my mind would be set at rest. However, there she was – back against the lamppost, dressed like an 80's heavy metal parody, looking up at my window and smiling at me. I darted back to my bed, stayed there and caught whatever sleep I could manage.

The next day followed almost exactly like the one before; Darren King annoying me on the train, Louise D'Souza giving me another odd, possibly judgy look, a serious chat from Mr Claypole about the lack of appointment with my Dad and another evening of tense bedroom-window-peek-aboo with my apparent stalker. This time however she wasn't smiling and just kept ushering me to come down with head nods and hand gestures. Not a chance.

The third day was the real shitter. I did manage to get the train to college without being in the same carriage as Darren King but that was about as good as my day got. Firstly I had Louise D'Souza being weird around me, but it had escalated beyond her uneasy staring. The first mistake I made was listening to Sgt Pepper on my Alba wannabe-Walkman and absent-mindedly whistling along to 'Fixing A Hole' while typing up my latest lacklustre piece of course-work. Like a troubled dog sensing a careless paperboy approaching a noisy letterbox, Louise sprung up on high alert.

'Is someone whistling the Beatles?' she asked, addressing the room but staring an unfixable hole through me. 'Is it you?' she continued directly at me, but barely audible as the cascading shower of harpsichord notes that introduce 'She's Leaving Home' filled my ears instead. I chose to ignore her and kept my head down as she tried in vain to get a conversation about the Beatles going with the rest of the room. Every so often she'd try to catch my eye, clearly hoping that I'd leap to the Fab Four's defence and help her sell their merits to the small-town clubbers she associated with but frankly, what's the point?

A little later, while waiting for the afternoon's session to begin on the cramped and crowded staircase outside the classroom, she tried to spark up a conversation with the Darren King clique about Star Trek or The Next Generation or whatever it's called these days. Naturally, that lot weren't having any of is, so as she babbled on about Klingons and various characters that I would imagine have bumps and protrusions coming out of their faces, I found her eyes trying to meet mine. Like I'd know the slightest fucking thing about any of that! I present two middle fingers to the energy I seem to put out into the universe. Things really needed to change, and fast. It's bad enough that everyone thinks I'm a goth but I draw the line at people presuming I'm a Trekkie.

I then had to endure a train ride home with Darren King and his friends' voices booming through the carriage. I was sat far down the other end with my denim jacket draped over my face, attempting to have a quick nap. They hadn't figured out I was on the train which I initially felt a blessing until it warped into a terrible curse. Their giddy chatter was the usual inane barrage of ear-piercing nonsense that I would, in other circumstances, drown out, however one name popped up that piqued my interest in the worst way.

'Do you know something about that Friday?' Darren said, in a steady authoritative tone which cut a path of silence through the chatter. 'Deano had his car nicked while he was in JJ's. Turns out though he had an inkling who did it. I'm not saying who but you can probably guess. All I'll say is it turned up in Sheppey. So him and Jon Miller went and got it back on Monday night. Turns out things got rough but they got away with the car, the only thing is Jon hasn't heard from Deano since that night.'

My mind trailed off, remembering the breadcrumbs of information Kelly had given me about her bad date. My heart sank – was she involved in all of this? Dashing over to the Isle of Sheppey and forcefully retrieving a stolen vehicle from someone or some people that even Darren King's big mouth dare not identify? That's not the way Kelly is, I hoped and prayed that she wouldn't be involved. Unfortunately, her name was then mentioned, but not the way I was expecting.

'I tell you something else about that Monday night,' Darren continued, in a tone that sounded like a salacious grin spreading across his big, stupid face. 'Before Jon went off with Deano, he was with a girl. And do you know who it was? It was only Benjamin Cooper from our course's sister.'

There were howls of amusement over this development but it didn't stop there. 'And I tell you something else, she wouldn't have normal sex with him because she's scared of getting pregnant so he talked her into taking it up the arse.'

There were awkward chortles from the girls and fevered cheers from the boys, one of whom cried in celebration, 'what a dirty bitch! I bet that's not the first time she's done it either. It's no wonder Alice is such a weird tosser.'

Great, so that's my sister labelled a 'dirty bitch' and the depressing realisation that my secondary school nickname of 'Alice' Cooper had made its way to Canterbury.

The evening was long and apprehensive; I wasted time and energy avoiding Kelly by hiding in my room for long periods and lurking on the landing when needing to traverse to a different room. I had no doubt that the gossip about my sister was untrue but was she aware of the word going around about her? How does someone raise the subject of anal sex with their little sister in any circumstance, let alone when she's the focus of it? Maybe I've led a sheltered life, maybe it's best I stay there in the shelter and ignore it. Yet the taunting and the arrogance of the gossip lingers in my gut like plastic in a fire, melting and mutating into a state of deformation but never breaking down or diminishing.

The envelope addressed to my Dad containing the letter from Mr Claypole sat ominously on the bed. It sat unopened with what I presumed would be a very matter-of-fact letter inside about my failings. As I stared at the unopened letter and considered the drama its contents would unleash, its ominous form appeared to throb and hum threateningly. It would have to go. The bins had been emptied the day before so I knew I could sneak it out of the house, dump it at the bottom of the wheelie bin and put today's waste on top, leaving it as good as buried. Mr Claypole would of course chase up the situation, but with my

Dad at work all day it would prove impossible for any calls to reach him. I could hold off Mr Claypole with excuses about my Dad being too busy with work until at least the summer holiday, giving me a bit of a breather from all the escalating tension and hopefully a chance to get my assignment scores up. Yep, into the bin the letter had to go.

But I pondered about my stalker – what if she was out there, standing by the lamppost staring up at my window again tonight? Surely she wouldn't be. Dark clouds had descended upon the heat wave, teasing the clear blue sky and a heavy rain was almost guaranteed. Aside from that, the novelty should have worn off by now. Surely she wouldn't be there and yet, of course, she was. This time dressed up like some kind of scary doll or a European cabaret clown or something. With a startling, creepy smile on her face she gave a slow wave. Not using her wrist but with a gentle movement of her fingers. Who does something like that? What was that about? My instincts overtook my reserve and I screamed at her an order to 'Fuck off!' The double-glazing probably soaked up most of the volume from my declaration but I'm sure my point had been made.

Christine:

This really shouldn't have been as difficult as it was. Most normal teenage boys would be out of their front door as soon as they had their tea but oh no, not this one. Night after night pottering about in his impenetrable bedroom. Even if he didn't fancy me, (believe it or not, many don't) he'd welcome the company, right? I tried wearing my KISS 'Creatures of the Night' t-shirt on Night One. I presumed he'd be into that, he looked the sort, but he barely even glanced at me. Night Two, I thought I'd just be me and play it casual. I would have thought he'd at least have been curious about who I was, but again, absolutely no interest. So I figured Night Three would need something different than my usual box of tricks. Maybe my style wasn't his bag. He looked like he should be a goth, metal head or even just a double-denim rock kid but maybe he wasn't? I decided to try looking like a *pretty girl*. Now, given how I struggled to look like a *pretty girl* even when I was a real, live teenage girl, this was going to be somewhat of a challenge. I had been tempted just to sack the evening off. It looked like it was going to piss it down with rain and I had discovered that Bates had a pretty tasty-looking collection of Star Trek VHS tapes including some new Deep Space Nine stuff from his stateside connections. Maybe, I thought, I should just have a night off and watch a bunch of them but I really needed to get this introduction off my to-do list. I had already found a bunch of *pretty girl* clothes and make-up in a suitcase under Bates's bed when I snooped around a day or so earlier. The garments were possibly a little dated but still girlie. I made as good a go of it as I could and made my way to Woodberry Drive. I tried hard to look cute and smiley; I even tried a little feminine wave, but he hated that. Reading his lips I think he even told me to 'fuck off'. It was nice to see a little fire lurking beneath the nervous icy disposition I had seen previously. That could certainly come in handy down the line, but I wasn't getting anywhere as a *pretty girl* and I felt the rain begin to descend.

Standing by a lamppost night after night and staring up at his window wasn't working, it was clear I'd need to switch things up.

· · ·

Benjamin Cooper:

It took until the hour hand on my clock began to creep towards midnight for the rain to stop. I was sure the downpour must have chased away my stalker and to my heavenly relief, I walked to my window and found she was gone. With one less thing to worry about already lifting my spirits, I decided to remove another burden – time to get that letter in the bin. With my Dad and Kelly all tucked up in their beds, I tore the sealed envelope in two and quickly descended the stairs, softly unlatched the front door and made my way to the wheelie bin. I dropped the two halves of the accursed correspondence in and watched them land crumpled at the bottom.

I started to make my way inside but became distracted by the sky. The rain had passed but the storm remained. Dark clouds and a persistent pressure lingered in the sky, still unsatisfied despite the weight of the water it had shed. After a couple of stumbling, distracted steps backwards I swung around expecting to find the front door. Instead, I saw two eyes, glistening with a yellow glow. Here I was, face-to-face with my stalker. It appeared she had grown tired of the lamppost and had instead decided to lurk on the raised area surrounding my home's front porch.

Wet from the rain she smiled insidiously at me revealing her pointed fangs. 'At long last we meet,' she said. 'We have so much to talk about.'

CHAPTER 4

DRINK THE ELIXIR

TESTIMONY: CHRISTINE AND BENJAMIN COOPER REGARDING THE first minutes past midnight of the 9th June 1995 and the busy afternoon of light stalking and petty vengeance that followed

CHRISTINE:

Finally, there he was - a child *of lineage* alone and approachable. Well maybe not approachable.

'At long last we meet,' I said in what I presumed to be a friendly, inviting manner. 'We have so much to talk about.'

But he wasn't having any of it.

'No, I don't think we do!' he muttered before snaking past me, running back inside and bolting the door. I realised that securing his talents was going to be harder than I thought. This was going to take time, and information. I began to wonder about the contents of the letter he'd just thrown in the bin.

Benjamin Cooper:

I began to wonder if I'd ever be free of her. Maybe I should have just asked what she wanted with me? Though it's hard to believe that anyone with yellow eyes has harmless intentions. And what's the deal with the yellow eyes and fangs anyhow? She's clearly a goth type and I just have to hope its part of the dressing up nonsense that lot do. Maybe it's all a prank at my expense. I could imagine Darren King encouraging one of his former Westlands classmates to honey trap me for a laugh. It had to be something like that. I can't deal with any paranormal theories right now, there's already far too much plain-normal stuff going on at the moment.

Helping me through these testing times was the mixtape put together and left on my bed by Kelly. She'd titled it 'Britpopping' and quite charmingly had used her four-colour Bic pen to turn the 'o' in Britpop into what I had always called the RAF circles but Kelly quickly corrected me that it was in fact something called a 'mod target'. There had been one superimposed on that NME front cover where Paul Weller may or may not have looked like a horse. I had wondered what the NME were trying to symbolise by including something I had previously associated with Airfix Model kits of Spitfires but it just goes to show that if you wait for a while most things will eventually make some kind of sense.

The mixtape had served me well on my journey into college and I looked forward to enjoying the imminent weekend that, according to my calendar, was free of plans or obligations. My happiness was short lived as I waited for the classroom to open and saw Darren King stroll towards me. To my horror I realised he'd caught me with my backpack open as I adjusted some of the contents within, his eyes were full of intrigue and I could guess what he was going to say. After letting out a flurry of his usual coughs and snorts he cleared his throat and asked me, 'Alright there Mr Cooper? I don't suppose you've got any of those 'arvest Crunch Bars in that there-backpack-there do ya? I had a rough night and need something to line my guts.'

Darren King liked nothing more than getting hold of my Harvest Crunch Bars. It's partially my own stupid fault as I'd made the mistake at the beginning of the year of letting him have one. With his casual way of asking for stuff as if taking items from other people's packed lunches was the most normal thing in the world, and the jeering faces of his clique surrounding the situation, I caved in and handed him one. At the time it didn't seem that bad as I had a spare one left over from the previous day but he continued on an almost daily basis to have a sniff around the contents of my backpack like an unwelcome dog at a picnic.

'No, I don't,' I declared, as I fumbled to close my bag, leaving a window of optical opportunity.

'What's that wrapper in there then?' Darren asked, trying to stick his face in like a beaky bird.

'A Wagon Wheel.'

He was a little disappointed but still satisfied, 'Yeah, that'll do. Can I have it?'

'Well, no. I mean, it's my lunch.' A fair refusal I'm sure you'd agree.

Darren started to get a bit huffy at that. 'Yeah, but you had other stuff in there, mate. No need to be greedy. Like I say,

I'm totally hangin' this morning'

'No, it's mine,' I asserted.

'Come on, don't be a cunt about it. It's just a Wagon Wheel!'

One member of his platonic harem, a bullish girl called Becky Hollis, then piped up. 'Yeah he's feeling really sick. Don't be a wanker all your life.'

And then, like the mindless sheep his crew truly are, they all started bleating at me.

'Come on! It's just a Wagon Wheel.'

'Seriously, what's wrong with you?'

'You're such a weirdo. Just be kind, you know he's got an alcohol problem and he's really hung-over.'

Ah yes, Darren King's 'Alcohol Problem'. A situation that was twisted into whatever conversational form best suited his little clique's mood of the hour. A source of great amusement on Friday afternoons and Monday mornings when it's all about the pre and post weekend clubbing analysis. The mid-week lull however brings about a change to the way they like to bang on about it. Suddenly the amount of pints Darren King puts away on a daily basis becomes an ultra-serious, mature-tones-only talking point where all involved like to drive their facial expressions southwards in a race to see who can look the most concerned the quickest. All I know is he must be a highly functional alcoholic to arrive at the station every goddamn day on time and hassle me for free food. Was he an alcoholic or just a teenage pisshead? I know how I feel about the subject but it appears the jury's still out on that one.

In the end it was easier just to give him the bloody thing, which he took and devoured in two bites.

'Ah, that's better. Don't suppose I could have some of that-there drink to wash it down,' he asked, peering into my backpack at a can of Sainsbury's own brand Lilt rip-off.

I was just explaining that it was a can, could only be opened once, couldn't be closed and I'd be needing it for lunchtime when thankfully the door swung open and our tutors started ushering us in.

My initial joy at escaping Darren King's lunchbox larceny was diminished almost instantly as I was pulled aside by Mr Claypole and marched off to his little office. To my surprise I wasn't the only student there and to my slight dismay, amongst that number, was Louise D'Souza. I was beginning to actually resent her increased presence in my life. It was an intrusion of sorts. Like someone sitting in the same aisle in the cinema even though there's plenty of other seats available, or a vague acquaintance leaving a building at the same time and walking beside you instead of doing the decent thing of holding off and pretending they're waiting to meet someone. It's rude and aggressive in my opinion. Don't threaten me with a conversation. I was, however, surprised to see her there as she normally got top distinction marks on her assignments and it was clear by Claypole's furrowed brow that this was going to be an end of Year One bollocking for the shitheads. And lo and behold, it was. Claypole was very animated about it all, with his arms gesticulating wildly and his reedy voice being pushed into near operatic tones to stress how badly we were all doing. He said we had until the end of term to hand in revised pieces of failed course work or we wouldn't be coming back in September. I was already in a bad mood, what with, well, EVERYTHING that had been going on in the past few days and Claypole's finger wagging had really pushed me into being fully pissed off so I chose not to hear Louise calling after me as I stomped back to class.

I knew that things were unlikely to improve and they didn't. On the notice board as you enter the classroom there's an awkward class photograph of everyone on my course. Earlier in the year someone had decided to write 'demon' above my head in pencil. It was an odd development as I hadn't really interacted or pissed anyone off at that point. I mean if someone had taken a look at my pale skin and pointed teeth and decided I look like a gothic creature or something – I get that, but even so, it seems a strangely bold and unnecessary gesture to write it. After noticing it, I had braced myself for a bunch of ribbing from my fellow students about it and for my tutors to raise it, but nobody said anything. Not a damn thing. Day followed day, month followed month and nada, not one damn care about it in any capacity. For a while, I had considered that either my mind was playing tricks on me or that I was so much of a nobody that no-one ever looked at my section of the photo, but today proved that they clearly did, as above the word 'demon' someone had written the word 'anal'. This was clearly a bit of mischief at the expense of both me and my sister, unless the words are meant to be read together. I can't see any reason for that, though Anal Demon would make an excellent name for a pedantic thrash metal band.

Later on, while typing some of the least inspiring Travel and Tourism college work to ever be half-heartedly typed, I felt a growing anger begin to bubble. I don't get how people can have a pop at me for not giving up items from my packed lunch or failing to understand what was required for course work but hassling me for food and turning a blind eye to people graffitiing my photo is all a-ok. The fury began to surge through my body and my mind drew upon the aggressive pulsing riff of the Supergrass track that opened Kelly's mixtape.

Lunchtime arrived long before my temper had calmed and I felt its persistence influence my thoughts towards self-preservation and payback. The scales weren't balancing and I needed to tip things back in my favour, but how? I searched my churning gut to see what was stuck within it. What exactly was pissing me off the most? Well, I knew for starters that *he'd* be down by the entrance doors – Darren King, gasping down dirty, fingertip-yellowing smoke from his B&H snouts and looking to secure my can of pop to wash it down. I thought about taking the can in my clenched fist and smashing it hard and fast into his fore-head repeatedly until I split skin and caused a gash so harsh it dyed his hair blood-orange. This, of course, was a foolish idea. Far too many witnesses, far too much drama. His gaggle of cronies kicked up enough of a stink when I refused to gift him my Wagon Wheel, lord only knows what they'd throw at me for attempted murder. Plus, it'd probably give Claypole just the ammo he needed to kick me off the course and out of college for good. Violence would be an excellent release but in the grand scheme of things it would prove unsatisfying. I pondered what it was I was actually looking for from an act of revenge. It wasn't recognition – I now realised that, nor did I crave a visible scar to act as a trophy of my superiority. No, I wanted a very specific display of power; control hidden within my secret smirk, an invisible lingering victory. I wanted to be the master of a game with rules existing far beyond everyone else's vapid comprehensions. Darren King was going to ask for some of my fizzy drink, of that I could be certain, so what if I gave it to him with a little something extra on top? I thought about gobbing into it but it seemed a little too obvious and with the amount of drinks he's taxed off others, surely a bit of backwash is an occupational hazard. I needed something deeper, darker – more taboo. With my heart pumping, my cheeks burning and a rare giddy excitement racing through my veins, I found myself in the toilet cubicle relieving my bladder and my emotional frustration straight into the opened ring pull of my drink. I didn't go crazy with it, just one little warm amber squeeze. I swilled the can around to allow the notes and tones of my wastewater wine to blend with the sugar and carbonated water of the fizzy pop. I grabbed some discarded bits of bog roll from off the floor and patted the rim of the can to remove any tell-tale drops where my aim hadn't been as accurate as I hoped.

I swung the bog door open feeling full of vim and vigour ready to serve up my bitter cocktail. Thankfully the toilet area was empty which was a relief as I could have sworn I heard someone lurking around in the cubicle next to me.

With the can clutched in my hand I bounded out of the building and walked past Darren King and friends trying to avoid his glance.

'Mr Cooper! Oi! Over here, give us some of that-there drink,' he predictably hollered.

I sauntered over, feigning reluctance and faking a swig. 'Here you can finish it off.'

I handed him the can and watched him raise it to his tobacco tainted lips as he began to knock back half of it in one gulp, stopping only to pause for a quick cough and a burp before finishing it off. I didn't linger on the scene but watched long enough to feel the satisfaction of my golden payback invading his organs as it slid down his throat, clinging and clutching while making its way through his body.

There were two hours to squander before I had to be back in class, so I headed through the doors at the rear of the college main block and hit the Student Union café. It was a bit of a grubby affair there but they had a jukebox and they sold Unigate chocolate milkshakes at a very reasonable price. Double denim rockers and the metal-heads infested most of the right side of the café. They didn't seem to like me very much, which is odd because you'd think they'd jump at the chance of having someone who apparently looks like a demon amongst their party. It does make me laugh, how the Metal-heads bang on about being outsiders and individuals when they hang out in large groups and all wear the standard uniform of denim, leather and band t-shirts. To be honest, I am a little jealous of the conformity and convenience of being in that crowd. I never know how I'm supposed to dress as an ABBA and Beach Boys fan or indeed what my cultural tribe even is. I suppose there was now Britpop in my life, I wondered if indie bands did patches you can sew on to jeans and such like. Or perhaps something like the RAF and/or Mod target thing that seemed to be all the rage these days. So with 'Lenny' by Supergrass kicking off Kelly's Britpoppping tape, the sound filling my ears and amplifying my heightening smugness over the vengeance of the fizzy piss, I quickly picked up a chocolate milk, threw an ironic yet celebratory devil horn hand gesture at the Metalheads and made my way out of the campus and towards the Indoor Market.

One of the great student and tourist hotspots in Canterbury, the Indoor Market was situated towards the end of St. Peter's Place on the edge of Westgate. It was a mecca for second hand vinyl; bootleg CDs, t-shirts, cheap posters and all the paraphernalia required for someone to express themselves through pop culture.

I made my way to the back and was confronted by a shop-keeper of some kind. He was a tall bloke with hair that was far longer on the sides and back than it was on top, almost like the strands were in a race with each other to escape the top of his scalp. Still he wore it well, with enough hairspray, hair dye and rattling, silver jewellery to distract from the less busy area.

'Can I help you, chief?' he called out in an accent that sounded like a Scotsman pretending to be cockney or possibly vice versa.

'Just looking,' I muttered, preferring to help myself. After all, it was only a small section of the store and I did have eyes that work.

'Patches, right?' he continued, pointing around the shop. 'Right up here on the display boards.'

'Thanks, I can see them,' I supplied the response to act as a full stop and even circled my right arm slightly, pointing at the four walls around me covered in patches, but still he continued

'Lots to choose from, we've got loads of band stuff up there covering all the Metals: Rock, Classic, Thrash, Speed, Death, Black, Prog. We've also got Punk, Hardcore, Goth, Industrial.'

I had very little clue about what he was talking about but I didn't like the idea of any of it. My eyes then caught a patch at the back of the store featuring the round circular RAF and/or Mod target I was after. 'This one please!' I asked as the Shopkeeper of Some Kind peered around to see what I was pointing at.

'Ah, so you're more of a mod, are ya? You like a bit of Quadrophenia, yeah? Great album, great film n' all.' He started to ramble on about The Who peaking, being too young to have gone to fights in Brighton and a salacious tangent that was surplus to requirements about 'young Leslie Ash' while I was itching for him to hurry up and put the damn sale through the register. During his earthy ramble I must have been too distracted to hear the door open and another customer enter, so I was slightly shaken and jumped back when I felt someone tapping me on the shoulder. For a split second I shuddered, fearing it would be Little Miss Yellow Eyes but then I heard the voice attached to the prodding and it was one I was more familiar with.

I spun around and saw Louise D'Souza's face beaming at me. 'Hi there,' she said. 'It's me, Louise. From college.'

'Erm, yes I know' I responded trying to curb an eye roll by offering a smile. The awkward seconds of silence that followed felt like an eternity.

'I'm not surprised to see you in here. I knew you liked good music,' she eventually said, 'like the other day with The

Beatles.'

I really didn't want the bloody Beatles, especially rumpity-bumpity brass band Sgt. Pepper Beatles being brought up in this den of denim screams and studded fists. Another period of silence lingered as The Shopkeeper of Some Kind handed me my change and the patch.

'Nice Mod patch,' Louise chirped, nosily looking at my purchase. 'I love Quadrophenia. Have you seen the film?'

'No,' I snapped. 'OK, I'll see you back at college.'

'I have!' blurted out The Shopkeeper of Some Kind leaning forward keen to gain Louise's attention. 'Great film, great album n' all.'

Lovely, I thought to myself. *The pair of them can talk about whatever the heck Quadrophenia is together and let me go on my way* but then I felt Louise grab my arm.

'Wait a minute, listen.'

She pointed to some musty brown speaker held high in the corner of the store, it was playing some yelping echoey goth silliness from the 1980's that had descended into just drums and someone making scratching noises on a guitar. She proudly declared something through an unintelligible vocalisation that sounded like 'Bow Hows'. I couldn't fathom what she was trying to express to me but with the Shopkeeper of Some Kind excitedly bobbing his head along with her I assumed it was the name of the band making the racket. I went to leave the shop and let the pair of them talk about The Bow Hows or whatever they were called but she followed me out of the shop and, despite quickening my pace, began to follow me.

'I'll walk back to college with you,' Louise perkily asserted, without asking my thoughts on the matter. 'I bet you were surprised to see me in a shop like that.'

I really wasn't, I hadn't even given it a single thought, but I threw a 'Suppose' into the mix if only to break another silence before it happened.

'Everyone thinks I'm a girlie-girl because of the way I look and all that but I'm actually a bit of a rocker and into sci-fi and horror and all that. Y'know, the sort of stuff you like.'

I'm in to none of that stuff. Absolutely none of it. She saw my Walkman equivalent on my hip and stuck her nose in again, 'What are you listening to today?'

I would have loved to have told her it was Bucks Fizz or Kylie or something else completely displeasing to her apparent sensibilities (and on any other given day it could have been either of those artists) but I told the truth. 'It's a sort of Britpop-indie tape someone made for me.'

I'm not sure if it was the concept of someone making me a tape or the genre of music but this news rattled her slightly and threw her cheeriness into a more uncertain approach. 'Oh right. Yeah, yeah, indie music's cool. I mean, I like stuff like Suede and Pulp and of course the Manics.'

A period of curious quiet followed as we walked through the high street, past the Great Stour River and towards the Library. There were several occasions where it felt as if Louise was about to say something but instead changed plans and decided to moisten her lips or chew her finger.

Eventually she spoke. 'I wish someone made compilation tapes for me. My friends aren't really into bands and stuff, y'know. And I don't have a boyfriend or anything.'

'Right,' I answered, a little bluntly but in a polite, sympathetic tone. Even though she'd forced a walk and a conversation on me, my desire to be rude to her had faded slightly. I got the feeling she was lonely and upset. I mean, I'm not a complete arsehole.

'I'm guessing you know I went out with Darren?' she asked with a sense of hesitation.

'Yeah, I heard.'

'It was only a date. I only went because my mum kept going on at me about how a pretty girl like me should have had a boyfriend by now. I asked Darren out because I knew he'd say yes. I never fancied him.'

'I wouldn't stress about it. I doubt in the grand scheme of things it's a big deal. I mean, it doesn't really matter much to me,' I offered with a shrug.

Louise's face brightened, 'It doesn't?'

'Nah, I mean I've never gone out with anyone so I don't know how it works but it's clear the pair of you are hardly the love of each other's lives or anything. I don't mean to be rude but there's zero chemistry between the two of you.'

I'm not sure what my words did but they brightened Louise's mood considerably. 'I feel I should apologise for my friends earlier. When they started on at you about the Wagon Wheel. I don't know why Darren does stuff like that; he doesn't just do it to you. He does it to everyone.'

'It's partly because he needs to feel we're all looking after him because his Mum's left and his Dad's too busy with his umpteen businesses and partly because he likes to say stupid stuff like *It's good to be D. King* with an accent like he's from Africa or something.'

'He's stopped that now,' Louise informed me. 'Sarah told him it sounded a bit racist and it all got a bit heated. He changed it for a week or so to It's good to be Daz King using a kinda German-Dutch voice but I think he got an inkling that some of the girls were secretly mocking him because of it on the little notes they make during lectures. I shudder to think what they write about me.'

'You seem too smart to be a sheep,' I sighed wearily, 'why do you hang around with that lot?'

'I suppose it's because at the end of the day you've got to have friends.'

'Do you, though?' I asked with a shrug.

Christine:

All I know is, I spent most of that day in a bin. Not like a bin full of rubbish and tissues or whatever, it was one of those big bins situated within the campus of Canterbury College. Y'know the kind they normally put salt in. I think it's salt or maybe it's grit, is grit the same as salt? I dunno, either way, it was one of those big bins they put the anti-snow stuff in. Luckily, it was empty. Whether that was because it was June and snow was unlikely or because the college hadn't been arsed to fill it in the first place is a debate for other people to indulge in. All I know is that I was in a bin, avoiding the sun, trying to find a way to make a fuller acquaintance with Mr Benjamin Cooper.

After being so rudely blown out by him the previous night, I decided to take a gander in his recycling bin to see if the paperwork he'd just cast aside could present me with some further clues about his identity and hallelujah, I got his full name and a good handful of information about his current academic pursuits.

Making my way out of his front garden and with plans to head home, I noticed Deano's car remained parked by the alleyway where I had consumed the life out of him. It was crazy to me that his missing body (hopefully now in small pieces, travelling around in the bellies of a thousand evil rats) hadn't created a wealth of concern and even more baffling that his car had been sitting there for days unlocked, without being chored. I figured if nobody else wanted to steal it, I might as well have it. Bates had previously introduced me to some scoundrels he knew in Canterbury who could get plates changed and give the vehicle a fresh coat of paint to throw the local police off the trail. A plan formed in my mind – nip back to Bates' place, grab his cold bag with his travel syringes full of blood, drive off to Canterbury through the night where I'd put the car in for a facelift and then hide out at the college with a view to finally getting to chat with Mr Benjamin Cooper.

The morning was spent hiding in the bin with my ear to the plastic; scanning, researching and trying to identify his voice whenever I could hear that pure lineage heartbeat approach. Daylight was, of course, going to be an issue – hence all the hiding in the bin. I knew I'd have to make a dash into the college building, shielding myself with my coat over my head. I'd then pull him into somewhere windowless, like the bogs, and declare our shared destiny. The syringes of blood borrowed from Bates' gaff would give me a little bit of a boost to survive and/or heal from the effects of the sun. I only had about ten of them in that cold bag but he had good connections and stored some pretty potent stuff.

It felt like I was in that damn bin for years, listening to all the inane wittering from passing students. Were my fellow teenagers and I this annoying back in the 80's? The thing about vampires never growing old isn't strictly true, you see. It's more a case of the world rolling on without you while your body and personality remains stuck. Eventually, I heard Benjamin approach and took the opportunity to launch myself out of the bin. Shaking off the sizzle of the sun, I tossed my big, black trench coat over my head and made a dash to follow him inside, but calamity struck when some nonsense kicked off about Wagon Wheels. I felt the lacerations begin to tear through my skin and had no other option but to leg it into the college before him and dive into the toilets. The wounds on my skin stung and within them creation's light burrowed through my blood and bones, attempting to snare each molecule and vigorously corrode them out of existence. Without hesitation, I quickly sucked down a full syringe of blood which began to ease my physical suffering, although in my head and my heart one of my deepest, darkest fears reared up like a savage beast and bared its teeth. An untameable thought on the loose once more; the concept of being stranded outside, banging on locked windows and doors, daylight as the hunter descending, the pain and sorrow of being slowly burned out of existence.

The heady mix of Bates' prime stock and my phobia merged, healing my body and spinning my mind until the thoughts arriving and leaving crashed into each other, leaving a fidgeting scattershot collage. My mind was consumed; too much information, too much to consider. The guilt of the past, the pleasure of the present and the fear of fate. The friction of their collisions rattled my mind until I fell into dreamless sleep.

When I eventually came to, I heard that familiar heartbeat. I pressed my ear against the cubicle wall to be absolutely sure it was Benjamin in the toilet beside me. I went to knock on the cubicle wall and try to strike up a conversation but the influence of the blood was still strong and I slipped, causing a crash and bang. I think this spooked him as he left pretty sharpish. By the time I got to my feet and out of the cubicle he was gone. Feeling nervy, I made a dash back outside while it was quiet and got back in the big bin with my skin covered in yet more burn marks. I knocked back a further syringe to ward off the effects and lay in wait for Benjamin to draw near.

Benjamin Cooper:

The walk back to college felt longer than usual with my every step weighed down by the conversational expectations of having Louise walking beside me. We eventually made our way into the grounds of the campus and I began to put my patch into the front pouch of my backpack.

'So where you going to stitch that patch?' Louise asked.

Several students from our class were eyeballing the situation. I wanted out of the moment as soon as possible and in my haste, answered without thought, 'I dunno, I can't sew. On the arm of my jacket I guess.'

'I can stitch it on for you, if you want,' she verbally presented her help in a casual tone but her grabbing hands towards my patch felt more like a demand. My mind raced to find a way out of this loose proposal but the stress of being observed by our peers conspired against my usual talents of social avoidance. She gestured at the denim jacket I was wearing and an excuse found it's way to my lips, 'Oh hang on I'll need this for the way home. What if it rains or if I need to keep the wind off me.'

Typically the sun was out, brighter than it had been all week and Louise started banging on about a heat wave approaching. In the end I had to concede and hand over the jacket. I hoped that would satisfy her need to intrude into my life but still she continued, 'So if you give me your number I can call you when it's done.'

Oh hell no, I don't hand anyone my telephone number; lord only knows what people might do with that sort of information. I mumbled an excuse about our phone line being down. She then offered to just 'drop it round' on Sunday – I wasn't having that either. I'd had enough uninvited guest trouble with old yellow eyes lurking about every evening so I suggested we meet up the following evening around 9.30 at The Ypres Tavern in Sittingbourne. As I knew it's a bit of a popular place for the Westlands lot I figured it'd be a busy spot on a Saturday night and I could grab my jacket and then, as politely as possible, lose her in the crowd and get back home to my bedroom.

While I was clearing all that up I saw Kelly standing by the grit bins near the block's second entrance. It was an unexpected appearance and it distracted me as I was waving off Louise who seemed confused about the arrangement and asked what date it'd be so I clarified, 'Yeah. Tomorrow night: 10th of June. 9:30. Don't be late.'

I walked over to see what my little sister was doing lurking around my humble sixth form college when she was clearly on the path to A Levels at her Grammar school, then University and into a lifetime of achievements I didn't even have the scope to dream of.

'Hey Kells,' I hollered as I approached, 'what are you doing here?'

I had spoken loudly and confidently, hoping to shake any questions she may have had about my interaction with Louise. It didn't work. 'Who was that you were talking to?'

I tried to shake it off quickly, acting ignorant without contemplating the bullshit cul-de-sac it would leave me in, 'Eh? Oh I dunno.'

'But you just gave her your jacket.' Kelly quizzed, quite fairly.

'Yeah, I mean, she's on my course. She's going to fix my jacket. Because it got ripped in class. I don't really know who she is,' I flapped as altered truths ran from my mouth like unruly children escaping a flustered child-minder. What I was struggling with in this interaction, I had no idea. I guess it's just hard to explain a situation you've found yourself in when it's not one you've had any hand in creating. I mean, is it my job to present Louise D'Souza to the world? Can't Kelly just go up to her and ask who she is? Why did I have to be the middleman in all of this?

'Oh right,' said Kelly in a confused, muted tone. 'Well, she's very pretty whoever she is. Are you going to ask her out?'

Everyone bangs on about how pretty Louise is but I've never got the appeal. I think everyone rates her looks because she's got a tan, a little perky nose and smiles a lot to show off her white, straight teeth. She just looks very presentable, like the daughter in a commercial, maybe that's the appeal but I've never felt moved by her apparent beauty.

'No,' I replied to Kelly's question, 'I'm not going to ask her out.' I mean I had arranged to meet up with her but that's hardly the same as asking her out.

Kelly drummed her fingers on the grit box. 'Fair enough. She'd probably turn you down anyhow. I was going to ask if you wanted to come to the Penny Theatre tonight? It's an Indie and Alternative night, I've got a date and Dad said I'm only allowed to go if you're there.'

I agreed to go. I'm not sure why – The Penny Theatre was a nice little venue but I always felt a bit like I was on the outside looking in when I tried to hang out there. Maybe it was the thought that the brave new world of Britpop might make it seem like a fresh playing field rather than trying to integrate myself into long established social circles. Also, why's my little sister got another date already? It had been less than a week since all that nonsense with Jon Miller and the rumours that followed that. I glanced over at my class-mates pointing and giggling at Kelly and I began to worry about who exactly she was going on a date with that evening and what he may have heard about her.

Christine:

I had the best intentions. My plan was to hide in the bin, rationing the syringes until night fell, then I'd go pick up my newly reborn car and drive home. However, the lunch hour dragged on and I found my naughty fingers teasingly begin to roll a syringe back and forth in the cool bag, which eventually rolled into my palm. I figured a little extra scarlet at lunch wouldn't hurt but then one led to another and then another. My mind began to swim through the darkness of the bin, exploring its depths and considering if it extended beyond the construct of the bin. Voices that sounded both familiar and new began to penetrate from outside and for a while, a rhythmic beat pattered overhead and patches of deep mauve and blue blossomed and folded as my eyelids opened and closed. I finally nodded off until I was woken by a less artistically stimulating knocking sound. This wasn't the pitter-patter of fingers' tapping; this was a threatening fist ratta-tat-tatting.

The bin's lid was flung open and instinctively I cowered, fearing a flood of sunshine. Luckily, it was pitch black apart from the light from two torches. Holding the torches were two boxy looking security guards with faces defined by looks of shock and horror.

'Careful, Jonesy,' said the guard on the left, 'I think she's one of *them*.'

One of them? I panicked slightly, fearing that-they might be vampire hunters.

Jonesy cast his light around the inside of the bin and barked, 'what's all this then? Have you been doing needle drugs?'

Needle drugs? What? I stifled a chuckle, cleared my throat, brushed some of the now-empty plastic syringes off of my lap and replied, 'Yes. I have been doing needle drugs. Nothing I love more than my daily dose of needle drugs.'

'You a student here?' Jonesy asked, peering deep into my pinpoint pupils.

'Absolutely,' I beamed before adopting a more apologetic tone. 'I'm doing an arts diploma. My work is extremely personal and today it was all getting a bit intense so I hopped in here for some needle drugs to take the edge off.'

'Well, the college is closed now. I suggest you get out of here before I report you,' Jonesy swept the light from his torch like a broom towards the direction he wanted me to go.

I could have murdered the pair of them and had a cheeky night on campus. My mission to secure the patronage of Benjamin Cooper had failed again and I could have done with a bit of rule-breaking, establishment-shaking mischief to help cheer my spirits. I was wise enough by now though to know that I'd already drunk far too much blood that day and would be likely to make mistakes and leave evidence. I certainly wouldn't be of sound body and mind to drive home in my spruced up car. So I hopped out of the bin and left Jonesy and his mate to their flashlights. I wondered and worried about the Benjamin Cooper situation. Turning up at his home had been unsuccessful, turning up at his college had been unsuccessful – that's two approaches that hadn't worked. Some might say, 'third time lucky' but I couldn't conceive when and where that third time might occur.

CHAPTER 5

Happenstance = (How to escape the straitjacket of constraint)

Testimony: Christine and Benjamin Cooper regarding the evening up to 23:18 on the 9th June 1995 and the 49 minutes that followed

Benjamin Cooper:

Kelly and I loitered around the centre of Canterbury for a good couple of hours before making our way to Northgate and arguably the city's most notable live music venue, The Penny Theatre. It wasn't the largest of places but it seemed to attract all of the country's biggest tribute acts and budding young alternative types putting their first tentative step on the bottom rung of the showbiz ladder.

On the way in, Kelly urged me to 'be nice' to her date, which immediately made me want to be anything but. She told me she'd liked him for ages but he'd been in a long-term relationship that had just hit the rocks so now he was free and single. I pondered how she knew all these guys and how she'd been in a position to like someone for ages – she was only sixteen and he'd been in a long term relationship, just how old was this bloke going to be? Alarm bells were ringing and upon entering the venue, the din was proven justified as I saw my fresh-out-of-fifth-form little sister head straight over to some fully grown six foot man with a sandy little beard and a ponytail, wearing DM's on his feet and a blazer on his broad-shouldered Alice In Chains t-shirt covered torso. He over-shook my hand and told me his name but my mind just dubbed the phrase Grunge Tosser over the top of it. I knew it'd be only a matter of minutes before he did something to reveal how shallow his 'deep', artistic leanings were and after a bit of a nod along to the band playing in the adjoining room's stage area he pulled out a leather-bound notebook. Kelly failed to observe the gesture so he made a big deal of thumbing through the pages and readjusting the ribbon bookmark attached to its spine.

'Sorry, one moment, I'm just making sure I don't lose my place.' He continued to fumble with his book, leaving a space for Kelly to ask the question he was desperate for her to ask. She remained oblivious.

'Started on some lyrics on the way down here that I might want to pick up on later,' he made squinty but stern eye contact with me, as if he supposed we were in some kind of tortured artist, alpha-dog power play. I felt like holding my hands up there and then, declaring my lack of interest in such nonsense, setting his mind and ego at rest whilst rescuing my reputation from the world of photocopied fliers and gigs where there are more people on the stage than there are in the audience.

Kelly's interest was piqued and she took the bait, 'Ooh, lyrics! I didn't know you were in a band.'

'At the moment it's just me and Gavin jamming out a few ideas,' Grunge Tosser proudly declared, as if we knew who the fuck Gavin was. 'The lyrics I'm working on here are for a potential song called 'Locust'. It's quite free-form at the moment, very Burrows. My current reading habit is to flick through The Naked Lunch on the bus and make the text part of the journey; it's my companion, the driver, the very road itself...'

On and on he went. It seemed he was more interested in trying to bore my sister to death than getting her knickers off so I left them to it and decided to investigate the bands playing in the other room. The first band were an absolute state. They were pretty old – definitely in their thirties, and the singer was familiar to me. I'd see him walking around Canterbury with his eyeliner leaking into his crow's feet and the purple hair dye doing more to stain his scalp than the thinning hair sprouting out of it. Unlike the Shopkeeper of Some Sort at the Indoor Market, the Thirty Something Frontman didn't seem to own his look. He looked ill at ease with his sartorial choice, backed into a stylistic corner, sad that the role he'd defined for himself had passed its sell by date. I realised at that moment that growing old with a style is a tight rope act – I'd have to tread carefully with my jacket patches or I'd end up like that poor old fucker on the stage, trying to twist his old stolen Bowie shapes into something that could compete with the younger guns on the scene but ultimately ending up looking and sounding like a pantomime dame doing a Suede pisstake. Christ, it didn't seem fair, I'm already eighteen – a legal adult and I don't feel like I've lived a young man's life yet. Maybe I could work out how to avoid growing old and Peter Pan my life away. More realistically, perhaps I need to face the stark reality of just how short human life is and start enjoying these final teenage days rather than sulking them away.

Christine:

Sobering up after a long day on the syringes is a miserable experience. Especially having missed out on my eight hours of day-sleep while stalking a possible patron who was incredibly, annoyingly evasive. My head was nagging me to indulge in some delicious disobedience and my heart was yearning to have someone else's blood pump through it. I was caught between a rock and a hard place; drain some fool and continue the buzz or go through hours of aching, dizzying discomfort until I was sober enough to drive home and get some rest. I decided the best approach was to taper the withdrawal by hiding out behind bushes in the Dane John park, scout out a victim, get them alone, take just enough of the scarlet stuff to take the edge off and then pick up the wheels from Bates' mates and take it slow and steady westwards on the A2 until I reached home.

The problem was that it was initially hard to find someone who really deserved draining; everyone was just too humble or attractive or (in the handful of people that bumped into me while I was lurking) just too damn polite to murder. Where's another Deano when I need one, eh?

The time was just shy of 21:15 and the sun hadn't quite set, but was dim enough, buried within a cloudy sky, for my skin to only feel slightly prickly when I couldn't keep to the shadows. I was about to give up on pursuing a feed when I heard a loutish voice drowning out the sound of a frightened heartbeat. I spun my head around and saw a short, sweaty man in his early twenties intimidating and berating his even shorter, not-at-all sweaty girlfriend who looked well into her late teens. She was a cute-as-a-button brunette and, despite our age difference, I would have loved to have swung in there like an old-timey matinee hero and rescued her from this brute but I learnt a long time ago that my actions are rarely viewed as heroic and often quite rightly so. Also, I gave up on chasing after straight girls a long time ago, even the curious ones. Window shopping is always better than buyer's regret; there's always so much drama after the deed, too much chat I don't want to hear, too many words in letters I don't want to read, too much gossip I don't want to be part of, none of it leading anywhere useful – 'What happened between us happened and I like you but not in *that* way.' Really luv? Too late, you came. And all that was before I became *of the night*; I'd hate to throw my fangs into that mix. These days I'm mostly celibate. Mostly.

The Short, Sweaty, Shouty Man continued to holler at his better half. Blaming her for his shortcomings, accusing her of being paranoid, demanding money from her for lord knows what.

I stood static against a bush with my fingers crossed that he'd take one more little step forward over the moral line so I knew for sure he was an utter bastard that the world would be better off without.

'And let me tell you, Stacy, if you aint got that hundred quid for me tomorrow, you'll be in for it. It'll be your fault what happens, believe,' he barked while theatrically clenching his fist to make an alarming point. Whoomp! There it is!

With his cards now marked, I observed from a distance, trying to plan how I could quickly, cleanly and without witnesses burst one of his veins and get myself a cheeky little stiffener. I then saw a black shape flicker and flap above me, the image appearing larger as it descended down towards me. What the fuck was Igor doing in Canterbury?

We exchanged pleasantries; it turned out he had just come from a crazy night out at the Annual General Meeting of Kentish Bats, held in the belfry of the Cathedral. I, in turn, mocked my familiar about his species' rather naff sense of humour and he said I was just jealous because I don't get invited to anything these days. He was probably right. Either way I told him to keep track of the short, sweaty man and report back as I followed from a distance in the shadows.

We eventually tracked him to the alley behind the London-bound platform at Canterbury East train station. I guess he was either about to deal drugs or was hoping to hop over the railings and get on board a train without a ticket, so basically a criminal, right? No guilt required. I'm actually freeing up police resources by ending him. We pulled an old favourite double-combo on him; Igor emerged from a dark corner ahead of our prey and flapped about in his face while I snuck up behind him and chomped down hard and fast. We timed it perfectly with the rattle and chug of a freight train speeding through which buried his one shrill scream and gave me enough cover to drag his corpse through the alley and into the overgrown sidings beside the track.

Benjamin Cooper:

After a frankly abysmal start, my evening at the Penny Theatre had begun to pick up. The Thirty Something Front-man's band had finally finished their set (where they raided Bowie's box of tricks but forgot to nick any of his melody or style). As they packed up, the DJ span some great tunes. I recognised a few of them from Kelly's tape. By the time the next band hit the stage, I found myself three pints in. Slimfit were a significant improvement over the previous lot. They were younger, faster and to be honest, drew a more attractive audience. In particular, I managed to find myself in a casual exchange of smiles and glances with a pair of girls. While they were certainly attractive enough, I wasn't entirely sure whether I proper fancied them or was simply drawn to the attention. I think their feelings about me were equally muddled but for whatever reason we found some form of temporary salvation in sending segments of clipped conversation to each other. With our words fighting their way through the sound of the band to get there, I failed to hear most of it but nodded along to the muffled declarations. I think they told me their names but they were amongst the sounds that became lost in the noise and it felt too futile to ask them to repeat them during the band and too rude afterwards. Between songs I discovered they knew the band from Worcester but were merely acquaintances and had only come to Canterbury because their friend wanted to come to track an ex-boyfriend who'd moved here. After Slimfit had finished, the three of us found ourselves nodding along to some Stereolab song or other and talk turned to the music of the Human League. Like a two-way relay they took it in turns to head to the bar offering to buy me drinks each time. Soon I was returning the favour and found myself six or seven pints deep quickly, with important concerns such as making it back to the station in time for the final train home or saving my sister from Grunge Tosser lost to the fog of festivities surrounding me.

I wondered where this situation with the two girls was going. Both seemed keen on my company but neither of them pulled forward from the idling lanes of mild flirtation and giggling into something that would indicate a definite interest in me. Would I have to make a move on one of them, if so which one? Both of them? Or even neither of them? I mean did I even *really* want to make a move on either of them? As it is I'm not much of a make-a-move kinda guy and besides anything this might have been just a friendship thing. Perhaps that's all that this truly was; one wild, stolen night of platonic friendship before I went back to Sittingbourne and they went back to Worcester and we never saw each other again. Who knows what this was but it felt nice. When you've been sad for such a long, long time it becomes the only way you know how to feel. It becomes normal, it becomes all there is to such a degree that you stop even identifying it as sadness. It's only when something good pushes that feeling out, you realise just how you've lost touch with yourself and how far you've drifted. A long lost feeling swells in your heart and for a few blessed seconds you remember what happy feels like.

Naturally such contentment rarely lasts and, as such, I found Kelly tapping me on the shoulder with two pieces of disconcerting information that brought my freewheeling evening at the Penny Theatre to a screeching halt. The first was that she was going to share a taxi home with Grunge Tosser and his friends later that night but there wouldn't be room for me. The second was that it was coming up to eleven o'clock so if I wanted to get the last train home I'd better make a move, pronto.

There was no time to scream and panic; no time to fret over my sister's wild deviation from my Dad's plans that I chaperone the evening. I bolted straight out of the Penny Theatre and fled through the city as the summer sky chilled and drizzle began to flick my cheeks. Like a Converse-shoed Cinderella, I ran and ran and then ran some more, my chest sore from air and my feet feeling worn. Through Westgate, past the Cathedral in all its evening splendour, down a side road to the high street and past the clock tower sternly alerting me that the time was 23:04. Just fourteen minutes remained until the last train departed and I'd be stuck sleeping rough until I could catch the milk train early the following morning.

I increased my pace and made good time as I darted along the city wall above the Dane John Park and over the bridge to the station. Bursting through the doors, I observed the big yellow digits on the rectangular clock read a relief-inducing time of 23:15 – plenty of time to briskly walk through the tunnel connecting the two platforms and prepare for my homeward journey. But then a speaker crackled and a voice dryly pushed into my ears, 'We regret to announce that the 23:18 train from Canterbury East to London Victoria has been cancelled due to an incident on the line.' Seriously, someone gimme a break already, though incident on the line? Sounds like some poor sod's body hit a train. I can't imagine what must have happened for someone to end up like that.

Christine:

Well I had to get rid of the body somehow. Our victim may have been short (and sweaty) but he was also surprisingly heavy and hard to carry. Or maybe I was just too tired and dizzy from all the peaks and dives of the blood binges and withdrawals. Either way, I wanted rid of his chewed-on torso and with the lights of an oncoming train approaching I saw my opportunity. Selfish? Perhaps, but ultimately it got me where I needed to be.

Benjamin Cooper:

Naturally with the last train on a Friday night cancelled, all of the taxis in the area were quickly booked up and a long, futile quest for transport home threatened to burst the bubble of my post-Penny Theatre glow. Having Kelly's tape in my wannabe-Walkman helped but I knew it's recharge-able batteries were unlikely to last much longer and the sunny skies of the daytime were now a bruised rich purple which darkened by the minute, strangling traces of starlight to make way for another night of violent storms. I began to feel the drizzle turn to rain and lamented my situation, but suddenly I saw a taxi of some sort coming towards me. I stuck my arm out and to my initial joy it began to slow, offering salvation.

Christine:

I couldn't believe my eyes when I caught Mr Benjamin Cooper in my headlights. I wondered what he was doing waving his pasty arms about but it turned out he thought my car (well, the car I'd stolen from Deano,) was a taxi. This must have been down to the chequered wrap Bates' mates had placed across the bonnet, roof and boot. I thought it had given the car a sort of retro cool New Wavey, Cheap Tricky vibe but it seems it could also, apparently, double up as a minicab.

I've rarely seen a face drop from elation to deflation as fast as I did when I rolled down the passenger side window and offered, 'fancy a lift?'

He wasn't keen and, admittedly, my initial pitch was a little too eager. I decided it was time to keep it as simple as possible, 'Look. I'm a vampire, you're a vampire. We should vampire together.'

Benjamin Cooper:

When the window rolled down and I saw my stalker sitting there with a cat-that-got-the-cream grin on her face, I'm pretty sure I told her to 'Fuck off!' and turned away. She crawled the car along the kerb beside me, begging me to listen. I wondered just why she was so interested in me, what the deal was. Was she a long lost sister? Or a maverick goth solicitor chasing me down to discuss a substantial inheritance from some distant aunt? I feared for a moment that she might be the only person I'd ever had sex with presenting me with a baby but the young lady in question looked completely different. Eventually, after introducing herself, my stalker – apparently named Christine – revealed that she, like me, was a vampire. She moaned about using the term as she felt it was derogatory to our kind but said it was the easiest way to break the news. I protested, I told her that it was bollocks, that she was just a goth searching for some kind of persona to hide behind and I was just some small town loser cursed with pale skin and British teeth.

She argued that a non-blood sucker would surely be freaking out about a creature with yellow tinted eyes and fangs turning up at their house night after night. She reasoned that as I saw her as little more than a nuisance it must be because I knew deep in my heart that we were both made of similar stock. Standing in the rain with nowhere to stay and no way of getting home, I gave up arguing and got in the car.

Christine:

In the end I-explained that he was *of lineage–* one of the most powerful beings in Kent – and he could and should have all the sex and power he could dream of. That got him in the car, all right.

We drove along the A2, back to Sittingbourne, listening to the latest Siouxsie album. Our heads bobbing along to the beat broke some of the ice between us and the beginnings of a bond presented itself.

We shared a little small talk. He bitched about some grunge tosser his sister had copped off with and we had fun laughing at the lyrics of Pearl Jam's Jeremy. My chest was full of light and laughter the whole journey home. It was a relief that he wasn't as uptight as our initial meetings suggested – the promise of a successful working relationship bloomed. The night's sky cradled the road ahead of us, and the storm within it began to shrug itself away. It felt like a birthday and Christmas coming at me all at once.

Benjamin Cooper:

It turned out that Christine was actually a bit of a laugh. Maybe I'd been too quick to dismiss her. I wasn't convinced about all her vampire talk; I mean, for every believable point she made there'd be some bollocks about being able to talk to bats or something. Either way, it was a very pleasant journey and as we drove through Faversham the skies cleared, leaving a feast of stars shining sharply in a clear, navy blue sky. One in particular caught my eye and I kept my gaze upon it all the way home. The light from a dead sun reaching out from the past to become part of the present. I was honoured to carry its sparkle home, occasionally closing my eyes to allow its light to dance about in new colours and shapes in the darkness behind my eyelids. Eventually we reached Sittingbourne and Christine dropped me off at the top of Keswick Avenue. She wanted to meet up again soon and tell me more about being a vampire. I figured that as I already had to meet Louise there to get my jacket back, I might as well invite Christine along to the Ypres Tavern too. Maybe one would scare the other off and I'd be down to having just the one stalker in my life.

It had been an odd evening but in the best sort of way. There were strange new acquaintances to be considered and a few long-forgotten feelings that had returned. I thought back to the two young ladies I'd met at the Penny Theatre that night. I knew now for sure that I didn't really want them in any kind of romantic or carnal manner but there was that moment of happiness I experienced being around them. I dwelled on that joy and let it burn brightly once more in my stomach as goose bumps formed on my arms. I threw on my own personal Human League Best Of tape and collapsed onto my bed. I kept my window open wide that night. I wanted to keep this intriguing night with me as I slept and let the midnight hour breeze flow into my room and wrap itself around me like a blanket taking me through the night until the morning came.

CHAPTER 6

THE STARS THAT PLEASE THE NIGHT

Testimony: Christine and Benjamin Cooper regarding the alcopop drenched evening of the 10th of June 1995

Benjamin Cooper:

Saturday had been a waste of a day. Between nursing my hangover from the night before and dwelling on the arrangement to meet both of my stalkers at the Ypres Tavern later that evening, I didn't really have the spirit to get much done. I found myself wondering what the benefits of turning up tonight would be. Firstly, there was Louise D'Souza. She seemed lonely and keen to break away from Darren King's college clique so I knew providing her some alternative company was a nice thing to do but, being honest, just wanted my jacket back. Then there was Christine apparently-no-surname and apparently-a-vampire. Looking at my reflection in the bedroom mirror, I ran my fingers over my fangs – they were certainly sharp and unusual. Thinking about it, I always thought vampires weren't supposed to have reflections yet there it was in the mirror, my washed out ugly mug staring back at me. It was

79

one of my many queries I'd have to confront Christine with. I felt increasingly conflicted by her declaration, it sounded mad to say it out loud but it would certainly explain a lot; the pale skin, the jagged teeth, the widow's peak hidden via a centre parting and my general dislike of garlic bread. She was keen for us to 'vampire together'. I had no idea what she meant by that. Did she mean just sitting about in dark frilly clothes listening to dreadful music, or literally going about killing people and drinking their blood? The question churned in my stomach. It shocked me that I took greater discomfort from the former option than the latter.

Christine:

It was around 9 o'clock in the evening when I burst majestically through the pub door, away from the dust in the breeze and the litter of the street outside and into the beermat and ashtray-decorated world of the Ypres Tavern. It was an establishment I was very familiar with as it had not only borne witness to many of my own lamentable underage drinking misadventures in the early 1980s but had recently become my local since staying at Bates' flat.

It wasn't the most glamorous of places, but it was reasonably priced and had a jukebox that was as eclectic as the clientele. Most of the music on there was the usual fare, y'know – a bit of Queen here, a bit of Meatloaf there, some Celine Dion for the homely types, a couple of Now! comps for the tyre kickers but there was also a small but significant scattering of slightly more left-field stuff like The Cure, early B-52s and niche alternative compilations with the likes of Jellyfish on them. The U-shaped layout of the pub seemed almost geared to cater for this with the side off to the left being mainly favoured by the rockers, goths and indie kids and the earthier types favouring the right-hand side, with the pool tables and easy access to the gents. It always felt a bit of a gamble going in there as you could never be sure what kind of crowd would have dominance. I made the mistake of going in a couple of nights ago where it was full of scowls, thick necks and tattoos taking part in a couples darts competition. They didn't take to my ways at all and I kept my fangs hidden lest I get staked with a broken pool cue or something. Luckily I heard the twangs and warblings of Rock Lobster on the way in, which usually indicated that the freak kids had control of the jukebox for the night.

I saw Benjamin Cooper sitting neither with the kids on the left nor sharing his East Sittingbourne roots with the bellowing geezers and birds on the right. Instead, he sat slap-bang in the middle, alone at a table by the door.

Benjamin Cooper:

Christine came clumsily bustling through the door in a frankly ridiculous manner. She was wearing a dark table-cloth like a poncho with a huge floppy black sun hat on her head, looking like Speedy Gonzales at a funeral or something. I squirmed a little at the sight of her, inwardly terrified about how the locals would take to such a figure.

Christine:

It was at this stage I discovered one of Benjamin Cooper's lesser attributes; his lack of empathy for my struggles with sunlight. It's pretty typical for those *of lineage* not to grasp how lucky they are and show little to no empathy for us lot. So yeah, what with it being the middle of June and during a heat wave no less, I had no option other than to cover myself up as I strolled through an evening determined to take its sweet time to merge with the night.

Benjamin Cooper:

We exchanged a few pleasantries and almost immediately she went straight to vampire chat. I panicked and urged her to ssh-it-up but she just grinned. She reckoned that there was a spell over the pub that allowed vampires and such-like to talk about the occult and black magic. Apparently, to anyone who wasn't *of the night* or *of lineage* it would just sound like general chitchat. I thought that it was almost as ridiculous as her claims about being able to talk to a bat but when she proved her point bellowing, 'I'm Christine the Vampire, back in Sittingbourne and I'm here to drain all your cunting daughters' without even a single, 'You wot?' thrown in our direction I had no option but to begrudgingly accept the 'magic spell on the pub' theory.

Christine:

The Conversational Cloak spell? Yeah, it was Bates' doing. When my old master fled town, Bates brought in a Warlock to make things a bit easier for my kind. Nothing too heavy, just a cheeky little incantation at the Ypres that makes it sound, to blood bag normies, that we're talking about whatever they presume our type talk about. So they hear us nattering on about stuff like Red Dwarf or Warhammer 40K if we mention anything about the supernatural night-time world.

The Warlock in question was supposed to do all the pubs in the area but the poor fucker chose The George in the high street next. His purple shirt adorned with gold leaf moons and his ratty ponytail didn't exactly endear him to a group of sports casual-wearing, Bulldog Breed louts drinking in there, who literally kicked him out of the pub singing, 'You can stick your bell and candle up your arse' to the tune of 'She'll Be Coming 'Round the Mountain When She Comes.'

I asked Benjamin to accompany me to the jukebox and pick out some tunes. I figured it would be a way to break the ice and get to know each other a little better. I find I can gather more about someone's character during a couple of minutes flicking through the yellow and white index cards housed in a jukebox than from an evening of small talk and bullshit about their day-to-day dullness. Sadly, the process of choosing five mutually agreeable songs for a quid wasn't the walk in the park I was hoping it'd be. To see him turn his nose up at the likes of Sisters of Mercy and The Jesus and Mary Chain but eagerly push for bloody Ace of Base really made me doubt my decision to seek him out as my new Blood Lord. Things perked up when we reached The Cure but when he started moaning that the peerless Staring at the Sea compilation didn't have Friday I'm in Love on it I knew better than to waste a declaration of love for Charlotte Sometimes on him.

Benjamin Cooper:

We tried to share a round on the jukebox but it was tricky, as she'd just keep shooting down every suggestion I had, sometimes with a shake of the head and sometimes with a scowl. Her proposed song choices weren't any better. I'm sorry but I don't know what 'Some Candy Talking' is and I'm not prepared to waste 20p finding out.

Despite our differing tastes, there was a little Venn Diagram overlap in the dry ice roaming realms of fist pumping power ballads and bombastic pop metal. As the auto-selected track that had been playing began to fade, signalling our first selection was on the way (with a tasty line-up of Heart, Bonnie Tyler, Freiheit and Alice Cooper to follow) Christine offered to go to the bar for drinks while I went back to save our table and await Louise's arrival.

Christine:

So there I was at the bar about to order us some drinks when the door to the pub swung open like the golden gates of heaven itself and there, soundtracked by the opening of Eloise by The Damned no less, stood its archangel. Framed by the heat and dust escaping the summer-stung paving slabs from the street outside, stood the most beautiful human I had ever seen. She looked like a vision in a dream. Like a work of art carved from stardust and a solar storm. Like a blonde Beth Brennan from Neighbours. And she was of the Goth persuasion – dressed in a Bauhaus t-shirt with the sleeves cut off, a wrist full of bracelets rattling rhythmically as she crossed the threshold. Admittedly, the lace choker and dark lipstick were maybe a little too try-hard, but it was pulse-risingly unbelievable to see such an exquisite creature in a place like this. I didn't know where to look – I tried to look away but my eyes were drawn like paper clips to a magnet. I bit at my lips to stop an over-eager smile. Everything about her lit my fuses – her posture, the way she ran her fingers through her hair like a comb as she surveyed the pub, even the great big, dorky River Island shopping bag she had with her was kinda hot, what with it being held in her sure-to-be soft hand.

Eventually, her eyes fell on Benjamin Cooper and I realised that she must be the girl he was meeting here tonight. I should have felt jealousy and envy and all those silly human emotions but I just felt glad that I'd be spending the evening with her in any capacity. I didn't want to cheapen a moment like this with something as tacky as pursuit. A beauty as rare as this must be nurtured explored and understood before seduction.

Benjamin Cooper:

While Christine was off getting the drinks, Louise turned up with my jacket. She'd done a good job stitching on the mod target patch and I thanked her accordingly. She then pulled up a chair and made herself comfortable before being invited, which I thought was a bit presumptuous.

'I'm glad you asked me out for drinks tonight,' Louise beamed.

'Well, I wanted my jacket back,' I answered truthfully, though Louise seemed to think I was joking.

Louise continued, 'You're much funnier than a lot of people know. I've wanted to get to know you better for a while now but at college you're always so distant whenever anyone tries to talk to you.'

Seemed a bit rich of her to be having a pop at my ways. I wouldn't dream of parking myself at her table and start banging on about any of her shortcomings. 'I don't mean to come off rude or anything,' I shrugged, ' I mean, I'm only distant with people I don't care about.'

'And look here you are, talking to me,' Louise smiled and leaned forward across the table. I think she was trying to reach my hands and hold them or something. Instincts took over and I recoiled back in my seat, drawing my hands up close to my chest. An awkwardness hung in the air as neither Louise or I knew what to say or do next.

Thankfully Christine arrived looking pleased as punch and carrying drinks, though not the drink I ordered.

'What's that?' I asked as she slid a small misty green bottle towards me.

'Alcoholic lemonade!' she declared, proudly. 'Just like you asked for.'

'I asked for a Fosters with a lemonade top!'

'Oh, like a shandy? Sorry I thought you meant like an alcopop thing and the barmaid recommended these.'

I looked at the label before taking a gulp – it read 'Two Dogs' and reiterated the brand with a picture of two mutts. It was a little earthy and a tad bitter but kinda zingy and fresh. One mouthful wasn't enough and I soon found myself taking another. Each sip was increasingly moreish; I should have known there and then that the evening would get messy.

Christine:

After a couple of cumbersome prompts, Benjamin Cooper eventually introduced me by name to his friend Louise D'Souza. Her name buried itself into sighs and longings that would have to wait for another day as I could sense from the look on her face that my presence at the table was a source of great displeasure.

'I didn't know that anyone else would be joining us tonight,' she stated, though threw it at the both us in quite an accusatory way, clearly looking for an answer. I wondered if she thought her and B.C. were on a date, and then I wondered if they *were* on a date? He was an oddly clueless boy in many regards. I wouldn't put it past him, inviting a vampire along on a date as a plus one for the benefit of freeing up an evening later in the week. Either way I didn't want her to get pissy about me being there and bolt out of the door never to be seen again so I decided to set things right.

'Oh, don't worry about me. I'm not here to intrude; just a friend passing through... more of a family member really, like a cousin, a distant cousin. It's a blood thing. I'm not his girlfriend or anything, so if you are worried about that – don't be.' Inexplicably, a panic took hold and my brain began churning out a ramble of half-truths and, before I could apply the brakes, a yearning declaration. 'If anything you'd be more my type because I'm, y'know, like mega queer. And stuff.'

While the silence that followed was incredibly awkward it was nothing compared to what happened as the evening progressed.

Benjamin Cooper:

One of the reasons I distance myself from people is that they seem to enjoy generating drama completely out of the blue. All I'd wanted out of the evening was to have a couple of pints of lager, get my jacket back and be persuaded that I was an actual vampire. And yet here I was drinking alcopops, having my jacket being held hostage by a girl who's gone from being over-keen to hostile in less than a minute and a vampire coming out of the closet.

I tried to clear the air by setting things straight. I went along with the spiel that Christine was just a distant relation who was back in town and wanted to meet up with me. I thanked Louise for sewing the patch on my jacket and said I was glad to be getting to know her better as a friend and then after quaffing the last mouthful of my bottle of Two Dogs, I offered everyone a round at the bar. Which seemed more than fair.

Christine:

With Benjamin Cooper off at the bar, I took the opportunity to wangle my way into Louise's world. Benjamin's declaration that he wished to know her better as a friend had clearly hurt her feelings and upon soft interrogation, she revealed that she had thought it was a date and that he had seemingly confirmed as much. I think this miscommunication had occurred while I was hiding in the college salt bin and I cursed myself for not gathering a true account at the time. Benjamin returned with drinks; worryingly, he'd bought himself an extra bottle of Two Dogs because in his own, slightly slurred words they 'drink so easily'. Then something caught my eye that alarmed me greatly and I knew I'd have to ease back on the drink in order to play the evening just right.

Benjamin Cooper:

Maybe it was the alcohol helping the situation but once that initial awkwardness had faded, the three of us began to have a rather enjoyable night. It turned out that, despite our differences, we did share a certain sarcastic and self-deprecating sense of humour and could quite happily sing-along to the jukebox if the right song popped up. It was during this happy haze that I glanced up towards the bar and saw some sparkling eyes staring back at me. It was hard to gauge whether they were blue or green as their appearance was changeable depending on how the light caught them. If I squinted, I could see the owner of these eyes in full, dressed in a red and black plaid dress and Converse baseball boots. She looked a little shorter and younger than me, but not by much. She stood leaning against the bar; fidgeting with a strand of her mid-length blonde hair that refused to remain tucked behind the ear she kept placing it behind. Before I had the opportunity to lose my nerve and break eye contact she began to send me casual smiles across the room.

Christine:

I knew the minute I saw that girl walk into the pub that trouble was brewing. I couldn't be one hundred percent sure but I had a strong feeling about what type of girl she was and, if correct, it's the last thing I needed interfering with my blood-drinking plans with young Benjamin. And there the pair of them were, instantly making goo-goo eyes at each other from afar. Vile. I'd have to play this just right if I wanted to get rid of her and keep him.

I went off to the toilet to pee some of the booze away and consider my next move. On the way there a bit of conversation caught my ear, 'Oi Jon! Jon! You seen Deano around?'

I slid over to the shadows to observe. A rabble of lads were huddled on the right-hand side of the bar, holding court and talking shop.

'Nah mate,' replied the tallest and rattiest looking member of the cluster, 'haven't seen Deano all week. He was supposed to be coming with me to Sheppey tonight, to do a little business. To be honest, I could do with a bit of backup if you fancy some cash in hand.'

It transpired that they were looking to head to the breaker's yard on the Isle of Sheppey to take part in something illicit. Deano's disappearance didn't seem to bother them in the slightest. I wondered if they were too inconsiderate to care or too careless to consider it.

I took myself off to the bogs and thought about my own evening's tactics. Getting Benjamin away from boning and into blood-drinking was of paramount importance tonight. He was clearly the kind of boy who's hopeless with the opposite sex so all I had to do is propose we move on elsewhere and get him away from Princess Plaid before she ruined everything but, to my surprise and dismay, I came back from the toilets to find her already at our table, sitting in my chair, laughing and flirting away with him.

Benjamin:

'Excuse me,' the girl at the bar called out as she approached, 'but you look really cool, can me and my friend join you?'

You look really cool? I thought that was an odd thing to say. I mean, it's a bit of a strange introduction and cool isn't really an adjective I'd use to describe any aspect of my life. She shrugged as if she'd heard my thoughts, 'There's not many cool people in Sittingbourne so we have to stick together, right?'

'I guess.' I wasn't sure how to answer. Luckily she broke the silence immediately with an introduction.

'I'm Eliza and this is Kate,' she said, ushering her friend away from a group of lads by the nearest jukebox. Kate looked like a junior version of the singer from the band Powder, a little detached in demeanour with dark hair held in place with daisy hair clips. Kate seemed a lot less interested in my supposed coolness but obliged her friend.

I got a little lost assessing the situation, leaving a pocket of quiet that may have been perceived as rude but Eliza chuckled, 'And then you're supposed to tell me your name...'

'Oh, my name is Benjamin.' I felt weird to leave it there so I continued, 'Benjamin Cooper.'

Eliza found this amusing. 'Why do you say your name like you're James Bond or something?' I pondered for a moment whether James Bond isn't the suave alpha dog he's presented as and introduces himself like that to mask his own social failings. This train of thought produced another gap in the conversation for Eliza to step in and save.

'And what about your *friends*?' she asked, pointing at Louise and throwing a thumb towards Christine's poncho and hat hanging on the chair. She used the word 'friends' in the same way Louise had earlier, perhaps fishing for relationship statuses rather than details about the people themselves.

'I'm Louise, and Christine, who had been sitting in the chair you've just taken, has just gone to the toilet.'

There was an assertive, almost territorial tone in Louise's voice, which I'd never encountered before. The stuff about the chair was served with a generous extra order of salt. Considering how standoffish she'd been to Christine when they'd first met less than an hour earlier, it was amusing how Louise was getting protective over my vampire friend's chair since she had rebranded herself as my lesbian cousin.

'I think you live near me, right?' Louise continued like a boxer letting out a flurry of lefts and rights. 'Burley Road? I see you during my sister's school run if I get a lift. You still go to Westlands, yeah? How old are you? Fourteen? Fifteen? I wish I'd been allowed to go out to pubs when I was your age.'

'It's fine, I'm allowed in here. I'm sixteen but my birthday's in September so I'm closer to seventeen. Finished my GCSEs so I'm out of Westlands now, I'm off to Canterbury College to do art.'

'Me and Benjamin are already there. I'm going to help him with his coursework over the summer.' Louise pounded that information out like an office clerk stamping an official document.

While it was nice to have two young ladies throw a bunch of words at each other while I kicked back, relaxed and got on with enjoying my bottle of Hooch (they'd run out of Two Dogs after the last round) I was a bit surprised by the last bit of info. I don't recall there being a discussion about Louise helping me with coursework.

Louise saw the confusion on my face. 'Sorry that's what I wanted to talk to you about tonight. I was thinking that we could help each other with all the coursework we need to re-do before the end of term.'

I would have shuddered over the idea a day or two ago but Louise was certainly bright, I had an ungodly amount of work to catch up on and I was in a devil-may-care drunken frame of mind, so I agreed.

'So you two aren't girlfriend-boyfriend, just college friends?' Eliza asked with a smile while, like a cowboy firing a pistol only to find its barrel was empty, Louise realised she had run out of words.

Eliza answered her own question with a declaration. 'I'm glad.'

Christine:

I arrived back at the table to discover that my seat had been taken and things had escalated far beyond my expectations. Benjamin was like a kid in a candy shop, adoring every quip and hair flip this Eliza girl produced and yet he was clearly too scared to make a move. Of course Eliza might be the type to instigate some physicality but I refused to let that happen. Meanwhile, Louise was sitting there looking longingly at Mr Cooper trying her best to get even the slightest bit of attention from him. And then there's me, gazing upon Louise, wishing I could swoop in and stroke her hair, caress her skin, hold her close to me and deliver to her the love she deserves, powered by the thunderous heartbeats she inspires within me – the kind she will never generate with Benjamin. Bloody hell, isn't it pathetic? I can't believe there's all this sexual tension in the air and nobody's going to fuck.

Benjamin Cooper:

Eliza and I chatted excitedly about all manner of things. It was a joy to find one conversational topic flow on to the next. She asked me about college life in Canterbury and I waxed lyrical about the joys of Parrot Records and the Penny Theatre. We talked about music and films. She declared an interest in indie and then sixties music – it was a conversation I could, for once, thrive in. It led to some banter about The Doors and Val Kilmer; I rolled out some moments from Top Secret and I think somewhere along the way we agreed to see Batman Forever. The alcopops kept flowing. Even Christine arriving with a sour expression couldn't stop it. For a brief shining moment it felt like, for once, I was going to win.

And then the first domino tipped.

'MISTER COOPER,' a familiar voice boomed. Darren King appeared, leaning on the section of wall beside our table. 'I didn't expect to see you out and about in the 'Bourne on a Saturday night. Thought you'd be at 'ome, 'aving a wank. Just kidding.'

Eliza sank down slightly in her chair, trying not to be seen, as he gave a nod towards Louise. 'Alright, D'Souza? You here hanging with Mister Cooper, then? Looks cosy.'

The confidence Louise had possessed early that evening drained away. 'I'm... well, I mean, we're just discussing coursework and stuff.'

'Righty-o,' Darren scoffed before bending down beside Eliza. 'And little Liza's here too? This is a very, very unexpected gathering. And you over there, Shakespears Sister! Who are you then?'

'Me? I'm more than you can handle so why don't do yourself a favour and fuck off,' Christine spat.

'Steady on, no need to be rude, luv,' Darren King hissed before sliding back to his friends at the back of the bar.

Being a little under the influence from an evening of alcopops and keen to impress Eliza I made the questionable decision to boast, 'Don't worry about him. I made him drink my piss the other day.'

Louise was shocked, Christine laugh-spat out the mouthful of cider she'd just taken and Eliza grinned, 'What!?'

'It's true. It's true. He's always bothering me, asking for a swig of my drinks. So the other day I secretly pissed in the can and gave it to him.'

'You wot?' One of the blokes Eliza's friend had been hanging around with overheard this and turned round to glare at me, 'You made a bloke drink your piss? That's not right, mate. Fucking disgusting.' He shook his head before turning back to his own group's bellowing conversation.

'I wouldn't normally encourage such behaviour but, all things considered, I think you deserve a medal,' Eliza beamed. Louise looked uneasy about the whole thing and made her apologies and left. I felt a bit bad about how Louise's evening had gone – I think she was expecting to form a stronger bond with me so she could escape Darren King's clique for good but I had been pretty rude to her and left her on the periphery. Maybe she felt like she'd gambled her social standing on a friendship with me and lost everything.

This guilt evaporated as Eliza leant forward and took my hand. She asked if I'd like to have my palm read. I was conflicted, as I wanted her to touch my hand but I was worried that my lines might indicate that far from being 'cool' I was actually 'a bit shit'.

She took my hand, started flattening out the skin and began her analysis. 'First of all let's start with the important one – the heart line. It's long but a bit flat.'

I didn't think that sounded good but she continued, 'It's not necessarily a bad thing. The flat line means you have a tendency to over-rationalise your romantic feelings rather than passionately dive into your emotions, but the length of the line indicates that those feelings are there and run very deep.'

Christine:

For fucks sake, I had to sit there nursing a drink on my own while all this bullshit palm reading stuff was happening. I don't think she was even doing it right, isn't one of them supposed to be about money or something.

All this hand holding and stroking wasn't a good sign. Luckily her mate Kate was lingering around, looking sternly at her watch and making motions that they should leave.

Benjamin Cooper:

Next up was my lifeline, which was apparently very short and faint. I thought this meant I didn't have long to live but Eliza explained it was indicative of a feeling of inner chaos and strife, which was fair. She then attempted to look at my head line and looked concerned. She flattened out the skin on my hand a number of times and held my hand up to the light, checking both sides. The look on her face was hard to read – she seemed both curious and jittery, making it hard to tell if this was from positive excitement or fear. I asked her if something was wrong and after some umming and eering she replied, 'Well, your head line is faint and cracked but stretches right across your palm and onto the other side. Which means...'

Eliza stopped mid-sentence as Kate grabbed her attention and began tapping at her watch and gesturing towards the door.

Eliza left her chair in haste and swung her small bag over her shoulder. 'Sorry. I have to go. I was supposed to be home fifteen minutes ago. It was lovely to meet you though, Benjamin Cooper. Maybe we could meet up again? I'll be at the college on Monday for an open day, so if you see me say hi.'

'Sounds good,' I replied, 'but wait, what about my Head Line? What does it mean?' My questions went unheard and unanswered though as my voice was lost in the clash and crash of the door opening and Eliza disappearing through it.

It wasn't how I wanted the evening to end but compared to most of my lonesome hours or social humiliations it felt like a win. A swell of butterflies and wonder filled my stomach and my head felt airy, light and for once, hopeful. Of course, with my life being as it is, that wasn't allowed to last.

'She might fancy you,' Christine's voice wormed its way to my ear as she moved next to me, 'but she'll never stay in love with you.'

The wonder vanished and the wings of the butterflies disintegrated, causing them to plummet into the sour pit of my stomach like lead.

Christine:

I'd observed Eliza for less than an hour and I already had a pretty good read on the type of girl she was. She was an unwelcome distraction for young Benjamin and would ultimately cause conflict and severely hinder his progress as a blood drinker, not to mention ruin my own plans to rest comfortably under his shadow. I had to nurture a little doubt and darkness to tarnish the dream. So I told him to imagine their future together. I assured him that it'd be all smiles and flowers for a while but that would wear out and then she'd need more from him. Commitment, reassurance and a consistent drive to make their lives together better. He'd need to make her proud as her choice of partner. I urged him to consider all of Eliza's friends and family members and his potential obligation to hold court with them and stand tall as at least an equal. Could he do that? Day after day, month after month, year after year? And if, in his heart he knew he could not, I asked him to ponder how could she possibly still manage to stay *in love* with him? Would the stars in her eyes diminish when her friends and family members carve out bigger, brighter and more successful futures than anything he could aspire to with his half-arsed college course certificate and his secret vampire heritage. And what if she wanted children? That would be an awkward conversation; he was *of lineage* and certain to pass on those traits to his offspring. I asked him to contemplate how Eliza might feel after a decade or so married to him; her youthful looks fading after wasting them on one man too early, living month to month financially, raising children destined by blood to be murderers, as her friends all transcend to picture-perfect lives of success and happiness. I asked him to consider just how much she'd resent him for stealing away the life she could have had. It would only be a matter of time before she'd have to take that frustration somewhere; it could be her hand down the thong of a stripper at a hen night, a dry hump with a fireman at JJ's or a full blown affair with that twat who called me Shakespeare Sister. I sold Benjamin a vision of a house decorated with hurt; suspicion, misery, anger, hatred. It hit harder than I had hoped.

Benjamin told me to fuck off before downing a whole bottle of Hooch and sinking down in his seat. He looked both furious and tearful. I had made a lot of that up on the spot, based on nothing other than my desire for him to stay away from that girl. I had gotten over dramatic and was venting a lot of my own baggage. I'd expected him to scoff at most of it and maybe feel a twinge of doubt, but it definitely struck a nerve.

Benjamin Cooper:

I was pissed off. I really thought for a few minutes that everything was going to be good but nope, it seems I don't get that in life. The worst thing about it all was that Christine was right. If I can't satisfy my own feelings, how on earth could I ever make a witty and wonderful girl like Eliza truly happy? What right do I have to steal her light and let it wither in my darkness?

Soul searching has never calmed me and this train of thought stirred up the wrong kind of fire in me. I was ready to push, pull, scream and scratch at the next person who came at me with anything other than the most positive of vibes. And as if on cue, Jon Miller was loudly mouthing off unaware that I was sat listening to every word.

Christine:

I saw that lad who knew Deano beginning to gather his crew for the nefarious antics at the breakers yard I had overheard him planning earlier. He'd had a skinful and was beginning to bellow and brag about this and that. I saw this display had caught Benjamin's attention and I asked who he was – turns out he was a young man called Jon Miller and my new fanged friend had no love for him at all.

Jon Miller was offering his flock of fiends a night full of revelry once the Sheppey job was done and dusted. 'All things being well we can get back to the 'Bourne before Aida Kebab shuts, grab some nosh and then head round to Mandy's and I'll treat you all to a deuce.' I wasn't sure what a deuce was but the way the word fell out of his mouth sounded pretty sordid. I asked Bates on the phone earlier today what he thought it might mean and he thought it was either new drug slang or old wartime brothel slang for a 'suck and a fuck'. Either way they were all very excited about it.

'How are you gonna pay for all of us,' one of the Miller Mob questioned. 'Win at the dogs?'

'Nah mate, I finally sold all that weak puff I haven't been able to shift. Y'know that grunge tosser we sell to in Canterbury? Dickhead bought the lot like a fucking mug. I tell you something though, I was talking to him this morning about what we're up to tonight and this and that and it turns out he took my advice and went out with that Kelly Cooper last night. He'll confirm everything I've told you about her, she took it right up the arse again. Total filth.'

Benjamin became enraged and stood up and sort of scowled at him. It wasn't very threatening. It looked a bit like Benjamin was going to cry.

He caught Jon's eye. 'Ooooh, looks like Big Brother's upset about something.'

'You need to stop lying about my sister.' Benjamin's voice was shaky but I have to admit he sounded a little unhinged.

Jon was more entertained than afraid though. 'Where's the lie? She takes it from behind and do you know what I reckon? You do too. The Coopers: a family full of arse bandits.'

With his mob cackling and laughing, Jon continued to taunt. 'I bet your family saves a fortune on toilet paper, what with the pair of you cleaning your arse on every cock in Sittingbourne.'

I'm not sure who lunged first but a brief scuffle broke out and Benjamin got the worst of it, being pushed backwards and tripping clumsily onto a table, knocking some random folks drinks everywhere.

Jon Miller and friends gave a quick snorting laugh at my fallen associate and left. Benjamin picked himself up amongst grumbles and jeers from all around. I decided to give him a pep talk and remind him that he was a blood drinker and one *of lineage* at that, and he shouldn't be the one on the floor. With that, Benjamin dusted himself down and headed out the door. By the time I'd grabbed my poncho, my big hat and his jacket and made my way outside, I could already hear loud voices and the shuffling clutter of fisticuffs coming from the small car park area behind the pub. Running around the corner the first thing I saw was Jon Miller's fist introducing Benjamin's arse to the floor.

BENJAMIN COOPER:

This was the first fight (and by that I mean a real fight) I'd been in and it wasn't how I expected a fight to be. It wasn't like the puppy-pile scraps I remembered from childhood, nor was it the choreographed cathartic release of a movie dust-up. This was someone continually hurting me while my punches apologetically wafted limply towards a torso unharmed by their nudges. I had already taken a few punches to my face before I felt a sharp jab to my stomach, which took the wind out of me and made me stagger backwards and fall to the floor.

Defeat did little to subside my anger and I found myself staggering back to my feet, calling out for more. My opponent mocked me and went to walk away but I swung a punch his way and it connected. Suddenly I had his gang all over me, grabbing me, pulling me about and eventually dragging me to the floor. Then I felt the kicks, pounding into my arms and legs like a shower of hammers. In between the shuffle of shoes and the thudding sounds of them bludgeoning my torso, I could hear them labelling me; 'pussy', 'faggot', 'wanker' and indeed, 'cunt'. One of the kicks found its way through my bunched up arms and legs and connected with my mouth, splitting my lip.

'I tell you something else, Jon,' said the guy who had been talking to Eliza's friend Kate, 'he's a right wrong-un, a real dirty bastard. He made another bloke drink his piss.'

'Is that right?' said Jon Miller, motioning for the kicking to stop before kneeling down beside me and grabbing me by the hair with his left hand. 'A right little pervert ain't ya? Fucking filthy cunt.'

I then felt a sovereign ring-enhanced punch drive itself into the left side of my head and I collapsed, humiliated, beaten and defeated. Lying there, depleted of all ego, I heard two sounds. One was that of hasty wheels crunching through pebbles and loose tarmac taking Jon Miller and my attackers far from the scene of the beating and the other was Christine's footsteps walking towards me.

'Well, that didn't go very well, did it?' she said, perhaps taking a little joy from my misfortune as she walked toward her car and opened the boot.

I sat up and dusted myself down. 'This is your fault! You said I had power! What happened to all the being *of lineage* stuff?"

'I didn't expect you to go straight after him like that.' I could almost hear her eyes roll in her tone, 'And besides, Popeye isn't really Popeye until he's eaten his spinach, is he?' With that, she pulled out a test tube full of blood, its rich crimson tones illuminated by the car's interior courtesy light emerging through the opened boot.

I caught a glimpse of the stars in the sky. Good old stars – no matter the weather, even if they're obscured by the darkest storm they continue to sparkle and shine. Pure and perfect. I wish I could be more like them. I try to be but there's always some storm or another raging through this town and maybe for once that storm should be me.

Christine:

Benjamin wasn't at all happy about having his ass handed to him, to be fair who would be? I explained that being *of lineage* wasn't enough. He'd need experience and practise to fully be an all-conquering King of the Night Time World, and before he even thought about such lofty ambitions he'd need to consume. Nutritionally, he was starved. I can't imagine the pain and exhaustion someone who's *of lineage* must be in if they've spent all eighteen years of their life without feeding on the red stuff.

I had a vial of blood in a cool bag in my car boot. He seemed a little reluctant to partake, maybe stung by the fact that I hadn't exactly led him into glory so far. But as he sat there, staring at the stars in the clear summer sky while gently licking away the blood on his cut lip, I felt his demeanour alter.

'I know where Jon Miller and his friends are heading tonight. If you want Round Two with him and his gang, I could drive you there. But you've got to show them who you truly are.' I handed him the vial of blood and urged him to drink. 'When life kicks you in the fangs, bite back!'

CHAPTER 7
> = < DISORDER > = <

TESTIMONY: BENJAMIN COOPER AND CHRISTINE REGARDING THE final hours of the 10th of June 1995 and the haze that followed

Benjamin Cooper:

I shut the car door hard but didn't hear the slam. Sliding into the passenger seat of Christine's car, I could taste the blood she'd given me. It lingered on my tongue and teeth while my anger and frustration began to burn through the emotional tinder that had built around my heart over the past eighteen years. Christine knew where to take me and I knew what I needed to do. The night was in motion.

Christine:

I didn't expect him, as a first time blood -drinker, to down a full vial in one go but he knocked it back like a champ. He had a sharp stare on his face, taut and distant like it was burning a hole through a steel wall a mile away. His eyes weren't fully yellow – that would come in time, but I could see light lemon tinted threads in his iris' between their shades of blue. He was so far gone, lost in his simmering rage and trying to keep a lid on all the released energy bubbling up from the sudden injection of another human's blood, that he didn't even notice or moan about the fact I'd popped in a Joy Division tape for the journey.

Benjamin Cooper:

My heartbeats felt out of sync, beating in an unusual pattern with my breaths finding it hard to catch up to their improvised dance, and time started to become hard to gauge. I had no idea how long it had been since we left the pub. I checked my watch and made note that the time was 23:05. The metallic notes from the blood I'd consumed repeated on my taste buds with a rhythmic haste; the pace of this sensation chased the tyres of Christine's car as they raced together on the tarmac hurtling towards unavoidable violence.

As the pace quickened, the separation between the stark white markings on the road ahead merged into one quivering translucent steady beam. Traffic lights peppered the roads with their flashing lights, the crimsons and emeralds shining brighter than the ambers as we passed through each and every one of them regardless of their threats and promises.

All the while, my heart was pounding full of dissatisfaction, urging my thoughts to linger on violent desires. Blood on my hands, blood in my mouth and all over my face. Jon Miller's blood taken from him by force, now belonging to me. I checked my watch again – 23:32. From behind a crimson veil, my eyes stared at his whimpering final moments, as he realised that his life had been short and mostly pointless. His eyes darted for a clutch of futile seconds, seeking salvation yet finding only death. The bodies of his associates lay around him, stained red and lifeless. I could feel the moment on my skin, the chill of the midnight air and the distant sound of vehicles washing across the roads like a wave repeatedly rushing against a pebble shore.

Time began to splinter in my mind like two separate reels of film spliced into neat sections, shuffled with care, mixed equally and compiled together into one disconcerting, dizzying fever dream. Were the earlier parts memories or the later parts desires – maybe even prophecies? Where amongst these experiences did the present dwell?

My watch read 23:15 and I was back in Christine's car, speeding across the Kingsferry Bridge, away from the mainland and onto the Isle of Sheppey. We were travelling at such speed that Christine nearly missed a turning to get us to the breaker's yard in Queensborough. As she slammed her foot down the squeal of the brakes bled into sounds of screaming. The frightened whimpers and hollers of Jon Miller's crew desperately trying to escape. They were boxed in tight against the yard's metal railings and I found myself on their car bonnet, pulling a body through its broken windshield while my fangs chewed a punctured neck, spraying blood around me like a broken hose.

With that victim drained I slid off the bonnet and made my way to my next prey – the lad who took umbrage with my piss-drink anecdote. It wasn't anything personal, he just happened to be nearest. I took great satisfaction in twisting him hard by the head and breaking his neck. Again, sounds merged and time shifted, the snap of his neck somehow being one and the same as the sound of Christine pulling up at the yard and clicking her handbrake up. The time was 23:27. Jon Miller and his gang were there, full of swagger in the beam of our headlights. They recognised us and were laughing and gesturing. I smiled my first confident smile in years, as I knew exactly how this was going to end.

Christine:

To be totally honest I hadn't expected much to happen during this confrontation. I figured we'd bare our fangs a bit, chase after them in a somewhat-slapstick manner, throw in a couple of jump scares and get them so piss-pants humiliated by the whole ordeal that they'd run off somewhere distant and stay hidden for the next few years. However, Benjamin's natural instincts took over. Like I said earlier, it's tricky to bite a neck and drink blood. It takes years of practice normally, but he was a natural. They were stood there taunting him and, without so much as a flinch, he leapt, landed and clenched down in one fluid motion. His lineage must go back a long, long way to pull that off.

He then noticed one of them had got back into their motor and was attempting to start the engine. Benjamin bounded onto the bonnet, stuck his arms through the glass and pulled the poor bastard through the windscreen before feasting on him too. Oddly it was in this moment I saw a glint of remorse in Benjamin's eyes, yet it did little to quench his thirst as he methodically went from one geezer to the next, draining them. Call me immature but all this unexpected violence gave me the giggles something terrible.

Benjamin missed one of them though; one sneaky sod was trying to scramble away on his hands and knees. I didn't need to feed but it seemed a waste to let him get away and besides, why should new boy Benjamin get all the treats.

'Please! Please!' Sneaky Sod whimpered as I pulled him by the back of his Spliffy jeans towards me. 'I have a family in Murston!'

A family in Murston? A FAMILY IN MURSTON!?! 'You've got a family in mourning, muthafucker!' I cackled as I bit down hard on his jugular.

I'd sworn that I'd outgrown such senseless violence and greed but here I was, giddy as an aunt, murdering fools and needlessly feasting on them while lost in the post-pub glow of meeting a beautiful, straight, teenage girl. A month or so ago I would have presumed I was better than this. I don't know what's got into me. I'm way too young to be having a mid-(after)life crisis, but here I am acting like an idiot.

I stood up and attempted to wipe the blood from my mouth but quite possibly ended up just smearing it across my big grinning face as I continued to chuckle at all the carnage. Benjamin paced around the fallen bodies; breathing heavily and snorting like a bull or something. Eventually I caught his eye and he just started laughing, softly at first but soon hysterically. We went from body to body, vein to vein draining every last drop of blood from them, getting more and more buzzed. Things around this point got a little fuzzy for me but I recall placing the corpses next to each other in compromising positions and possibly doing puppet-style shows with them. My last clear memory is popping them all in their car and setting it on fire before we pushed it down some sort of bank or slope. It was quite high and we cheered victoriously when the vehicle crashed to the ground in a frenzy of orange and yellow flames.

We then took off in my motor; it was very late by then well – into the early morning. Our laughter and our song briefly filled the early morning roads as we sped through them. I think we might have driven to the coast, maybe Whitstable, and hung out talking shit and listening to tapes by the sea until near sunrise. I'm unsure if that part was just a dream. I vaguely recall dropping Benjamin off at his home but have no recollection of getting home myself. Best night out in ages.

Benjamin:

The fire and violence faded and calmer recollections blended. My hand on the front door of my home, my hand on the handle of Christine's car. Gentle steps up the stairs in my house, Christine easing a cassette into her dashboard with a satisfying click. And then finally, as I collapsed on my bed, wide-eyed for a section of time that could have been seconds or could have been hours, my eyelids eventually fell and somehow, somewhere within that darkness, I heard Christine's car door slam.

CHAPTER 8
1 DON'T RECALL A TIME 1 FELT THIS ALIVE

TESTIMONY: BENJAMIN COOPER AND CHRISTINE REGARDING THE 12th of June 1995

Benjamin Cooper:

The sunlight from the brightest dawn of the year was the first thing to stir me from my slumber. I was laid out on my bed fully naked apart from my hands and face that were still decorated in dry, brown blood from the incident at the breakers' yard. Almost immediately, my clock radio alarm kicked into gear with the Boo Radleys pounding out of it like a parade of parping cockerels. My mind instantly alerted me to the fact that it was a Monday and, as such, a college day, but even that couldn't wipe the smile from my face. A contentedness and happiness flowed through my body, the likes of which I had never experienced before. Also, at the risk of seeming crude, I'd woken up with the biggest hard-on I'd experienced in a good couple of years. I was extremely thankful for this because the occurrence and regularity of fully-bodied, firm erections had deteriorated quite abruptly over the past year or so and I was starting to worry that I was going impotent early. All of this added up to a wondrous sense of ease. My mind was clear of worries and I felt so very strong.

With Wake Up Boo still pumping away in the background I leapt out of bed, threw some clothes on and began to dance my way out of the bedroom towards the stairs. I could hear Kelly in the kitchen and realised if I timed it right she'd helpfully make my tea and toast while she did her own. Luckily, I caught a glimpse of myself in the mirror and remembered I was covered in blood, so made a quick yet jovial detour to the bathroom to flannel myself clean, dancing all the while.

'Oh, so you're finally up,' Kelly remarked when I got to the kitchen. 'I was getting worried. I was about to call Dad.'

'What do you mean?' I asked, trying to lower the volume of my smirk.

'Lord knows what time you got in on Sunday but you've been asleep in your room ever since. I was worried you might have died or something.'

I became worried that she may have seen me nude and blood stained. 'Did you come and check on me or anything?'

'Nah, I was too nervous. I thought you might have company. Word was going around on Saturday night that you were out with three girls. I didn't believe it at the time but I heard you crashing about early on Sunday and didn't want to interrupt anything.'

'No,' I said, scratching my head and yawning a little, 'I was in there on my own. Just very drunk.'

'And what about the girls? I'm guessing one of them is that girl from college who you told me you didn't know. And the other two?'

'Well,' I hesitated, trying to work out how best to describe my relationship with Christine, 'I've become friends with a girl called Christine who used to live on Woodberry Drive years ago. She's, y'know... a goth, punky, metal kinda girl.'

'Oh yeah?' Kelly raised her eyebrows, under the misguided impression that a goth, punky, metal kinda girl would be my type.

'And she's a lesbian,' I added, 'It's purely platonic.'

'Alright, so who's girl number 3 then?'

'Oh, it was some girl who came to sit with us for a bit.' I didn't dare mention Eliza's name, I had a horrible feeling that Kelly might know of her and burst my bubble with some poisonous piece of gossip about her. 'She left after a drink or two. Anyhow, how do you know about what I was up to on Saturday?'

'Darren King was laughing about it in JJ's. He was calling you the Pussy Hound Pussy, banging on about how you act like you're not a threat to lure unsuspecting ladies into your thrall. He reckons you're a secret ladies man or something. I heard him roll that spiel out to at least five different groups of people. To be honest I think he's more obsessed with you than anyone with a vagina is.'

The thought of being the main character in one of Darren King's conversation starters filled me initially with frustration and then panic. If me sitting with three young ladies was deemed a noteworthy topic, then what of the pushing and shoving match with Jon Miller? Surely news of me getting pushed into a table full of drinks would have done the rounds? And if so, that could have major implications when his absence was noted. 'Any other gossip about me?' I asked, apprehensively.

'Not that I've heard,' Kelly shrugged.

'Great!' I replied, as my sky-high smile returned to my face. I grabbed some of the spare toast as it popped out of the toaster, threw my backpack over my shoulder and left for college.

Kelly's compilation tape had become a companion of both locations and emotions over the past week and today it especially seemed to share my joy. While there was some guilt and worry about my antics on Saturday night, it felt insignificant next to the sheer happiness I was feeling. Each song felt like a friend as the train went station-to-station, further eastwards. Nobody could steal my smile, not even Darren King, who was sitting in the same carriage with his two mates and gaggle of girls flocked around him. The train was pulling into Canterbury East and I passed them on the way to the door.

'Not surprised he's looking so chipper this morning,' Darren King chortled to his platonic harem as I passed them. 'Like I said, he had three birds on the go on Saturday. Three of 'em! It's always the quiet ones.'

'Him? Nah, shuddup!' replied Becky Hollis, as ever one of the louder and more assertive members of the clique. Her voice was coated with an abrasive chuckle of derision however her eyes began to look at me in a more ambiguous manner.

'You just wait until I tell you who the girls were.' Darren King continued. His voice was dripping in delight as he revelled in the opportunity to dine out on this exaggeration of the truth for the rest of the day.

Becky left her seat slowly, keeping her eyes on me but lowering her brow in contemplation and twisting her mouth like a toffee had become stuck in her back teeth. Being in a silly mood and unwilling to let her staring intimidate me, I decided to throw her a quick wink and a smirk. I'm not sure what message I was sending with that gesture but it felt better than being passive and allowing her intrusion to stand unchallenged. I had endured enough of these fools. Seriously, let them throw any heckle at me; I killed and drank the blood of seven of the most dangerous teens in Kent last night. Darren King and company are even more worthless. These bags of blood are just bumbling livestock; three cocks and a group of cows. They're one step below me in the food chain. They're prey and all their crowing and mooing is little more than the din of a slaughterhouse holding pen.

Christine:

I woke up around 10:00am on Monday feeling like a demon had taken a shit in my head. That wild Saturday night had been too wild, too fast. I really hoped Benjamin had done the wise thing of taking a day off because those early blood buzzes can really take one's ego to dangerous places.

Benjamin Cooper:

On foot between Canterbury East station and college, I realised that Louise D'Souza hadn't been on the train with her usual crowd. I felt a bit bad about how she left the pub on Saturday, although it had freed up the rest of the evening for Eliza's palm reading and Christine's blood drinking. I was eager to see both of them again; Eliza because my Saturday night shyness had been driven back by my Monday morning afterglow and I felt sure I could nail down a definite date to see Batman Forever at the cinema. And Christine, because I needed to know when we'd be out on the hunt again. It was around this time I realised I still had the massive erection I'd woken up with. I wasn't sure if this was excitement over Eliza or about going out on the kill again, but there it was, throbbing away with such steady conviction it felt like it might eventually stretch out with enough force to break away from my groin and start travelling across my tummy like an earthworm on wet soil.

While trying to shake off this distraction of uncomfortable arousal, I was accosted by Becky Hollis on the way into class. 'Is it true? You were with Louise in the pub on Saturday? And Eliza from Westlands?'

'Yeah,' I said bluntly, bored by now of this pretty low-interest story gaining a surprising amount of traction.

Becky wouldn't let it lie though. 'Did you have sex with 'em?'

'No,' the words came out surprisingly shaky and a little flustered.

'But you were with 'em, yeah? And some other gothic girl?' Becky's words, dressed in second-generation Estuary vowels, came hard and fast. Her vocal tone made her a tenacious interrogator and I was beginning to wish I had some sort of sordid confession to end the ordeal.

'Are they your girlfriends or something?' she continued.

'Nah I don't have ONE girlfriend let alone three.'

'But you were with them?' Her stern voice was like a spotlight in my face.

'Yes Becky, the rumours are true, I was with them.' I had no idea how to get out of this so I threw a little spice in her direction. 'What does it matter? You jealous you weren't there as well, or something?'

By this I was aiming to make a joke about her being jealous of missing out on the night in the pub and highlighting how it really wasn't anything that glamorous or scandalous. However my barbed comment seemed to hit her differently and she got flustered, 'Nah. Nah why would I be jealous, you weirdo? You're jealous if anything.'

I left it there and went into class. It's hard to combat a desperate retort without it descending into who's got the tougher dad territory and, judging by her presumably-inherited attitude, I reckon she'd win that argument.

Louise didn't come into college that day but her presence was felt in the form of whispered gossip that seemed to follow my movements like a vapour trail. All the while, I continually found myself the target of Becky's inquisitive glances.

Once class had finished, I threw my backpack over my shoulder and made my way to the Student Union Café. I saw a bunch of sixteen-year-old kids from Kelly's school nervously skulking around and realised that the open day must have started and that perhaps Eliza was on campus. I'm not sure if it was the thought of this or the anticipation of tucking into my chocolate milkshake and muffin but I became very aroused again. To be honest, my morning wood had never truly left but had been lingering between the semi to quarter mark in class, so I had presumed it was just about ready to give up and go back to sleep. But nope, there it was, perky as ever, pushing itself eagerly against the harsh denim and unforgiving bronze metal buttons on my flies.

Equally irritating was the fact that Becky had decided to follow me into the café and was continuing to fix me with an uneasy stare. It was like she wanted to find out something from me but wasn't even sure what it was.

I was so keen to get rid of her that I walked over and said the first juvenile thing to come into my head. 'What is it? What do you need from me? Why are you so fascinated with me today? Do you want to have sex with me or something?'

Becky stuttered a little and began to look a little flushed. 'You what?' she asked, softly.

It wasn't a no, it wasn't a fuck off – it was an intriguing direction. I felt like for once I had her against the ropes, with the ball in my court and all the other sporting analogies indicating that I was winning for once. 'I just mean, I know you don't like me. And trust me, I don't like you much either but truth be told I've woken up with a rigid erection that I can't shift so if you want to use it, feel free.'

I could see her fake-tanned tummy under her crop top, breathing in and out, beginning to rapidly increase and an uneasy curiosity burning in her eyes. Had I accidentally turned this into a pick up? These lines shouldn't have been working, but they were.

'I mean... perhaps,' she said, a little flustered but not un-eager. 'But...'

'Listen, it's up to you. You can hang around here pretending to laugh at Darren King's jokes or you come with me and get fucked happy.' I was clearly taking the piss at this point, just lost in the joy of seeing how lewd I could get before she told me to fuck off but oddly she was into it.

She took a step forward and whispered, 'Ok, but not here. We'll go to my dad's around the corner. Don't walk with me though; keep a good distance behind me. I don't want any gossip to start.'

And off she walked. I thought about just staying in the café but she gave me a glance over her shoulder and so I followed her. Perhaps I was concerned about being a dick and playing a trick on her but I think I was still a bit shaken by how vicious her scorn had been during the Wagon Wheel argument the other day. I had no idea what I was going to do when I got to her dad's house. Was I going to be all, 'Ha ha, not really!' or was I actually going to go through with it? Was I really about to have sex with Becky Hollis, of all people? I honestly found this to be one of the strangest and most surprising developments in my life, which is quite something for someone who unexpectedly went on a blood-drinking rampage two nights ago.

Eventually we reached a semi-detached house on a side street leading off New Dover Road. She gave a long, involved explanation about how her dad lived in Canter-bury but hadn't divorced her mum. She spoke quickly and I wasn't really listening so didn't take much of the informa-tion in.

As we made our way inside, she stated in an alarmingly casual manner, 'My dad's out until seven, so one quick shag and then back to college separately, ok?'

I felt like backing out there and then and confessing that I had said what I had said to annoy her, but before I could, she put a firm arm around my waist almost like she was trying to teach me to dance and I felt it easier to follow her lead. She kissed me – it was somewhat passionless and felt more like adhering to social convention. I sort of kissed her back but she broke it off quite swiftly as if that was all that was needed to satisfy etiquette. I did wonder for a second or two if she might have gone off the idea but then she proceeded to hold me closer and indulge in a little dry humping. She seemed more into that than the kissing and sort of purred, 'Come on then, let's go.'

I went to make my way to the stairs where presumably the bedrooms were but she insisted we make our way to the couch in the living room. I felt a bit uneasy about this; it was a nice, fresh-looking couch, straight from DFS (probably on a four year interest free payment plan). It seemed wrong to filth-up the upholstery but she was determined, pulling me towards her before hitching her skirt up and her tights off. I felt a little under pressure to keep up. It reminded me of being rushed through customs at an airport, trying to get all my metal goods in a tray while keeping pace with a fast-moving queue. Before I knew it she was popping open the buttons on my jeans and plunging me by the hips into her. It didn't feel very erotic at all; I think I put more emotion into putting the wheelie bin out. In and out and in again I went while she made all kinds of guttural noises. I really wasn't into it but I also didn't want to finish up too quickly lest that became the next hilarious anecdote bounced around the clique. My thoughts wandered and I found the jaunty pocket tapping music from Asda adverts playing in my head, perfectly in time to the steady bounce of the intercourse. My mind became fixated with the jingle playing on a loop over and over again, struggling to find its way to an outro like a little car stuck on a big city roundabout. I shook my head, attempting to focus on the task ahead, telling myself to try and enjoy it and be grateful for this rare carnal opportunity, but in doing so I awoke a different urge – a need to match the high of the bloodbath at the breaker's yard. If it had felt great sinking my fangs into Jon Miller's stubbly neck I couldn't begin to imagine what it must be like piercing an eighteen-year-old girl's soft, perfumed skin while her breasts bounced off my chest. Typically my dick hardened even more, causing Becky to gasp and throw her neck back, presenting a glorious, pulsating vibrant jugular vein. It was there on show, almost begging me to feed from it. I pinned her down harder and was about to bring my bite down upon her when a thought compelled me to stop - the thought of covering this beautiful new sofa in blood. Becky cried out, broke free of my grasp and dug her nails deep into my back while a feeling akin to being dragged naked through a folded silk curtain took hold of my loins and I began to pull out. The sudden switch from detachment to sensation was too much and a warm, watery ejaculation catapulted out of me.

Becky drew her knickers towards her using her foot and rolled them back on. 'Bloody hell, that felt good. But it was a no-strings, one-off, right? Don't tell a soul.'

Becky told me she was going upstairs to get cleaned up and wanted me to leave pronto and make my way back to college so I'd be back a long time before her.

While walking back to the college campus, I began to feel a little despondent about my fling with Becky Hollis. I felt hugely relieved to be out of Becky's grasp but also vaguely sad about the whole thing. I vowed to stay well away from flirting and sex until someone could explain the exact terms and conditions of the whole sordid ordeal in a clear concise fashion. In the midst of this confusion I caught a glimpse of Eliza on the other side of the road. She was stood there drowning out the darkness like the effervescent light of a summer moon, dressed in a Persil-white Suede t-shirt. Her eyes sparkled just as they had done the other night in the Ypres Tavern but this time not for me. She was laughing with tall, handsome, perfectly-stubbled young men who wielded social confidence that a boy like me could never muster. They were holding big folders, indicating that they were on the art course that she'd applied for and had probably shown her around the art block. A worry that my encounter with Becky had taken away an opportunity to reconnect with Eliza while leaving a space for better boys to occupy filled my stomach and made me want to vomit. I thought back to Christine's somewhat damning but sadly convincing analysis of the misery that might occur should I enter a courtship with Eliza. It frustrated me that she was probably correct. I suddenly wished my new vampire friend could hang around with me during the day – I felt stronger with her there. Feeling pathetic, I walked quickly past Eliza so she wouldn't see me. My ears picked up the muffled conversation of the group as I passed with a female voice pushing its sound over the top. It may have been Eliza calling my name, but I didn't dare look back.

I decided to sack the rest of the day off and head straight home. Another feeling of unease started to rattle my nerves. I had the strangest feeling that someone was following me. I glanced over my shoulders but the pavement behind me was empty. I looked towards the road and saw a hearse with darkened windows slowly crawling beside me instead of catching up with the traffic ahead. I stopped for a moment, hoping the car would simply continue to crawl onwards but it slowly ground to a standstill and lingered ominously beside me. Feeling alarmed, I quickened my pace only to find the car following suit. A nervous sweat broke on my brow and panic began to take hold. Thankfully the hearse's pursuit of me only lasted another half minute or so before it turned off to the right and left me startled but unharmed.

I tried my best to shake off the strangeness of the past hour and a half during my train ride home by burying my head in music. From an amazing start, my day had descended into an afternoon of distress. When I got home things weren't much better. My dad was home from visiting distant relations in Hertfordshire and had a right face on him.

'Look who's back,' he grumbled. 'I've had people looking for you.'

Jesus Christ, what people? Louise? Christine? The people in the hearse? Two of them I could possibly explain, the other I couldn't. I didn't really want to explain anything about my life at the moment, especially to my dad.

He handed me a pink Post It note with the name 'Gary Thrill' and a phone number written on it in scratchy black biro ink. 'He's a copper. He wants a word with you. I hope you're not bringing trouble to my doorstep.'

Shit! The police!?! What did they want? If I were to hazard a guess, a discussion about a burnt-out car with seven bodies inside would make for a pretty certain bet and was far beyond any trouble my dad would tolerate being discussed on his doorstep.

'The police?' I replied, feigning surprise. 'I don't know what that could be about. Did this Gary Thrill happen to say?'

'Nope,' grumbled Dad. 'It seems he spoke to your sister about it before I got back and when I questioned her about it she got all defensive and moody. She won't tell me what it's about. Bloody hell, I go away for three days and come back to all this. Whatever it is, sort it out. Quickly. Quietly. Like I say, I don't want any trouble coming to my door.'

And with that he rubbed his hand over his sunken face before stomping off to his room and slamming the door. I was left looking at the carriage clock in the living room anxiously counting the minutes until Kelly returned.

Christine:

I knew the sun was starting to set when I was awoken by the sound of the blood-drinkers' secret door knock. It's hard to explain but it's basically an approximation of Toccata and Fugue in D Minor, ratta-tat-tatted by hand. Like thump-thump-thump ratta-tatta-thump-thump.

Upon opening the door, I saw two familiar but unwelcome faces. 'Banks and Long Tooth, what a displeasure to see you again after all these years.'

'The feeling's mutual,' spat Banks. 'You've got some nerve coming back to the 'bourne.' Long Tooth made one of his usual grunts in agreement; he rarely spoke on account of his ten-centimetre-long snuggle-fang that could scrape against his tongue and lips unless he kept his mouth still.

The pair of them were two of my former master's foot soldiers and had served him for many years. After he had been driven out of town, they swore to carry on his malevolent work and uphold his brutal regime but, to my knowledge, they'd mostly spent the past five years driving about in a hearse and listening to Eric Clapton tapes.

'Yes, I'm back. What of it? Swear to god, if you're going to force me to listen to that fucking awful Unplugged version of Layla I'll tap out now and leave town.'

'Very funny,' Banks replied. 'I just want you to know we're watching you. I've never liked you; even back when you were our master's favourite new pet, and I like you even less now. I see you've found some new boy to hide behind. *Of lineage,* is he?'

'He's SO *of lineage* that any slight against me would stain your reputation considerably,' I bragged. 'Why embarrass yourself? He's the strongest blood-drinker in town and he's on my side.'

'Is he now?' Banks puffed his chest out before giving Long Tooth a whack on the arm, indicating they were leaving. 'Just know that we'll be watching you, and this boy. The moment the pair of you slip up, we'll be taking action.'

They began to walk away from my door but then Banks turned around, 'Oh yeah, and don't disrespect Clapton. Slowhand is my life.'

'Slowhand? Yeah sounds about right for you two,' I replied, flapping my wrist to and fro, giving him a listless take on the wanker gesture before slamming the door.

After the revels of the night before, I could have done without that pair trying to piss on my chips. They weren't much of a threat but were still some threat, nonetheless. I heard a familiar (no pun intended) flapping noise at the kitchen window and was relieved to see Igor hovering there.

'Did you see who just came around?' I asked, opening the window. 'Do us favour Igor; keep your sonar on for me, will ya? Anything suspicious, let me know immediately.'

Benjamin Cooper:

Kelly eventually came in just past ten. She carried a medicinal, slightly spicy odour about her, which along with the clattering noise she made as she dumped her handbag to the floor, alerted me to the fact she was probably very drunk.

'Oh, you're still up,' she slurred, peering her head around the living room door. 'Something you need to tell me?' She was smiling but it wasn't a nice, friendly smile, it was the kind of smile that I could tell was going to theatrically drop into a scowl to highlight how angry she was.

I didn't answer, partly out of fear but mostly out of a numbing uncertainty regarding how to diplomatically handle the wide range of possible answers, depending on what she may or may not know about.

'Something you need to tell me about Jon Miller, perhaps? Something you need to tell me about certain rumours about me going around town? Something you need to tell me about getting into fights over it?'

'I wasn't getting into fights. I was just standing up for you,' I said, trying to bring a little context to the room.

'I don't need YOU, of all people, to stand up for me. You're a fucking joke in this town,' Kelly jabbed her index finger towards me to highlight her point.

'Oh so what, I just sit there while everyone spreads lies about you?'

'Maybe they're not lies. Maybe I just like sex. I'm sixteen, I've done nothing wrong and I'm not ashamed. It's people like you, with your hang-ups. Yeah, you're not better than the rest of them getting all caught up in it. Maybe, instead of sticking your nose into my business, you should go and have sex with someone. It might make the act of fucking less of a disconcerting alien concept to you.'

I mean, she was wrong, I'd literally had sex a few hours ago and the concept of fucking had never felt more alien and disconcerting to me. I felt the urge to clarify. 'You don't understand, Jon Miller was there bragging and laughing about how you take it from behind.'

'So what? From behind! Whoop-de-hoo! I've seen wilder stuff in More magazine's Position of the Fortnight! Christ, you're like an old vicar or something.'

I'm wasn't sure if this meant she had or hadn't taken it from behind and whether or not the phrase was exclusive to certain body cavities or whether there was an element of poetic licence when it came to gentlemen's bragging rights on the matter. I didn't want to raise this with her but my thoughts felt an inclination to ponder upon it.

Kelly, however, interjected in a way that made sexual position trivialities the furthest thing from my mind. 'Anyhow. He's dead. Jon Miller. They found his body in the wreckage of a burnt-out car. So you won't have to worry about him anymore, will you? Happy?'

'Oh... I... ' I wasn't sure how to respond. I wasn't shocked by the news of course but being suddenly confronted with how a wild, dreamlike night translates to the stark reality of the following day made me terrified.

'Oh... Oh...' Kelly angrily imitated me. 'Christ, you're spineless! How comes you've got nothing to say now? I know you didn't like him but sometimes your coldness baffles me. Like, do you even have any feelings? Any thoughts? I can't believe you'd just stand there with nothing to say, your mouth open like a fucking goldfish.'

I wondered where this was going. I mean, she made it pretty clear the other morning that she agreed with my negative appraisal of Jon Miller's character. Why was she this angry with me? I don't think she expected that I, the spineless virgin vicar, was the one that killed him so I knew this wasn't about that. No, this was something else.

'It was the same when Mum died. You said NOTHING to me. NOTHING!'

Ah, there it was. Kelly's furious eyes darted as she spoke, as if she wanted to stare a hole through me but also couldn't stand the sight of me.

Desperately wanting peace between us again I rushed my answer. 'Well, I had nothing to say.'

Kelly gasped, angry tears emerging in her eyes. Shit, it was a terrible choice of words. I meant to say that I was lost for words. I was shocked, stunned, unprepared, too devastated to put that whirlwind of hurt into a pit of conversation. I didn't have the vocabulary for anything like that. I barely talked to anyone about anything back then, let alone death. I had no experience of adult conversation so it seemed a bit of a bold move to kick off my first attempt with my step-mum's passing.

'Seriously? You're seriously telling me you had nothing to say? My mum loved you like you were her own and you felt nothing? Fuck you, Benjamin, fuck you.' Kelly paced the living room as I tried to explain but to no avail.

'Well, anyhow,' Kelly said, taking a deep breath and drying both of her eyes with the palms of her hand, 'That copper Gary spoke to me about it all. He knows all about your fight in the Ypres Tavern with Jon and wants to talk to you about it. So you better find some fucking words for a change.'

I tried to apologise but it was no good, I'd been too thoughtless and Kelly was in the height of drunken cathar-sis. She stormed upstairs and slammed her door shut. I'm guessing Dad must have been earwigging because he didn't have the nerve to moan about the amount of sleep he needs and the noise that was interrupting it. Maybe tomorrow I could smooth things over, although it always feels a bit rich having people telling me off about my lack of talking. If anything, there's too much talking going on in the world – some of it's useful but perhaps the smaller scale grumbles and judgements just make things worse. I think maybe if things were a bit quieter everyone would have the space and clarity to find the answer within.

I was left alone in the living room, uncertain of where to place myself in the house after everything that had just occurred. I felt unwelcome, and stepping from my spot of shame may have been seen as a disrespectful act. Thoughts of tomorrow invaded with the realisation that I'd have to talk to that policeman about the death of Jon Miller. The severity of the situation was beginning to dawn on me. I'd murdered a group of people in less than five minutes. Each with hopes and dreams, troubles and triumphs. Their friends and families would have been weeping at the news of the burnt-out car today. There would be funerals to arrange and trauma that would echo through a generation in their households. What right did I have to cause so much sadness?

I collapsed onto the sofa, exhausted and bewildered. The headlights of a passing car illuminated the yellow eyes and toothy smile of Christine standing in the front garden.

I opened the window and stuck my head outside. 'Are you coming out to play?' she asked, knowing I couldn't resist. The scent of the night air was far more appetising than the guilt and complications of four walls and family ties around me.

CHAPTER 9

I'M NOT THE HERO I COULD BE (BUT NOT THE DOG I WAS)

TESTIMONY: BENJAMIN COOPER AND CHRISTINE REGARDING THE final hours of the 12th of June 1995 and the three days that followed

Christine:

I had decided to take a moonlit saunter down to Woodbury Drive and check in on young Benjamin out of little more than boredom, but when I saw how crestfallen he looked, I was glad to have made the journey. After persuading him to come out and get some fresh air, I led him down through East Street, past the cinema and towards my favourite hang out. As we walked I gently drew information from him, pushing where needed but always giving him space to talk about his worries. He was reluctant to talk at first but eventually words began to fall from his lips like slow falling snowflakes kick-starting an avalanche.

Benjamin Cooper:

I would question, over the days that followed, how words and actions came so easily when I was around Christine. I wondered whether she used some form of vampire dark magic to control me, but ultimately I think it may have something to do with her being bound to the night. There's a certain separation between the day and night and to talk to her about bad sex, unfulfilled crushes and my difficulties coping with grief seemed easier when it was a world away.

Christine:

I was extremely disappointed to hear that the first thing he'd done with his new found powers was to rush off and go in raw with some local scrubber, and even more so that he was still mooning over that Eliza girl, but very intrigued to finally find out more about his sister. In all my excitement in discovering the wonderful prospect that was Benjamin Cooper, I hadn't stopped to discover whether there were more lineages to mine in that house. Sadly it turns out she was just a stepsister, which would explain why I hadn't picked up on her blood signature. The dad was the common parent of the two of them and I hadn't detected anything unusual from his blood either, so it must have been his birth mother who carried the blessing and the curse of being a blood-drinker. I was fascinated to know more about her – after all, Benjamin's antics at the breaker's yard indicated that his blood carried an almighty legacy. Benjamin, however, seemed to know very little about her and almost every question I asked bounced off his blank face as if he never even pondered it. He was a very peculiar boy; I understood how his stepsister could get frustrated with him.

Benjamin Cooper:

I know I promised Becky Hollis I wouldn't tell anyone about our liaison but I didn't mention her name and it wasn't like

Christine would be hanging around the college, gossiping. I think I was trying to get Christine to go along with my current, 'sex is overrated' philosophy to let me know that it was normal to feel so little about it all but she just shrugged her shoulders and started asking questions about my birth mum instead. I had few answers for her. I mean, like I'd know – I was tiny when she died.

Christine led me through the graveyard of St. Michael's church and showed me how to get up onto the roof of the mecca for frozen food-lovers, Iceland. She told me how it was a great place logistically to stalk the night but I think it was mainly because she liked being near the graveyard, like a big old goth.

Christine:

Sitting on the roof of Iceland, gazing out over the restful cool of the neighbouring graveyard, I thought it best to take him through some of the accursed lore of being a blood-drinker. After all, he confessed he was worried about catching sexually transmitted diseases off that girl he went with which is odd considering the lack of concern expressed as he showered himself in a bunch of wrong 'uns blood outside the breaker's yard. I explained to him that 'vampires' *of lineage* are as good as a variant species to humans and infused with olde darke magiks. Part of the benefit of drinking normal homosapien blood is that the erm, biological information it contains confuses the body and as far as I understand it puts a freeze on cells dividing during consumption. So any viruses or lurgies can't jump in and take over during the cell reproduction cycle before spreading through the body. Add to that, being *of lineage* meant he held a higher immunity system and a lower body temperature than human-humans, so I told him that the more blood he drinks the less likely he'd be to ever get ill or indeed age.

As for me and my *of the night* kin, well, technically we're almost dead, with our cells frozen in the moment we were bitten and the rest of our DNA kept alive as facsimiles of those that turned us. The blood we drink provides us with nutrients and oxygen for our organs and tissue. Or something like that – I don't know, I'm not a scientist. Heck, I didn't even pass O Level biology. So it wasn't a textbook explanation but it was as good as I understood it from the various times Bates tried to explain it all to me.

Benjamin Cooper:

I don't think she totally knew what she was talking about but I felt inclined to entertain some of the information provided. Essentially, unless I get shot, set on fire or decapitated I should be pretty much invincible. And the more blood I drink, it seems, the slower I'll age. If I play my cards right I'll live forever. There's a lot of talk about the new National Lottery but it feels like I've already hit the jackpot.

Admittedly, the fact that there will have to be victims is a bit of a buzzkill, so we discussed blood drinking and morals. Christine wisely counselled me towards drinking stolen donations rather than murdering folk.

It felt a bit like a hypocritical slap on the wrist coming from someone who was quite happily enjoying the blood bath on Saturday night, but it made sense. The fewer bodies lying around with fang marks on their necks, the fewer worries I'd have about coppers, guilt and what not.

· · ·

CHRISTINE:

After the first few feeding sessions, murdering people can quite easily become the new normal. It always starts off with 'Oh, I only drink from criminals and people who won't be missed' but before long it's, 'Well, that toddler was looking at me funny,' which will only draw the ire of Scratch and no amount of immunity from virus can save a night-dweller from his harsh punishments. I've seen many a new blood-drinker fall into that trap, so I urged Benjamin to stick to the test tubes and transfusion bags for a bit. He looked a little heartbroken about this but I promised him that IF nobody was around, and IF we caught someone who was clearly a menace to society, then YES, we could munch on them. I was looking over the edge of the rooftop across the street as I spoke and my mind travelled back to how the high street had been a decade or so ago, when I was growing up. Hulburd's department store was long gone but part of me remembered being the little girl running up and down the middle of the store during shopping mornings with my mum, before being treated to cake in the café at the back. The store seemed huge when I was little – these days it was a hollowed out husk, crudely converted into units, half-filled with smaller shops and used as little more than a short cut to the Sainsburys. It seemed a sad fate for a store that survived and flourished through a century and a half's worth of queens, kings, two world wars and a whole heap of social change. It was a sobering reminder that nothing lasts forever, no matter how unstoppable we may feel during our salad days.

Benjamin Cooper:

Christine was staring off into the street. Taking a look to see what she was so transfixed by, I noticed the black hearse from earlier in the day slowly making its way down the High Street. It appeared to catch Christine's attention too so I thought I'd mention my encounter with the vehicle earlier.

'Oh don't worry about them,' she said, 'just two local blood-drinkers. Couple of dickheads – they like to try and make out they're a big deal, intimidate us night-timers. You've got nothing to worry about though, they're just *of the night* and you're *of lineage*. They wouldn't dare go against you, and if they did they'd come out of it second best.'

I asked Christine how many blood-drinkers there were in Sittingbourne and she said there were a good handful, probably about thirty or forty but most kept their heads down and kept quiet, especially since someone called Scratch kicked her former master out.

I asked her about her master and this Scratch character to which she replied, 'Well, Scratch is like the full stop at the end of the sentence. Never mind good or evil, right or wrong, fair or unfair. He's got rules, standards, and plans within plans. You play around with him and you get burnt. You'd do well just to keep well away from him.'

'And your master? Is he the one who turned you into a blood-drinker?'

Christine paused for a moment, ran her front two teeth over her bottom lip in contemplation before answering. 'Yeah, I don't really want to talk about him right now.'

Christine:

I can't deal with talking about my master, I don't even like to conjure up his name in my head. The atrocious cruelties of my time in my master's service still make my stomach churn. I may swing about town like a blood-bound bucca-neer but I never wanted to become this. I had a happy family life – yes, I suppose my mum would have preferred if I had remained the happy little girl skipping through Hulburds in a dress rather than listening to "devil music" in "boy's clothes" and yes, I did keep my sexuality hidden from everyone but I was happy at home. He took that away from me because, in his own words, he 'liked the way I looked.' I spent the first month or so in his service terrified that he was going to force himself on me but then I quickly realised that he was more turned on by power over others and blood-drinking than sticking his cock into people. Still, the awful acts he'd make me carry out in his name and the twisted abuse he'd inflict on me forever taint any trace of happiness I experience. Eventually, my master got too ambitious and while lost in his delusions of grandeur, began to lose track of many of his servants, including me. Like an idiot he tried to usurp Scratch. Some say my master died, some say he fled, some say he was so ravaged by the whole ordeal his followers had to bury him in a grave twenty feet deep to avoid even the slightest drop of sunlight from finishing him off. Either way, while Scratch is about, he wouldn't dare come back. I'm safe and should be able to laugh about all of this but he's still there, in my blood. No matter where I go or what I do, he is forever my master; the original – the blueprint from which the creature I am today was created.

Benjamin Cooper:

Christine seemed keen to change the subject, so she broke out some of her test tubes and we knocked them back. We got giddy talking about music we liked and gently heckling each other when our tastes diverged. Christine asked after Louise D'Souza and wondered if I'd seen her since she left the pub on Saturday. I told her that I hadn't and Christine seemed a little concerned about it. She reckoned I should be nicer towards Louise. For a second or two I wasn't sure if she was indicating that I should ask her out or something, but then I could have sworn I saw a shy sparkle in Christine's eyes and I got an inkling of where her interest might lay. I didn't call her on this; it was clearly just post-blood chat. I was new to all of this but had already experienced how things can get a little loose during a post-consumption glow. The stuff we drank wasn't as strong as the stuff on Saturday but I could already feel my mind drifting, like it was urging my senses to chase the essence of a light breeze passing through the night. It was a fun hour or so, sitting up there, far away from all the daytime dramas.

We agreed to meet on the roof in future, rather than have Christine walk all the way to my house and then back again. Before we parted company for the evening, we agreed another night out was in order and decided to meet at nine in the Black Griffin pub in Canterbury.

Christine:

Before we left the rooftop, I saw an unwelcome figure loitering by the traffic lights. One of my master's most loyal night soldiers – a six foot seven savage called McArthur. He was a big, muscly bastard, always in his metalhead denim and leather get up. He was no victim; he had actively sought out my master and begged to be turned into a blood-drinker. It was in 1989, arguably the peak of the metal years in this town, and perhaps he knew the road to old age and cultural irrelevance lay ahead, so by being bitten, he could stay twenty one for life. Unlike me, McArthur took to our master's bidding with delight and, from what I'd heard, had continued on ravaging the Garden of England even though he was free to live a more peaceful life. I spotted him but I don't think he spotted me, so I quickly wrapped up the evening and pushed to meet Benjamin in Canterbury next time. The increasing presence of my masters' favourite cronies wasn't a threat but certainly a concern. I figured it was best for us to keep our night time rendezvouses away from the 'bourne for a while.

Benjamin Cooper:

Tuesday was a bit of a nothingy day. Grey clouds had barged their way across the sunny skies of the previous week and there was a general malaise in everything and everyone. Mr Claypole only half heartedly nagged me about the outstanding college work, Louise D'Souza was still absent and even Darren King couldn't be bothered to harass me for snacks or make jokes about my presumed cocksmanship. Becky Hollis pretty much blanked me the whole morning, only occasionally looking at me with a mixture of contempt and curiosity, I think once she realised I hadn't said anything to anyone she relaxed a little but like I say there was a weird, lethargic mood smothering the campus and nobody could really be bothered to fulfil their usual roles. I treated myself to a copy of Melody Maker, a Greggs burger pasty and a can of Top Deck lager 'n' lime for the train ride home and decided to try and sort my life out a bit during my spare afternoon.

The first thing I thought I better get a handle on was the interest some copper apparently had in me. I should have been shitting myself – after all, they were looking to solve multiple murders and I knew I was the culprit, but it mainly just felt like a massive inconvenience. I did ponder why I wasn't more worried about all of this. Maybe I took some comfort from the fact we surely burnt all our fingerprints off of the corpses and car, or perhaps I felt like I could just bite the fuck out of any arresting officer and go on the run like a sexy outlaw. Who knows? Either way, as soon as I got back home I dialled the number on the pink Post It note by the phone and within three rings I got an answer.

The voice on the other end wasn't some bloke called Gary but instead seemed to belong to a middle-aged woman. 'Sittingbourne Police, how can I help you?'

I attempted to shake the surprise out of my voice and regain my cool. 'Oh I've been told to speak to someone called Gary Thrill.'

'Gary Thrill?' the voice on the other end of the line answered with a raised and scratchy intonation.

'Yes, Gary Thrill,' I reiterated in a humble manner.

'Do you mean DC Gary Thrill?'

'Yes DC Gary Thrill,' I stated again, a quiet pause followed before I added, 'Please, if you don't mind. Please.'

The scratchy female voice returned, 'Thrill?'

'Yes please, DC Gary Thrill'

'Thrill,' she repeated for the umpteenth time. I wondered if having the word Thrill continually repeated at me over the phone was some kind of modern method of tricking a confession out of me or something.

A scoopful of silence followed that I presumed meant it was my time to say his name but I decided to play things differently, 'So can I speak to him?'

'Oh, he's not in at the moment. I'll have to get him to call you back.'

I left my details and hoped that would be that. The next thing to cross off my list was to try and reconnect with the memories of my biological Mum. Christine's questions about her had sparked something within me to build a fuller picture of who she was.

I had a rummage in the attic for old photos, letters or ideally a diary but there wasn't much up there. My dad wasn't one for keeping stuff like that; Christmas cards were thrown out by Boxing Day. 'Use it up and chuck it out' was his catchphrase when we were younger. That being said, he had kept two massive piles of old Titbits magazines from the 60's and 70's, which were nowhere near as porny as the title may have you believe. As enticing as vintage celebrity photo shoots and articles about stately homes may seem, I was far more interested in the large wooden box that lay beneath them. After removing the magazines I slowly lifted the lid and peered inside; to my shock I found a double-barrelled shotgun in there. I raised the weapon out of the box, held it in my hands and inspected it. It seemed a little longer than similar guns I'd seen on TV and it had ornate silver plates mounted above the trigger area that had pictures of woodlands and children dancing and stuff on them. Y'know, Swiss Cuckoo clock vibes.

'I'm here to clear the air,' a voice boomed through the attic, taking me by surprise and making me almost drop the gun. 'I was drunk and in a weird place. That's no excuse though.'

It was Kelly. I was glad to see her but wasn't sure why she was apologising – there was a lot of truth in what she said, perhaps too much truth. 'There's no need to apologise. If anything, it should be me. Sometimes I don't put a lot of thought into the way I go about things. I hope you know I do really miss Mum.'

'It's fine; you and I deal with things differently. I don't like the way you're distant but it's not really acceptable for me to scold you for it,' Kelly rolled out those twenty-eight words like a full stop. It was clear that she hadn't totally forgiven me and perhaps didn't even believe me, but it was a relief to know I wasn't about to get another earful and it left enough space for a new foundation to hopefully build on.

I was surprised that she hadn't mentioned the weapon in my hands. 'So then, look at what I've just found up here! What's this all about, then?'

'Oh yeah, Dad's gun, right?' Kelly's response was surprisingly nonchalant.

'What? You knew this was up here?'

'Yeah, he showed it to me once, years ago. I think he picked it up when he was backpacking through Europe in the 60's or 70's,' Kelly shrugged, 'I don't think it's real. Just a daffy souvenir.'

I let the gun's weight rest in my hands; it felt pretty real but indeed did look like something picked up at a tourist spot. I thought about asking him about it later but didn't want to enter an awkward conversation about all the Titbits magazines. Kelly told me she was heading off to the Ypres Tavern that evening and asked if I wanted to join her. I politely declined because I really didn't want to make any small talk with her friends and also thought a restful evening might do me some good before hanging with Christine the following night.

When I arrived at college the following day I was pleased to see Louise D'Souza had made her way in. What with all the chaos of the past week and the revelation that there might be thirty or forty vampires running about Sittingbourne I had begun to grow a little bit worried for her safety. She seemed pleased to see me in my jacket, in fact the first thing she said to me was, 'Nice to see you've got the jacket on. Did you like the job I did on your patch? You didn't look at it in the pub.'

She had indeed sewn the patch on extremely well and I complimented her on her needle and thread skills accordingly. The way 'pub' had been presented as the last word of her sentence felt like it was my duty to address how we'd parted company that night.

'Yeah about the pub on Saturday,' I squirmed, 'it was a bit of a wild night, wasn't it? Next time, make me have a water break every couple of alcopops.'

'Oh, so there'll be a next time then?'

'Yeah, I mean, if you fancy joining me I'm going to the Black Griffin tonight.' The words slipped out a little loosely so I quickly added, 'Christine will also be there, just so y'know.'

'Ah yes, Christine, your "lesbian cousin" right?' Louise sardonically said, emphasising the quotation marks with her fingers. 'I bumped into your sister in the Ypres last night and asked about this lesbian cousin and she didn't know what I was on about.'

'Kelly? How do you know Kelly?' I asked, a little on the back foot.

'I've known her through friends of friends and hanging out at JJ's for most of this year. I didn't know she was your sister until last night though. Anyhow, stop changing the subject. What's the deal between you and this Christine? There's something going on that you're both lying about, I can feel it.'

'She is sort-of my cousin. A distant cousin. I haven't told Kelly yet because, well, we have different mums and sometimes that seems to be an issue.'

'Riiiiight,' Louise smirked, ringing every drop of askance out of one word to let me know she didn't believe me.

The college day rolled on in a pretty easy fashion and by lunchtime I realised that not only had I spent the entire morning in Louise's company, but also I was quite enjoying it. She seemed a lot more relaxed than our previous encounters. I'm not sure if it was because a lot of ice had been broken in the pub on Saturday or, if compared, her barrage of warm smiles and chats felt a lot more welcome after the lunch break of shame with Becky Hollis and the character-assassination bollocking I got from Kelly.

Another perk of having Louise by my side meant that I got all my work done by the end of the day. She totally spun my world around by explaining that I should focus on mentioning stuff from the marking criteria at the back of the assignment pack, rather than ignoring all that and trying to answer the actual question in my own misguided way. It's easy when you know how, right? I had been too quick to dismiss her last week; in retrospect I was glad she'd forced herself into my life. It was just a shame that I wasn't attracted to her as she would be perfect girlfriend material.

Christine:

The clock had just struck nine when I made one of my famously epic entrances through the doors of the Black Griffin. It was an old pub, which seemed a little pokey on entry, but sprawled a fair way back, eventually leading to a garden. I was in clover to see that Benjamin had brought along Louise. Luckily, with introductions already made, I was able to play it a lot cooler. She wasn't all gothed up this time, just dressed pretty casually in a Gap sweatshirt and jeans. She must have come straight from college. I found her choice of attire hot, in its own odd little way, as it was like a cheeky, candid, behind-the-scenes glimpse kind of thing. About halfway through our second pints of snakebite and black we were nattering away like proper, actual friends. It was taking all the willpower in the world not to push through the gears and start trying to get proper flirty with her. I kept searching for clues that she may be into girls or at least willing to consider the option, but nothing was forthcoming. She was playing it a lot cooler than on Saturday but her blatant crush on Benjamin was still there, living through her glances that followed him whenever he went to the bar or off for a piss.

While Benjamin was away Louise leant forward and asked me earnestly, 'So, what's the real deal between you and

Benjamin? I know you aren't cousins. What is it? Are you drug buddies or is it a kinky sex thing?'

Christ, I wanted to tell her the truth. I wanted to proudly declare that I was a twenty-eight-year-old lesbian stuck in the body of an eighteen-year-old vampire and all I truly wanted in the world was to grab her around the waist and kiss her until the stars fell, but I couldn't. There was too much at stake (no pun intended) so I just reiterated the party line, 'No it's true. Me and him are distant cousins on his mum's side.'

'Riiiiight,' Louise said, clearly disbelieving me.

Benjamin Cooper:

Once again, lost in the peak of the evening, the three of us had a great time; chatting about music, singing along to the jukebox, taking the piss out of life. Is this what having friends is like? Like, proper friends? It felt nice but also troubling, like the safety of isolation had been torn from my day-to-day routine, like a band-aid plaster from skin leaving a tender wound exposed. I decided to trust the development; chances were that I'd probably piss them both off by the end of the evening and I'd be back on my own again anyhow.

The evening was going swimmingly until my ears picked up a loud, boastful voice that was familiar to me. As I looked I saw Grunge Tosser pontificating with some other bloke. His mate was a tall, wiry type, with short fair hair gelled up to try and convey a little edge.

While I was examining the pair of them, Grunge Tosser's eyes met with mine and it was clear that an acknowledge-ment of some sort would be required. For one sweet moment I presumed we'd both get away with a nod and a muttered, 'Alright?' but then he leant forward. 'Alright mate, how's things?'

'Yeah, yeah, Good.' I said, hoping that'd be enough and I could get back to my pint.

Unfortunately, that wasn't to be. 'Cool. Cool. So yeah, what about Jon Miller and all that?'

'Yeah I feel bad for his family but to be honest, me and him weren't exactly friends.'

Grunge tosser clearly wanted to vent. 'Yeah, horrific stuff but he was a complete arsehole. The little rat-fucker sold me a load of bad skunk the other day. Blew all my savings on that shit.'

'Wait a minute,' chirped Christine with a big Cheshire Cat smile spreading on her face, 'Jon Miller was bragging about that in the pub. He called you a Grunge Tosser!'

'Really?' I said, stifling a laugh and a little shocked that my dearly departed enemy and I were on the same page when it came to giving nicknames to dickheads.

'It's Aiden actually,' Grunge Tosser said, puffing out his chest.

'Consider me corrected,' Christine beamed. 'Nice to meet you, Aiden Actually,'

'Fine,' Aiden Actually The Grunge Tosser said, knocking back his last swallow of Guinness before turning to his dodgy-looking mate. 'Right, I'm going. Are you coming to the Penny Theatre?'

'Nah,' his dodgy-looking mate answered, bathing Christine in a salacious glance. 'I think I might stick around here and see how the evening goes.' And with that, he slid into a small space on the bench beside Christine.

Christine:

I couldn't believe the gall of this bloke. He looked ridiculous enough with his t-shirt and waistcoat combo adorned with a bunch of tacky pendants, beads and bangles from the Indoor Market, but he also liked to be very animated with his mouth, continually smiling and gurning showcasing two rows of very off-putting little sweetcorn teeth.

'So, before I get you a drink I'm gonna need your name, sweetheart,' he drooled, trying and failing to slip his arm behind me as I blocked his approach by pressing my back and shoulders hard against the wall.

'I'm fine, thanks,' I replied, turning my attention back towards Benjamin and Louise.

 Sweetcorn Teeth seemed to find this amusing; 'Ha ha, I'll just call you Little Miss Difficult then.'

'She's not interested, mate.' Louise stepped in to my rescue and I swear I damn nearly swooned like an olden days, silent movie damsel-in-distress or something.

'No need to be like that. None of you lot know me,' he declared, and started to roll out a load of guff about being a musician, a handy drug connection and all manner of stuff that only served to make him even more unappealing. We tried to ignore him but he lingered on the side of our table for the rest of the night.

Just after the bell rang for last orders, I started to feel a bit icky. Not drunk but like I had an upset tummy or something. This wasn't ideal because the locks on the doors in the bogs were broken. Either way, I felt the urge to sort myself out and headed for the ladies toilet. Turned out it was just a bit trapped wind, but as I was about to leave, the door to the cubicle was forced open and in strode Sweetcorn Teeth.

He seemed surprised I was still on my feet; he'd probably slipped something in my drink, which would explain my gut ache. Still, he was relentless. 'Come here often? Just kidding. I know it's awkward because you're with your friends but they aren't about in here. Nobody would need to know. How about a kiss, eh? You know you're up for at least that.'

And with that he was trying to mount me, attempting to thrust his sweetcorn-toothed snog towards my mouth. I turned my head to the side and attempted to push him off but lost my balance, falling back on to the toilet. He was a thin bloke but surprisingly heavy and with my hands all tied up pushing his ghastly lips away from my face, I couldn't get enough purchase to push his torso off of me. This wasn't going anywhere good so I just thought, 'Fuck it,' and launched my fangs at his neck. Typically I missed the veins and just chomped down hard into a patch of skin and sinew.

Sweetcorn Teeth screamed out in pain, 'What the fuck was that, you dirty bitch?' His temper flaring and an adrenaline release increased the pressure of his push. The cubicle door then swung open once more, revealing Benjamin, who spent only a microsecond analysing the situation before diving in and biting straight into the vein on the other side of Sweetcorn Teeth's neck. Our victim began to cry out so I silenced him with my hand and, with a more measured attack, tucked into the vein nearest to me. We knew this wasn't the ideal place for a kill so we attempted to drain him as quickly as possible. Lord knows what anyone outside of the cubicle made of all the intense, fast paced sucking noises but needs must.

Five minutes later we staggered out of the booth, dizzy from the feast, with bloated bellies and hazy heads. To my shock we saw Louise standing there. 'Holy shit, you're vampires? I bloody knew you two weren't cousins!'

'Listen Louise, we can explain,' I said, trying to sell an explanation in exchange for her silence on the matter.

'You don't have to. I know what you are now. Real life, blood-drinking vampires.' Her shock turned to a grin, 'And I want in.'

CHAPTER 10
I TOLD HER EATING PEOPLE WASN'T PLEASANT

Testimony: Benjamin Cooper and Christine regarding the final hours of the 15th of June 1995 and the week (or so) that followed

Benjamin Cooper:

I couldn't believe that Louise had caught us in the act and was even more baffled by her response. She 'wanted in'? She wanted to *join* us? What did that mean? Did she want to become a vampire or just straight up join in on the feasting and go at the corpse like a cannibal? Before I could stammer over an improvised excuse, Christine jumped at Louise's interest like a dog at a Frisbee.

'Great! So the first thing we've all got to do is get this guy out of the bogs and away from the pub.' Christine said this in a casual, cheery manner, as though arranging a birthday party.

A plan was then devised where she and I would place Christie's trench coat over our victim and lead him through the heaving crowd saying stuff like, 'Come on mate, let's get you a taxi.' Louise would then go and find the awkward bloke working the bar to tell him that it was her friend's time of the month and she needed some cleaning products to sort out a spillage in the toilet. This would enable Louise to scrub a good amount of the evidence away without murder even being considered. Our vigorous, controlled, speed-sucking ensured that it had been a pretty clean kill all-in-all, a bit of Mister Muscle and a J Cloth would sort the few splashes and dots right out. We'd all meet up by the river in Westgate Gardens where we'd weigh our victim down by placing stones in his pockets and stick him in the water, where hopefully his carcass would be eagerly consumed overnight by zombie fish. It was a great plan but I didn't have too much faith in the last part, zombie fish? In the River Stour? I'm not buying it. I could only presume that the zombie fish were mates with the talking bat she claimed to know. Was Christine full of bullshit or lost to delusion? I guess time would have to tell.

Christine:

Bon voyage, Sweetcorn Teeth! It was very satisfying to watch him sink down in the water amongst the reeds, used condoms and zombie fish. Bringing Louise into all of this was a risky move but she played a blinder. She was taking so much casual glee in the disposal of a drained body that I did wonder if she might be an actual psychopath, but her steady stream of questions revealed a truth that was possibly more alarming – she was a vampire fangirl. She was giddy about the fact that blood-drinkers existed, elated that we didn't age and damn near squealed with joy when I confirmed that those *of lineage* can turn normal humans (like her) into blood-drinkers (like me).

She didn't waste any time and almost immediately yanked down the collar of her sweatshirt to expose her neck. 'Go one then, I'm ready for it. I've wanted this to happen since I was little.'

'Oh, you're asking the wrong person,' I said, throwing a sideways nod towards Mr Cooper. 'He'd have to do it.'

'What?' Benjamin trilled, less out of shock but more to highlight his reluctance to the idea.

'But he shouldn't.' Luckily for Benjamin, I applied the brakes. 'You don't want to be like me. It's all right for him with his lineage perks, walking about in the sun, not being beholden to a master. If he bites you, you'd be stuck indoors all day and he would have all manner of control over you.'

Of course, I would have loved her to have been bitten and turned, her inimitable youth allowed to walk through the years untarnished by the tides of time. We could be daughters of the darkness, surviving and thriving together all nested up in a home of lace and candles. Who knows where that could lead? But I realised my desires were running away with themselves. It would have been too much, too soon, to turn her then. And besides, having Louise as an underling would have powered up Benjamin's abilities as a blood-drinker and he's not ready for that yet either. For his own sake, I haven't even told him about some of the stuff he might be able to go on and do should he become a master. He massacred a group of lads and banged some random girl after his first taste of blood; lord knows what he'd do if he knew by siring a servant he could learn to fly.

Louise looked disappointed with that news that she'd be going home human, so I qualified, 'Listen we want you around but take it from me, you don't want to go running straight into being a blood-drinker. I'm not saying you shouldn't ever be like us but you shouldn't straight away. Live your human life for a bit.'

It wasn't what she wanted but I invited her to hang around with us during our dark-skied shenanigans. I said we should be a secret gang, meeting when the sun went down, and christened our fellowship the 'Creatures of the Night,' after my favourite KISS song. Benjamin looked disgusted at the branding but didn't challenge it. Louise scribbled her address and phone number onto two pieces of powder-blue paper torn on from her diary, before handing them to us. Now I knew where she lived and it took Academy Award levels of acting to prevent my face showing how excited I was about that.

Benjamin Cooper:

I had mixed feelings about Louise joining us. I had begun to enjoy the time Christine and I spent together. We were bound by our blood-drinking, what was Louise going to do while we quaffed the crimson? Sit about being enthusiastic? Also, Creatures of the Night? I didn't want to be in a gang called that. I'm not a goth, or a metaller or any of that Tim Burton circus folk, clichéd bullshit. But, I did need Louise's help with my college work and she was now in on our crimes, as a witness. It was probably more prudent to keep a close eye on her. So, a Creature of the Night it seemed I must be.

The following evening I met with Christine on the Iceland rooftop. She turned up wearing a faded but still ridiculous looking T-shirt with a drummer boy and all kinds of magpies, rainbows and shit on it. She saw my eyes being held hostage by its visual assault and misinterpreted my horror as interest. 'I know, right?' She was oddly proud of it. 'Vintage Marillion t-shirt. They're like, my third favourite band of all time.'

'Ah right, the Scottish heavy metal band. Kayleigh and all that.' Indeed I knew of the band but was keen not to encourage Christine to try and increase their presence in my life. 'They're a bit before my time I'm afraid.'

'Before your time?' she grumbled, 'they're still around, in fact I think they've a new one out at the moment. I don't suppose if I gave you the cash you could run down Woolies and get it on cassette for me?'

'Ah yeah, Afraid of Sunlight?' I was aware of the album's name from ads in the music press.

Christine glared at me and answered with a curt, 'You what?'

I explained that I was clarifying the title of the new album rather than mocking her Achilles' heel. Christine was very excited and tried to hand me a filthy twenty quid note peppered with crispy brown spots that appeared to be either dried blood or dried shit. I didn't dare touch it in case it was the latter and I told her it was on the house, for all the free blood she'd sourced me. The following evening I handed her the tape and her face lit up like a child on Christmas day. I was dreading having to sit through the damn thing as the soundtrack for our evening drives but actually it was a bit more indie rock than I expected with some occasional 60's homages. She then, however, tried to get me to listen to some seventeen minute B-side called Grendel but I drew the line at that.

Christine:

For the next week or so, our evenings were fun and passed without incident. Benjamin, Louise and I would normally take my car out to Whitstable or deep along the back roads of surrounding villages. We'd chat, sip a little alcohol and listen to music. Nobody got murdered and blood-drinking was restricted to stolen donor bags. I hoped our excursions away from Sittingbourne would be enough to curb the rising prominence of my master's old foot soldiers but McArthur, Banks and Long Tooth continued to patrol through Sittingbourne on a nightly basis. Igor would often swoop to my window with dispatches. My furry, winged familiar reported that others increasingly joined them. The growing collective were full of vile biters with a long heritage of violence and pain; Barbarossa, Sheena, Turnstile, Baxter and erm, Wally. Ok, his name may not inspire fear but Wally's history of violence did. He was a brutal, animalistic blood-drinker; it was rare for him to use his fangs to feed. Wally was a messy eater and preferred beating his victims down with his abnormally strong hands before tearing out various organs to suck on. And then there was Turnstile, a master manipulator. I never liked to get too close to him. I'd seen him twist words and burrow into brains, make zealots defy their gods, turn saints to sinners. Still, not a single one of them was *of lineage*. As long as I had Benjamin Cooper by my side we were safe.

Benjamin Cooper:

The end of the college year was approaching and I still had a fair bit of coursework to get done otherwise I'd be booted off. Things at home hadn't been great, Kelly was still in an odd mood with me and I couldn't seem to do anything without getting my Dad in a hump before he'd storm off to his room. I think he felt I was dossing my life away and resented the fact he'd raised a loser. He had a whole thing about the fact that I was eighteen and by that age he had a job and a car and a girlfriend and to his mind, I was just lurking about my room or off doing who knows what with who knows who. But seriously, how could I explain to him that I was off drinking blood with a fellow vampire every night? I wanted to talk to him about my biological mum but the heavyset frown on his face let me know that it really wasn't the time. Amongst his grumbles, my dad was especially narked about the fact he was now receiving repeated calls from Detective Constable Garry Thrill.

'I don't like having a copper keep calling everyday. I don't like having trouble brought to my door,' he'd repeat. The trouble was, I was trying to call him but we kept missing each other.

On the Thursday of that week, I decided to accept Louise's invitation to go back to her house the following night after college and get all the remaining work done. She was very excited about all of this but had kept a pivotal piece of information from me about the night.

'My mum's really looking forward to meeting you,' she suddenly blurted out during the train journey back.

'What?' I cried out, trying to hide my horror at this. I sometimes forgot that most people my age don't have two dead mums and a dad who pretty much just hides up in his room. I couldn't hold it against Louise, of course her mum would be there and shit, probably her dad too.

'Oh yes,' Louise beamed, 'I've told her so much about you. Like how funny you are and how you're good at listening to me when I'm having a mope. Of course, I haven't told her *everything* we get up to but she's looking forward to getting to know you better during dinner.'

'Dinner? I thought we were getting all the course work done.' Foolishly, I thought she might suddenly remember the main reason behind my visit and then reassure me that the dinner aspect of the evening would at least be demoted to a possibility rather than a certainty.

Alas she was adamant. 'Oh, don't worry we will, but we'll have some dinner first.'

'And what about your dad? Will he be joining us?' I tried to will an answer of 'No' into existence and buried my crossed fingers in my jean pocket.

'Probably not, he'll likely be in his room or at the pub. He's not very social.'

Ah, thank goodness! Good old grumpy dads, I raise a glass to your services to young introverts.

We arrived back at Sittingbourne and began the walk to her house on Burley Road. My mind manufactured overworked thoughts and stress about meeting her mother. After all, one of Louise's main mopes (that I apparently so expertly counselled her through,) centred on the great expectations placed on her by her parents. Also, I was an East Sittingbourne boy entering a West Sittingbourne home, would there be some snobbery over that?

As we entered the front garden of her house, I noticed a motorbike scattered in various pieces across it.

Louise caught me glancing at it. 'Oh that's my dad's doing. He's a real petrol head. Always buying up old bangers and doing them up. I help him sometimes, we did that utility truck over there together.'

It was reassuring that a woman with a husband and daughter who were spending all his time and pocket money on old cars and coming into the house covered in grease possibly wouldn't be too judgemental and might look kindly upon my social flaws. Oh, how wrong I was.

Before we'd got to the front door it swung open and Louise's over-eager mum stood in the doorway. 'Hello, you two, come on in! Come on in!' As each syllable tumbled out her mouth I saw her look me up and down and up again while her jovial mask slipped to reveal an expression of heart-wrenching disappointment.

'Mum,' Louise beamed, 'this is Benjamin.'

'Yes,' the mum answered, leaving a space that said more than words could, 'yes it is. I'm Val. Come on in. Come on in.'

The house was modestly sized but Val the Mum had made the most of the space. There was, as they say, a place for everything and everything had a place. It was exceptionally neat and tidy and there was a pleasing hint of Mr Sheen and Shake & Vac wafting through the hallway. Sadly, it was doing battle with some very post pestle & mortar, tossed salad tones invading from the kitchen, which gave me fears about what kind of dinner I might have to endure.

'So,' Val the Mum said, suddenly bringing my sensory investigation to a screeching halt, 'my Louise has told me a lot about you. You're not like I expected.'

'You have no idea,' I muttered under my breath, running my tongue along my fangs.

'Eh?' she said with a polite smile.

'Sorry, I was just saying I have no idea what she's said about me. I hope it's good.'

'Oh, yes,' she replied, plastering a new superficial smile on her face, 'it is. All good things. Anyhow, you two get started on your work and I'll finish getting the dinner done. Louise's father won't be joining us as he's out looking at another car to buy.'

YES! Good old Louise's dad. He knows the score.

Just as we were about to walk up the stairs Val the Mum pulled Louise to one side and whispered, 'Door open, please.' I felt a certain relief over this, I'm not sure why. It just felt safer for all of us that way.

Louise's bedroom was an odd affair, created, it seemed, out of compromise and juxtaposition. The walls were painted dark purple and covered in posters of gothic fancies like The Cure and The Crow, however the walls were adorned with crisp white shelves proudly displaying medals, trophies and photos from Louise's past as a champion gymnast and ballerina while the posters had been framed and hung with nails and hooks and such like rather than the more teen friendly blue tack approach. It was immaculately clean and ordered; I could sense Val the Mum's influence strangling the life out of Louise's boudoir vision.

We immediately got going on the course work, Louise made me tear through the majority of the outstanding items at a hard pace and by the time dinner was served, we'd got most of it done.

Luckily, the dinner wasn't too frightening – just chicken in some kind of spicy dust, boiled potatoes and some green beans. Once I'd choked down the veg it was pretty plain sailing on the food side of things. Conversationally however, things were dicier. Val the Mum had decided against the grin-and-bear-it approach to me being her potential son-in-law and had decided to take that frustration out on me using barbed chat.

'So then, what star sign are you?' Val the Mother asked.

'Gemini,' I confessed, already aware that she'd probably have something to say about that.

'Oh, I don't usually trust a Gemini. It's a very two-faced sign. I've never quite known where I stand with them. They're never direct when questioned, it's always like they're hiding something.' Which was rich coming from the woman who nearly fake-smiled herself to death when I turned up on her doorstep.

'Oh well, I hope you'll forgive my birthdate, believe it or not I didn't get a say in when my parents' procreative efforts took place.' I hoped that was "direct" enough for her. She looked pissed off, Louise let out a little chortle, and I felt pleasingly strong. There was a time, even a few weeks ago, that I'd let a fool like her completely steamroller me but fuck it, she's old, in her forties or fifties even, and will most likely be dead in a couple of decades, long before me. She's already lost the war.

After that, conversation pretty much ground to a halt and, after some awkward plate scrapes and cup slurps, Louise demanded that we go back up to her room while Val the Mum tidied the dishes. She was frighteningly keen and pretty much pushed me into her boudoir with one hand and shut the door closed with the other.

I immediately reached for the safety net of Val the Mum's rules. 'I thought your mum said the door had to be open.'

'Never mind the door.' Louise's voice was clear and confident.

I needed to assert some control on this unexpected change of plans. 'Ok, shall we finish off that last piece of college work?'

'Never mind the college work,' Louise said, slowly pacing towards me. 'You know what I want.'

I panicked; this had shades of the obligatory sex encounter with Becky Hollis written all over it. I still felt odd about having been part of that hook up, I couldn't handle the weirdness of my sort-of friendship with Louise being thrown into a similar mix. She stepped forward and squatted down. I tensed up; worried she was about to grab hold of me or something. Instead, she reached under her bed and pulled out an old, musty brown leather book. This was totally not what I was expecting. She popped the book on top of her bed and then turned to face me.

She then threw me another curveball. 'What do you think about the clothes I'm wearing?'

She was dressed in jeans and a thin navy blue cardigan with a white vest underneath. In all honesty, I had very little opinion about her clothes and was unsure how to respond. Luckily she jumped in and let me know what the correct answer was. 'I hate them. This is what my mum makes me wear when I go to college. Do you remember what I was wearing at the Ypres that time? That's the real me.'

I didn't have the nerve to tell her I thought the cardigan and vest looked better. She slowly rolled the blue cardigan from her shoulders and threw her head back exposing her neck. 'I want you to bite me – make me like you. I'm begging you. I can't be trapped in the life my mum wants for me. I may as well be dead.'

I could feel the pulse of her vein, the rhythm of her heart. It'd been a long penance of feeding from donations and I missed the rush of fresh blood. It was there, offered willingly to boot but no, I realised it was a foolhardy fantasy to even entertain the notion.

'What, here? In your bedroom? I couldn't,' I said. 'I mean, think about the mess. What about your bright white vest?'

'Stain it,' she sighed.

'Louise, I don't even know how to turn you into a vampire. What if I kill you?'

'I've studied it. See that book on the bed? It's an ancient Italian book I picked up last year on holiday. I've been translating it at night, studying the world of blood-drinking. It says that you have to drink about a fifth of my blood volume and then leave my system to rebuild itself based on the DNA received from your bite.'

'I don't know about this. It all feels a bit sudden.'

'You have nothing to lose. Christine's not telling you everything about your potential. You're *of lineage*; do you know what that means? What that REALLY means? The more blood-drinkers you sire, the stronger you become.'

I must declare there was something in the moment. I wasn't sure if it was the closeness of our bodies or the way her fresh white vest clutched her body but the temptation to touch her washed over me, if only for a fleeting moment. It was as if she saw my moment of weakness and decided to play upon it.

'Kiss me, then,' she said. 'Let me make it easy for you, I know you get shy. We could be each other's firsts.'

I didn't have the heart to tell she'd be my third, but thankfully this exact thought reawakened sobering memories of how awkward my previous encounters had been. I applied the brakes. 'Louise, stop. I'm not going to bite you and I'm not going to kiss you.'

I hadn't really had time to consider how she might reply to my rebuttal or what my next moves might be after blowing her off. The first ten seconds were perhaps the worst; initially, she just stood there looking at me blankly. Then there was a look of questioning anger, as if she couldn't believe that I'd have the audacity to refuse her beauty. And then, the stern scaffolding fell from her face with a stream of steady tears chasing after it.

'Why not? So many other boys want me. Why not you? What is it? Don't you like me at all?'

'No, it's not that. I like you a lot actually, as in, I enjoy spending time with you and I care for you. That's why I can't do... all the things you want me to do. You deserve to give yourself to someone who properly loves you – someone who'll cherish your devotion.'

'What does any of that mean?'

I wasn't really sure myself and then foolishly decided to work through my own feelings out loud. 'I think... Basically, if I was to sleep with someone, it'd have to be with someone I'm unlikely to see again or someone I'd want to be with forever.'

This didn't help at all and she collapsed on her bed sobbing hard into her pillow. I hovered anxiously unsure where to go or what to do. Fortunately, I guess, she hollered an instruction; 'JUST. GO. HOME.'

I collected my stuff and tried to sneak down the stairs to avoid any family interactions on the way out. Typically, Val the Mum was there on the landing. 'You going? Good. I think you've done enough harm tonight.'

Done enough harm? Hardly! Considering the shower of tears and scorn decorating my departure it made me wonder whether I should have just fucked her, sucked her and chucked her for the sake of earning the hatred.

The journey home was a sour one. The moments in Louise's bedroom churned in my guts and consumed my thoughts which were only distracted when the sound of laughter and someone calling my name echoed out from a passing car

Before I could really consider that incident, I walked past a short, thin little goblin of a man, dancing about and painting the phrase 'A GOD CHIEN LAND IS HERE!' in rich red paint on the pavement. He was giggling to himself while breathing in and out quickly through his nose and licking his lips. He turned to face me, exposing an unnerving face that held the features of both a Mr Punch puppet and a Toby jug. I threw my gaze to the floor and walked quickly past him. Today had been difficult enough and I really just wanted to head home.

When I finally made it to Woodberry Drive, I saw a tall, handsome man leaning against the lamppost outside of my house, smoking a cigarette. He was blessed with what I called fantastically normal looks; everything on his face was in proportion. His teeth were straight and white, his hair was short and sharp and his light brown skin was free of blemishes, trapped hairs or shaving cuts. He was the kind of guy who looked like he could model menswear for Burtons if he wanted. My footprints caught his ear and he turned to face me, throwing his cigarette to the floor and extinguishing it with his shoe.

'Benjamin Cooper? I'm DC Gary Thrill. You got a minute for a chat?' His voice was steady, calm and confident as he flashed his warrant card.

'Erm, yeah, Yeah sorry. I have been calling but we appear to keep missing each other'

'Don't sweat it, I know you've been calling,' he said, whipping out a notebook and pen. 'I'm guessing your sister's already told you about the chat me and her had and what it's about.'

'Yeah, Jon Miller, right?'

'Yeah, the late Jon Miller. Just wondering what your relationship with him was like.'

'We went to St. Johns together but were in different classes. We weren't friends or anything.'

'More like enemies?' he asked, raising an eyebrow.

'Nah, nothing like that either. I mean, he wasn't exactly the nicest person to me but few were. There were a lot of cruel words and actions flung around in that school.'

'Tell me about it. I was there in the 80's. They found the colour of my skin *fascinating*,' he paused, aware of his candour, and course-corrected his patter back to professionalism. 'Anyhow, I believe you and he had an altercation the night he died.'

'He was mouthing off in the pub. Saying stuff about my sister. I stood up to him and lost. Look, it's all really embarrassing, he pushed me over a table, and then he and his mates beat me up in the car park. I'm not much of a physical threat am I?'

'Perhaps not.' Gary Thrill responded, giving me a quick look over. 'You ok though? No injuries or anything?'

I made a kind of 'nah' strange noise, somewhere between a grunt and a sight to let him know from my point of view it was all forgotten and forgiven.

'Ok, I think I'm satisfied but I might need you to come to the station at a later date and make an official statement. Stay safe and stay out of trouble. Your name was the first mentioned after the bodies were found. Hopefully this is just a wrong place, wrong time thing, right?'

'Right,' I said, throwing him a homely smile and slight nod, hoping this would be the end of it. I made my way back inside to collapse on my bed and dream my way out of the shitty day I'd had.

As I entered the house, Kelly was in the kitchen. She was spreading Fluff spreadable marshmallow and Nutella on toast and clamping them together to make some kind of outrageous dessert sandwich. I had to admit I was jealous and wanted one too. She seemed a little tipsy but, unlike our previous post-pub chat, she appeared to be on the happy side of drunk.

'Do you know some girl called Eliza or something?' Kelly asked, swirling her mallow covered knife around like a conductor's baton. 'Well, she was in the pub tonight and was asking me about you. She was saying she can't work you out?'

'So, what did you say?'

'I told her the truth. I told her that you find it difficult to talk to girls because you're a weird virgin.'

The day had been saved – Eliza had been asking after me! True, I had been labelled a weird virgin, but she had been asking after me. And she had been trying to 'work me out'. This was worth a thousand notches on the bedpost. The news was like the strike of a match in the dark and I carried its glow through the night.

CHAPTER 11
LET SOMETHING IN?

TESTIMONY: BENJAMIN COOPER AND CHRISTINE REGARDING THE escalating troubles following the 25th of June 1995

Benjamin Cooper:

My radio alarm clock flicked its digital display to 07:00 while a full bloom summer's sunlight kissed the glass in my windowpane. The glow greeted the sleepy, contented smile on my face. Life was good; most of my coursework was done, I'd survived questioning from Detective Constable Gary Thrill and I had word from my sister that Eliza had been trying to *work me out*. I wondered if the half-sketched plan of meeting up to see Batman Forever at the cinema still held weight despite having been cooked up at the Ypres Tavern weeks ago. The movie hadn't been released yet so there was still time to seal the deal. That is, if I could find her somewhere and not bottle out of talking to her. Christine's harsh appraisal of my long-term chances still heckled my heart. Also, considerations such as the dashing art-school boys she was associating with at College and the 'by the way, I'm a vampire' fang-tusked elephant in the room remained hurdles. It was going to be tricky but there was, at least, still a chance.

I made my way downstairs to grab breakfast and heard the crashing and banging of boxes being shoved around, mixed with drawers being violently opened and closed. This could only mean one thing; someone or something had upset Dad. I went into the dining room to find him standing in his pyjamas amongst boxes and boxes of stuff, all of it decanted from the attic and the garage. Alongside them sat a parade of plastic carrier bags, proudly displaying familiar logos, branding and slogans like a timeline tribute to the legacy of High Street shopping. Somewhat unnervingly, the weird Swiss shotgun was there too, not on display but tucked away to one side of the pile almost as if my Dad was trying to hide it in plain sight.

'Everything alright?' I asked.

He decided not to answer and skipped to the point. 'Have you been poking about in the loft?'

I wanted to broach the subject of my biological mum and how I was looking for any old artefacts, but Dad had the kind of faraway look in his eye where I knew I had to be careful to not send him off on one. 'Ah you know, just looking for old magazines and stuff, photo albums. Do... we still have any old photo albums?'

He made eye contact but it wasn't welcoming. 'From when?'

'When I was little?' I considered throwing in a dash of comedy squirm into my vocal delivery but thought better of it in case it came out wrong and was read as sarcasm.

He paused for a moment, clearly considering how to play the situation. 'Can I give you some advice? Whatever you're looking for in the past, you won't find it. There's no pearl of wisdom, no riddle-resolving truth. You might find a fragment of a memory but it ain't the truth. The truth gets redefined a minute after it happens. And then everyone moves on.' He sighed a weary sigh. 'I'm going to chuck out a lot of this stuff later this week, so feel free to have a look.' And with that, he took himself off to the sanctuary of his room and presumably only left for work after I'd gone to college and his coast was clear.

My day at college was slightly odd and stilted. Louise didn't turn up, which was to be expected, but even those that were there seemed a little distracted and distant. I drank a full can of Pepsi Max without generating even the slightest trace of interest from Darren King. In brighter news, I handed my huge wad of outstanding coursework to Mr Claypole who begrudgingly told me he'd have to mark it before being able to confirm my place on the course was secure for the final year. Whatever!

I continued to meet up with Christine over the next few nights, drinking blood and chatting shit. I was keen to get back to the pubs and high street of Sittingbourne, hoping to chance an encounter with Eliza, but Christine was adamant that we enjoy the coast while warm summer breezes rode the night. Louise's comments that Christine wasn't being entirely truthful with me were playing on my mind and as we walked to her car I tried to tease a little more information from her.

'Is there something you need to tell me?' I asked.

'Yeah, so, I've been talking to Louise on the phone. I know the pair of you have had some kind of weird falling out but... well, I like her.'

I wasn't sure if she meant "liked Louise" as in she fancied her or just liked her as a person. Either way, I jokingly said that I was pretty sure she was straight but Christine got all defensive and brought up an off-the-cuff comment Louise made about having a girl crush on Jet from Gladiators. So what? Who doesn't have a crush on Jet from Gladiators? Even my dad comes down from his room to see her flip her hair about, wrap her legs around a provincial town P.E. teacher hanging from some rings before yanking them off (so to speak).

Christine:

At first, I wasn't too concerned about Louise's absence from our night-time misadventures, but around the third no-show I decided to press Benjamin on the subject.

'What's going on with Louise?' I asked. 'Don't give me any of that "she's busy or tired" crap you've been rolling out over the past few nights.'

Benjamin was sheepish and awkward about it. I was worried that he might have had his wicked way with her and cast her aside like he did with that strumpet in Canterbury. This would have been the worst of all the worlds. While I would be secretly seething and jealous should they become an item, at least she would have remained in my life. If he'd fucked her and chucked her that would most likely be it - Game Over. I did have the safety net of her phone number from the night in Canterbury, but held off the temptation to call her for a day or two. Eventually I caved in and dialled the six digits of separation. All of my rehearsed opening lines went out of the window when a weary male voice picked up the phone and grunted, 'Hello.'

I presumed it must be her father – I forget that most eighteen year olds still have parental figures loitering about. I asked The Father if I could speak to Louise to which he simply huffed, 'Right,' drenched in an exhalation where the receiver was clearly pressed far too close to his mouth.

The sound of the receiver being carelessly plonked down on a table and the sound of footsteps and muffled chatter trailed. Eventually Louise picked up the phone – she was distant and sounded upset. All of my planned conversation starters felt too bold under the circumstances, so a five-minute feast of uninspired questions, one word answers and awkward silences followed. When the final 'take cares' and 'see you soons' had been dished out, it felt like a mercy killing.

I figured that would be that and prayed for a day when somehow, somewhere I should be re-acquainted with Louise, but to my surprise, she called me the following evening and was in a far more chatty mood. And then again the next night, on this occasion we chatted, laughed and borderline flirted for over an hour, only the sound of her Mum nagging her to get off the phone and my prearranged meet-up with Benjamin halted the call. We agreed to chat daily by phone leaving me giddy with anticipation for the phone to ring every evening at six.

Benjamin Cooper:

Over the next few days, my infatuation with Eliza built to frankly ridiculous levels. I'd conjure fantastical scenarios in my head about us bumping into each other again. It was maddening and pathetic; I hated myself for it and took myself out of the house on a quest to the D n' J Smith newsagent to grab a chocolate milkshake, some Wheat Crunchies and the latest music weeklies.

On the way there I saw that odd little man with the red paint again. His Mr Punch/Toby Jug-combo face was still gurning away with a variety of off-putting panting, licking and sniggering sounds coming out of his mouth, trailed by a slight whistle. Once again he was painting the phrase 'A GOD CHIEN LAND IS HERE!' all over the pavement and across some of the walls. Unlike the other evening, he wasn't satisfied painting it just once; he'd already got it down twice and was going for a third. Only this time, he'd messed up and the phrase had begun 'A GID CHOEN'. My internal monologue hankered to heckle him but he seemed thrilled with the error. He continued to paint the phrase incorrectly another three times and, as he did so, something caught my attention – the strokes of his brush seldom matched the letters they produced. It was less like he was slapping paint onto concrete clumsily and more akin to a child slopping water over a magic colouring book. The creepy little bastard then looked up at me, grinning and nodding with raised eyebrows as if seeking some kind of confirmation or approval from me. Before making his way westwards, he shook his face softly from side to side and started sucking the excess red paint from his fingertips like it was jam on a butter knife. I was glad my path home lay to the east.

As unsettling as The Little Man With a Paint Pot in His Hand was, it was a mere diversion compared to the unnerving sight that greeted me as I returned home. Detective Constable Gary Thrill was back outside of my home, waiting for me.

'Good morning, Benjamin Cooper,' he beamed before turning his tone several shades more serious. 'I'm going to have to ask you to come to the station.'

'What for?' I asked, trying to turn my shock into a laugh, hoping it was all a bit of a joke.

Gary Thrill's voice remained serious. 'To answer a few questions I have.'

'What questions?'

'You'll find out at the station.'

'Nah, I'm not going anywhere. I've got my music weeklies to read.'

'I'm going to have to insist.'

'Are you arresting me? Do you have a warrant? If not, I'm not going anywhere.'

It was a bluff, I'd seen this tactic on TV and in the movies and I was surprised it worked.

Gary Thrill's posture slumped and his assertive tone descended in a half-defeated sigh. 'Ok, so I can't force you to come to the station, but I have to ask – what's the relationship between you and Spencer Terrence?'

I'd never heard of him. 'I'm sorry, I don't know who that is.'

'That's odd because I have several eyewitnesses who said you helped him out of the Black Griffin pub in Canterbury on the evening of the 15th.'

'Oh him? I don't know him on a personal level. He just ended up drunk and sitting with us. He was hammered so we helped him out of the pub and got him a taxi home.'

Gary Thrill started to apply the pressure again. 'Well, he didn't make it home, did he?'

I urged myself to play it smart, confident and distant. 'Didn't he?'

'No, he did not. In fact, we believe we've just pulled his body out of the River Stour.'

Believe? That means the Police didn't know for sure; he was grasping. 'So you aren't certain it's him?'

'We're awaiting tests to be sure.'

'Well, like I say, we stuck him in a cab and sent him on his way, so it's probably not him in the river is it?' I thought I'd stick to the story until he got bored.

'It's hard to prove at the moment. There's not much left of him. Flesh wise, I mean.'

Gary Thrill paused, possibly noticing my distraction as I considered that maybe there ARE Zombie Fish in that river.

He continued, 'but I'm pretty certain it is him. Unless someone popped his clothes on a skeleton and dumped it in the river. You say "we stuck him in a cab". Who were you with?'

'Just some girls I met.'

'A bit of a ladies man are you, Mr Cooper?' Gary Thrill asked me with half a nod sold as a wink.

'I wouldn't know about that.'

'Yeah, it's a bit of a head scratcher, isn't it? The picture your sister paints of your private life is vastly different to that provided by a Mr Darren King. He seems to be under the impression that you have a handful of girlfriends on the go at the moment. Was Miss Louise D'Souza with you on the night of the 15th?'

'Bloody Darren King's an idiot, don't listen to him. Yes, Louise was at the pub but I was there to meet with a different girl.'

'Are you in a romantic relationship with either of these two young ladies?'

'It's none of your business but no, I'm just friends with them. I'm very single at the moment.'

'It's a bit odd, innit? A young man such as yourself, hanging about with girls all the time. No friends who are male. No romantic aspirations with the girls you spend all this time with. I hope you don't mind me asking, but are you gay?'

'No.' I replied, wondering where that line of questioning was going to go.

'So, what is it? I don't understand the company you keep or the associations you have. Is it a drugs thing? It's funny how Deano Barnes, Jon Miller and Spencer Terrance – three small-time dealers, all end up dead within the same month and your name keeps popping up in my inquiries. Help me out, Benjamin. Paint me a truth before someone else frames it.'

'Deano Barnes? Is he dead too? I don't know anything about that.'

'So you know about the other two then?'

'Only the same as what you know. I was in the same pub as them on the nights they died.'

'Interesting, isn't it? Just a coincidence, I suppose. And what about Mr Kincaid? What's your relationship like with him?'

'Who?' I had literally no idea who Mr Fucking Kincaid was, despite Gary Thrill rolling out the name like he was my next-door neighbour.

'Mr Kincaid. He was a friend of Spencer Terrence. He was with him at the Black Griffin on the night of the 15th.'

'Oh, you mean that Grunge Tosser?'

'That's not his name,' Gary Thrill declared, seeming a little pissed off that I was being so flippant during his interrogation.

I shrugged, 'Well, that's what I call him. It's what Jon Miller called him too. I reckon that's what everyone calls him.'

'His name is Aiden, actually.'

'Aiden Actually! Ha, that's what my friend Christine called him.'

'No. No. His name is Aiden Kincaid.'

By this stage, I had the giggles. I'd spent weeks nervous about Big Scary Police Detective Gary Thrill poking his nose into my night-time antics but it appeared that he was actually pretty incompetent. I decided to heckle him some more. 'Should you be giving me all this personal information? You're not very good at this, are you?'

Gary Thrill's exasperated mask dropped revealing his usual handsome, confident visage. 'Aren't I?' he retorted, throwing me a wink.

SHIT! I'd just accidentally given him a fuck tonne of information. He now knew I had more of a connection to Jon Miller than I had previously indicated. He now knew that we'd got into a bit of heated teasing with Grunge Tosser aka Aidan 'Actually' Kincaid and his fish food-fated friend. He now knew Christine's name. It all painted a picture far more colourful than, 'I happened to be in the area at the time.' SHIT! SHIT! SHIT! He didn't have proof, but now he knew he wouldn't be wasting his time to go searching for it. SHIT! SHIT! SHIT! SHIT!

Gary Thrill slowly walked backwards towards his car. 'I'll be keeping an eye on you, Mr Cooper. I'd keep a low profile for the next few weeks if I were you.'

I went back inside overwhelmed by the sinking feeling that I had well and truly fucked up my verbal duel with Gary Thrill. Things got even stranger when the evening began to roll in. I was about to get ready to go and meet Christine when the doorbell went. If it had been up to me I would have ignored it but Kelly, being Kelly, decided to open the door.

'Benjamin, it's for you!' she hollered up the stairs.

I made my way down the stairs as she made her way back up.

'Who is it?' I mouthed; pushing the words through as much of a whisper as I thought would remain inaudible.

'That girl you know,' she mouthed back.

I wondered which girl it could be; I briefly hoped it was Eliza who had by chance found her way to my neighbourhood and decided tonight was the night when she would track me down and 'work me out' but instead, it turned out it was Louise, bringing an awkward reunion and an envelope in her hand.

'Hi,' she said.

'Hi,' I replied.

It wasn't one of history's more verbose greetings. Both of our tones were chirpy but drenched in artifice, pretending the confusion and emotion burning behind the words weren't actually there.

'Can I talk to you outside?' Louise was nervous, I could hear it in the pauses between the words.

My initial instinct was reluctance but I dutifully followed her to the edge of the front garden. I stopped short of the pavement, keen to minimise my part in this uncomfortable reunion from the eyes and ears of the neighbours.

'I wrote this for you, ' she said, handing me the envelope. 'I wanted to explain a few things.'

Never mind the envelope, I had a bigger concern on my mind. 'How do you know where I live?'

'Christine told me,' she replied. 'I think she's keen for all the awkwardness to die down.' Louise was uneasy and would occasionally take a glance over her shoulder at a car parked far down the road. I guessed that Val the Mum must have driven her here and was keen to check that I wasn't doing anything else to drive her dear, darling daughter to tears.

'Anyhow, read the letter and if things are cool give me a call sometime. See you around.'

And with that she solemnly headed to the car in the distance and was gone.

Christine:

Later that night, Benjamin wandered down the road looking down in the dumps. I had hoped that by giving Louise his address, they might have patched things up and everything could go back to our three-way, thrill-seeking ways. Sadly, he revealed that she had given him a letter that he hadn't even bothered to read.

Benjamin:

After Louise's visit, I had gone back inside the house only to find Kelly in a talkative mood. After our bust-up a few weeks ago, it was nice to have her back on side. With her GCSEs out of the way it appeared she was focussed on building a collection of vinyl records. She'd picked up a batch and was keen to show them to me. During all of this I had placed Louise's letter in my pocket and forgotten about it. Well, not forgotten about it, but just hadn't got around to reading it.

Christine:

As we walked together past the cinema I began to egg him on about opening the letter.

'Maybe later,' he grumbled, making some weak excuse about why he hadn't read it yet. He was, however, interrupted when his ear pricked up and picked out a shuffling sound a split second before I did. The sound increased and we both followed it to our left, to see a group of figures approaching from the back of St Michael's Church graveyard. As they came closer their silhouettes became defined and I recognised every last one of them.

Benjamin Cooper:

At first I was grateful to have something break up Christine's nagging over the letter but as the shapes in the distance grew closer, I began to feel unnerved. There was a familiar heaviness in their heartbeats and, as the moonlight hit their faces, their eyes flashed yellow. They were like us. Only, they looked a hell of lot more furious than Christine and I ever did.

A clutch of around fifteen blood-drinking blokes moved through the darkness, striding around the crosses and tombstones that separated us.

As they approached, the large guy Christine had told me about, McArthur, took his steps a little faster and bounded up to us.

'So this is the new boy then, eh? The one you were bragging about to Banks and Long Tooth?' he barked, looking me up and down.

'Yes it is. And his blood is oh-so-thick and oh-so-strong, he walks through both day and night.' Christine kindly declined to reveal my name but began to introduce the main clutch of vampires starting to circle around us, 'So yeah, these are the local blood-drinkers. The one with the big bones and the big mouth, he's MacArthur. Old grey temples there goes by the name Turnstile...'

'And my name is Sheena Dafoe,' a smooth, sultry feminine voice trailed through the graveyard with its owner appearing through the crowd shortly after.

Christine:

Sheena Dafoe was the last person I wanted to turn up amongst this mob. She didn't like me much and never had. She'd searched and found my master willingly, a good couple of years before I was turned. She was a stunningly gorgeous creature; my master couldn't believe his luck to have her in his services. However, the problem was blokes would lose their nerve when she'd try to seduce them – she was just too beautiful and, quite perceptively, her prey would presume that someone as desirable as her must be a trap. Maybe in London or in a larger city, she could have brought in blood galore for our master but on a wet Wednesday in the 'bourne she just looked out of place. Me however, the goth tomboy, I was the kind of achievable challenge the drunk lecherous bozos round here cherished – in their minds they were doing a lonely girl like me a favour. As such, I became my master's chief asset and she was relegated to being a trophy girlfriend. She was besotted with him, so on paper this should have been her ideal place to be, however my master only truly lusted for blood and power. These were two things that I could help him obtain and Sheena would never forget that.

Benjamin Cooper:

'So you're the one they speak of. The new kid on the block, *of lineage* no less. Do you know how rare a quality that is in modern men?' Sheena Dafoe purred. 'Even though, based on first impressions, I'm far from impressed. You do realise you have the power to make me do all kinds of terrible, wonderful things? I could be yours completely if you wanted me.'

And I did want her. In the most superficial way possible, I mean she was undeniably attractive. She was an inch or two taller than I was, probably five foot eleven possibly pushing six foot, with an hourglass figure wrapped in velvet and lace dress. Her eyes were a piercing flash of sapphire and her high-cheekboned face was framed by long, jet-black hair, perfectly straight until the ends, which curled around in front of her breasts. My interest in her was a shallow pool and I resented my thoughts for paddling in it.

Christine:

Typically Benjamin reacted to meeting Sheena Dafoe in the most tragically hetero-bloke way possible – by staring at her tits. That being said, he's a bit of a short-arse, I reckon five foot eight on his tiptoes and she's pushing six foot so her chest was probably eye level for him.

'Right so we've all met. Is there any other business to attend to or can we all get on with our evenings?' I asked through a yawn that I could have suppressed but decided to unfurl for theatrical effect.

'Nah, we're far from done,' McArthur growled, 'we need to send a message to the new boy. We need to show him we don't yield to his lineage.'

'Send a message? What, beat me up? Beat him up? Are you mad? You know there are rules about this kind of thing. You wouldn't risk the consequences.'

'Ah,' Turnstile stepped forward, emerging through the sound of his own hushed voice, 'there are ways to make a statement without consequences. Mr Scratch would bear no mind to an incident of hurt if there was a degree of separation.'

'What's that supposed to mean?' Benjamin asked with an element of fear in his voice. I had a bad feeling that I knew what it meant and we needed to leave fast. I noticed that amongst my Master's old cronies, Baxter was missing. He was a brutal and tenacious killer but a complete loser, a needy, bleating sheep and a good-for-nothing hanger-on. He never missed group meetings and his absence here was suspicious.

'It means we need to stop wasting time with these goons,' I spoke confidentially, unwilling to blink. I grabbed Benjamin's hand and walked him away at a brisk pace, towards the west side of the High Street.

'I think they're going after your family,' I whispered as I led him to my car. 'We need to get there quick. They've sent Baxter; he's a big, bad bastard. We need to stop him.'

Benjamin Cooper:

It was only as Christine revved her engine that the words sank in. They were going after my family? How? Why? I mean, how would they even know where I live? Each thought became lost in a storm of questions and worries as Christine sped eastwards through St. Michael's Road.

'Shit! They're following us,' Christine yelled as I looked out of the back window to see a familiar-looking hearse speeding towards us.

The hearse gained on us, faster and faster until it swerved out to the right. Then, with swift acceleration, it manoeuvred alongside the car and attempted to barge into us. Luckily, a procession of oncoming traffic emerged, causing the hearse to brake hard and fall back into the left side of the road.

As we approached the roundabout by Clarke's Gym & Judo hall, the hearse made another attempt to ram us but Christine managed a handbrake turn around the corner, causing the hearse to miss. With her foot pressed hard against the floor, Christine swerved out to the right and overtook three cars ahead of us before turning off her headlights in an attempt to throw them off the scent.

However this flagrant disregard of The Highway Code attracted a different form of attention. Flashes of blue light circled around us and a siren rang out, 'Great, now the fucking police are onto us,' Christine hollered. 'I'll take us down the A2 and turn down Vincent Road instead. You jump out and save your family. I'll deal with the cops.'

With the cop car hot on our heels, Christine sped towards Woodberry Drive. My home was in sight, there at the bottom of a T-junction - just one right turn and I'd be there. However, just as Christine was about to complete the turn, the hearse emerged from the left like a battering ram and hit us so hard it spun the car off at a thirty-degree angle. Christine hadn't bothered with a seatbelt and smashed her head hard against the steering wheel. I attempted to rouse her but she was out cold. Through the car's wing mirror I could see the doors of the hearse opening. McArthur, Banks and Long Tooth all stepped out of the vehicle grinning.

My right arm and hip throbbed from the collision but I pulled myself out of the car. My rival blood-drinkers began to pace towards me but were halted by the arrival of the police car that had been following us. I dragged myself to the front of Christine's car and hid, while two uniformed officers ordered the vamps to put their hands on the bonnet of their car. A familiar voice joined them, shouting that they were under arrest – it was Gary Thrill. I wondered for a second about how to play this; Gary and I had built something of an association but I wondered whether this would grant me help or hindrance. My thoughts were interrupted by the splintering sounds of screaming and gunshots and I knew the only tactic I needed to immediately concern myself with was survival. I picked myself up and began to limp towards the lamppost outside my home. I peered over my shoulder to see one officer's body on the floor; his torso was facing down but his head had been twisted until its lifeless eyes stared at the sky. Beside it stood Gary Thrill, firing shots at Banks and Long Tooth as they fled. I glanced left to see McArthur pulling his feasting jaws away from the bloodied neck of the second officer before tossing aside the drained torso attached to it. Gary Thrill took aim and attempted to shoot but found himself grabbed by the lapels and slammed viciously into the hood of the hearse. I wanted to help him but my mind was focused on Baxter and whatever he might be doing to my family. I could hear Gary Thrill screaming as McArthur began to pummel him; his fate was as good as sealed. Compared to the carnage occurring at the T-junction my home was quiet and still. Almost too quiet and still – I held my breath as I gently opened the front door.

CHAPTER 12
...OR THROW SOMETHING OUT?

TESTIMONY: BENJAMIN COOPER AND CHRISTINE REGARDING THE dramatic culmination to the night of the 30th of June 1995

Benjamin Cooper:

Placing my key into the front door I leant forward slightly and heard a muffled noise emerging from the living room. It was a rhythmic rattling sound with some voices either talking or chanting in unison over the top of it. Peering around the doorframe I recognised the noise to be the track '2:1' by Elastica, which surely meant that Kelly had to be in there somewhere. I steadied myself and whispered a brief prayer for her safety. I say prayer, but in all honesty it was more of an eyes closed, fingers crossed wish than a proper all-the-trimmings Our Father bit of business but I figured it was better than nothing.

I stood still and listened - it was hard to gauge if all was well, what with the Elastica record playing and the curtains being blown gently to and fro by an evening breeze drifting through the opened window. The realisation hit me that

SHIT! The window had been left open. Baxter, a vampire who—had been described by Christine as a 'big, bad, bastard,' could and indeed probably *had* crawled through and must surely be in the house somewhere. But it was mostly still and mostly quiet, though perhaps too still and too quiet. Maybe Baxter had already been and inflicted some horrific act upon my dad and Kelly. Maybe he'd fled the scene or perhaps – my heart began to race as the thought crossed my mind– he lay in wait for me.

Approaching the turntable, I decided to lift the stylus from the revolving vinyl but as the crunchy guitar chords on the track repeated and built to climax, two figures came crashing through the double doors that separated our living and dining rooms.

One landed on top of the other. The one on the floor was my dad; I had expected it to be Kelly due to the Elastica record playing but oh no, it was my dear old father, desperately yet gallantly fighting for his life as a hissing, bowling-shoe-ugly vampire pinned him down with one hand and clawed away at his face with the other.

I sprinted towards Baxter and booted him hard in the head. It was a great kick but I had forgotten my hip wasn't in the best shape since the car crash minutes earlier and the pair of us tumbled off to separate sides of the room.

I screamed at my dad, 'Get up! Get the fuck out of here!' He scrambled to his feet and rather than leg it out the front door, made his way back to the dining room. I did wonder if he was heading to the garden to give the plants one last water or some other last bit of business that always needed doing before holidays but concerns over my dad's escape faded as I noticed Baxter rise back to his feet.

'Look at you, on yer arse! All the chat about you down at the pressing plant and this is all you are? What a fucking joke.' Baxter growled a little and bared his fangs, 'Gideon Lachand sends his regards.'

Before I could even question who the fuck Gideon Lachand was, Baxter hurled himself at me. He was strong, ferocious and totally taking advantage of my wounded state, pounding my damaged hip every time I was on the cusp of summoning enough strength to push him off me.

'Y'know, I shouldn't do this but fuck it, maybe if I drank your blood I'd be *of lineage* too', Baxter hissed. 'Who knows how powerful that might make me?' He began to lower his mouth towards my neck and I prepared to feel the piercing puncture of his fangs on my vein. Instead, there was a loud bang and what felt like someone throwing a pot of warm soup and boiled rhubarb all over my face. Only, I knew it wasn't either of those things – it smelt of blood and gunpowder. I peered over the bloodied stumpy remains of Baxter's neck and looked through the space where his head had been just seconds earlier. There stood Dad, with the weird Swiss rifle in his hands, reluctant to lower his aim.

'Is he dead?' my dad asked.

Baxter's headless body collapsed, flopping off to the side. 'Well I don't think he's getting back up again.'

I picked myself up and flashed a nod towards the rifle in his hands as he finally lowered it. 'I thought that was just an ornament? I can't believe you own a real, firing gun.'

'Oh yeah it definitely works; I once shot some sort of wolf with it,' he revealed, as if that was the most natural thing in the world to have an anecdote about. 'So you're a vampire then? I always had my suspicions. Your mum – your biological mum – had certain qualities, but never wanted to talk about them. I respected her privacy but I overheard things. I never raised it though; I mean how do you suddenly ask someone who's so sweet and so full of happiness if they drink blood on the sly? Speaking of which, that reminds me.'

He rummaged around on the table, picked up a photograph and handed it to me. 'Here you go, I dug this out for you.'

The photo was familiar to me, a woman in her mid twenties holding a baby in her arms. A thousand memories raced to show off in the centre of my brain. Echoes of colour and sound rebounded. Moments of laughter, love, yes – some pain, but also comfort. I remembered her pale skin, dark hair and piercing sapphire eyes and more clearly than I had for the past decade or so, I remembered who my mother was.

I went to thank my Dad but I was interrupted by the sound of sirens.

The old man gave a nod towards the front door. 'You better get out of here. Don't worry, I'll sort this mess out.'

Good old Biological Dad.

Grabbing the front door's handle I swung it open and was startled by a figure standing in front of me. In the blindness of shock my mind raced faster than my eyes and I presumed it must be McArthur but instead it was another familiar figure aiming a gun at me.

'Make one more move, I dare you. I don't know what the deal is with you or what the fuck's going on tonight but go on, step forward and give me an excuse to pull the trigger.' Gary Thrill's eyes were bulging, his hand was shaking but he was close to steadying his aim with his resolve.

'With all the shots you were letting off I doubt you have any bullets left,' I scoffed. I had seen this work on TV just like the arrest warrant thing. I wasn't going to let him out-bluff me.

As I took an over-confident step forward he lowered the gun slightly and squeezed the trigger, causing a bullet to bounce mere centimetres away from my feet. 'I reloaded,' Gary Thrill answered coldly, raising his gun once more.

I stretched my arms out slowly with my palms exposed. 'Gary, listen to me. There are plenty of evil fuckers in this town but I'm not one of them. Why do you think they tried to attack my home? How many bullets did it take to stop McArthur back there? Who do you reckon has a better chance of taking them down? You with that gun or me with my fangs?'

'Fine,' he stared at me for a few moments before lowering his weapon, 'Go, but make sure you finish this.'

I turned to run off into an uncertain night and saw Gary Thrill's attention caught by something behind him. It was Christine smirking.

Christine:

I think it was the gunshots that shook me from my concussion. Things were dizzy for a spell but I centred myself with an emergency blood sample from Bates' fridge that I had brought with me in a freezer bag.

I swung the car door open and slid out. Behind me I could see McArthur's corpse speckled and stained by bullets and blood like blueberries in a muffin, one bullet in his left thigh, two in his chest and one straight through his bollocks.

Looking towards Benjamin's house I saw some foolish plain-clothes copper waving a gun about, trying to be all intimidating even though he was clearly shitting himself. I had to laugh - he was hardly The Punisher. If anything, he looked more like an older version of a dorky kid I knew at primary school. I was about to mock him but when he turned around I was hit by the realisation that, while I wouldn't have grown any older, in the past ten years Gaz from Lansdowne Primary School would have.

'Christine?' he asked, shocked at my youthful visage. 'How? I don't understand.'

'It's complex Gaz. I would love to catch up but as you've probably noticed, shit just got real.'

Benjamin limped past him, still clearly injured from the crash, and joined me as I got in the car.

'Is this thing still roadworthy?' he asked. There was a simmering anger suppressed by shock and weariness in his voice. I didn't have a clue–but told him the car was fine, purely because he looked like he could do with some good news. He shot me a disdainful glance. It had been a while since he'd looked at me with anything other than warmth and it hurt. The car sparked to life and I swear I've never been happier to hear the sound of an ignition click into the purr of an engine. Sadly, despite this, the mood in the car didn't improve a great deal.

Benjamin Cooper:

We pulled away, leaving Woodberry Drive and headed back towards the centre of town. As we pulled away from the blood shed and sirens that had invaded my home the streets became filled with a disquieting stillness, which blended uneasily with the sound of Sparks' 'When Do I Get To Sing My Way?' coming from the tape deck. No plan had been agreed but it seemed only natural that we'd turn the town upside down looking for Banks and Long Tooth with our wants leaning towards vengeance and needs desperate to neutralise their threat.

Christine could see I was injured and weak. She advised me to down a couple of the tubes from a freezer bag sat on the floor by my feet to help me recover. They didn't sit easy in my stomach; a restless rage was stirring and I tried to expel it by hurling questions at Christine in an accusatory manner.

'Why did they come for my family?'

'They must be worried about you,' Christine replied briskly, trying to gently bat the conversation off before it could begin.

'You never told me about any of this, did you?'

'Any of what?'

'Don't take me for a fucking idiot. You never told me that there'd be others who wouldn't be happy with me being out and about in Sittingbourne, drinking blood.'

She shrugged her shoulders in an affected manner though it couldn't mask the discomfort in her eyes. 'I really didn't think it'd be important.'

'Is there anything else you didn't think would be important for me to know?'

'Nah. Let's just...'

'What about the powers I can apparently gain? What about how to turn humans into blood-drinkers? What about the bloke Baxter was going on about? Someone called Gideon?'

The mention of the name 'Gideon' threw her. She clutched the steering wheel and her eyes widened as she missed a breath. The name felt familiar somehow like I had been forewarned about it but I couldn't place when, where or how.

Christine remained silent while the space in our dialogue prickled and jabbed at my nerves, stirring my anger more. 'Well?'

She looked sad, uncharacteristically hesitant and more than a little lost. 'Let's just track down Banks and Long Tooth, yeah? Get everything sorted out for good.'

I remained on the attack. 'And what if we can't find them? What if they go back for my family?'

'It's fine; Igor can track them about town and report back. Then we...'

'FOR FUCK'S SAKE CHRISTINE YOU CAN'T TALK TO ANIMALS! I'm sick of your bullshit; the talking bats, the zombie fish, the blood-drinking. I mean, are we even actual vampires or is this just about drinking blood as part of some pathetic goth fantasy? Or are you actually nuts and truly believe that you're a vampire? My dad was almost murdered tonight in his own home because of you and this nonsense. After we track down that pair in the hearse, I'm done with the blood-drinking, I'm done with you, I'm done with all of it, you understand?'

Christine:

Benjamin was incredibly pissed off at me, though he kept calling us 'vampires' which I found pretty offensive actually, so I refused to take his scorn to heart. We must have circled around town two or three times before finally catching a glimpse of Banks and Long Tooth skulking out of a side road before dashing past Aida kebab, back eastwards towards the Ypres Tavern. I wondered if they might be heading to my current residence to send some kind of message to me but instead, they turned towards the car park at the back of the pub and lingered, looking at some short-arsed bloke with a paint pot in his hand, crouched down.

'Oh great The Little Man with Paint in His Hand is out and about too? Let me guess, he's an evil vampire too?' Benjamin snapped, as I slowly turned the corner and applied the brakes.

'I haven't a clue who that is. It sounds like you know him though?'

'Nah, I don't know him but I keep running into him. He's always painting some nonsense about a God Chien on the pavement and doing weird shit like licking paint off his hand. The letters don't even match the brush strokes, it's completely fucked up.'

My heart sank – this sounded like some warped warlock shit. 'And you didn't think to tell me about this?'

He shot me a glance that suggested I was throwing stones in a greenhouse, and after all my half-truths, I couldn't blame him. 'I just mean, are you sure it's paint in his pot?'

Benjamin's miffed face hadn't mellowed. 'Well, let's go ask him then.'

Before I could take the keys out of the ignition, he'd removed himself from the passenger seat, announced his arrival by slamming the door and given Long Tooth a punch in the stomach.

Banks looked startled for a second before barking like a Scottie dog confronted by a German shepherd. 'Come on then! I ain't bothered.' He scrunched his face up into an earnest gurn and began swinging his clenched fists about in a manner that I think was supposed to evoke bare knuckle boxing but more like a pig on its twos failing to control its own trotters.

After a blunt and brutal jab to the head, Banks found himself grabbed by the throat and hurled against the two large refuse bins at the end of the car park. The bloke with the paint pot looked delighted by it all.

Benjamin Cooper:

It felt great to relieve my fear by taking my frustrations out of Long Tooth and Banks. Though The Little Man with Paint in His Hand's excitement at my display of vengeful violence was more than a little unnerving.

'Ooh breathless, strong, yes? Hunger? Rage? Deepest joy for me, goody-goody goodson,' the little fella declared in his odd little voice, sizing me up and down before going back to his pot of paint and his quest to cover the pavement with it. 'Deliver the goody-goody.'

Christine and I made our way over to Banks, who was attempting to pick himself back up only to find his knocked-silly head caused him to collapse back down beside the bins.

A cut on his face had begun to run past his eyes and down his cheek. 'Your boy's strong Christine, I'll give you that. But he ain't nothing compared to Gideon.'

'Gideon's not around though, is he?' Christine declared defiantly. 'And even if he was able to return, old Scratch would finish him for good this time'

'Scratch? You've been holding onto Scratch as your insurance policy around here?' Banks began to cackle. 'You dappy cow. Scratch left this town two years ago, made his way through Canterbury to Dover and was last seen in France. He ain't going to help you.'

The Little Man began whooping and jabbering on at a heightened pace, painting faster and faster across the pavement and across the road into the car park. The phrase A GOD CHIEN became increasingly distorted as it made its way towards us. The letters swirled and shifted into a new order as The Little Man cried out in frenzied shrieks, 'Ooh GOODY GOODY GOODSON! GIDEON LACHAND IS HERE!'

I was confused, startled, and unnerved. 'What does it mean?'

'It means we need to get the fuck out of town,' Christine said as the street began to feel darker, almost as if the shadows were growing around us, 'NOW!'

CHAPTER 13
CAN I RUN?

TESTIMONY: BENJAMIN COOPER AND CHRISTINE REGARDING THE harrowing early hours of the 1st of July 1995

Benjamin Cooper:

Like ink invading blotting paper, the shadows swallowed the streets around Christine and I, grabbing at our ankles as we ran into the night. My mind had become a savage storm of revelations and ravages. I had no idea what was happening anymore; was this actual dark magic or just my mind playing tricks on me? The terror Christine experienced at hearing the name Gideon Lachand became contagious and the pit of my stomach began to burn with feelings of panic and regret.

Christine:

I couldn't believe he was back. Gideon Lachand, my former master. Well, I say 'former,' but by the laws of the night, he technically was still my master. I felt like a fool. How could I have been so sure of my plans and plotting when they had been founded on so many uncertain factors? That being said, how could Gideon Lachand be back? How could he have survived both the metaphorical and literal grilling Scratch had subjected him to? Why would Scratch just give up the vice-like grip he had on this town? None of this made sense.

Benjamin and I raced eastwards with dread chasing our heels, down the High Street. I grabbed Benjamin's arm and attempted to flee down a side road, only for the approaching shadow to crash around us and block our path, rising like a gigantic hooded cobra hissing and forcing us to turn back.

Gideon's followers began to march alongside the shadow, with the savage yellow burn of their eyes blistering the summer night. Benjamin and I turned back sprinting past the butcher shop's alluring bouquet of blood and sawdust and on towards the turning that would lead us behind the Co-Op department store and the back of the High Street. I had hoped to make it to the station; we were too late for any trains out of town but maybe there'd be a taxi lingering for late trade or even the police, trying to catch easy-win pissheads and stoners. Anyone would do, even just some witnesses to ensure that the imminent, inevitable cruelty wasn't erased by the lonely darkness of night.

We made it to the curb, with the A2 separating the edge of the high street and the possible salvation of the train station. However, we didn't dare cross it. The road was consumed with Gideon's shadow; lightning struck the sky causing the darkness to thicken into fog and smoke. Deep within the bleak mass blocking the road, Gideon's followers began to shine as the sound of excited inhalations and laughter barely concealed the noise of their footsteps approaching.

Benjamin Cooper:

The uninviting subway linking Sittingbourne train station to the Forum Shopping Centre was the last place I wanted to go at the best of times but with unnerving, supernatural smog approaching us it appeared to be our only option. It was a decision I'd come to deeply regret.

We raced down the wet, stone steps leading into the flickering unease of the underpass. I tried to focus on the ground anxious that one careless step and slip could seal my fate.

However, it was a sudden, sharp blow to the back of my head that caused me to fall, landing with a thump and finding myself disoriented on the grotty floor. While my nostrils were filled with the foul stench of damp bricks that had been marinating for years in urine and rain, a familiar but unwelcome sound took over my ears.

'Sir! Goody Goody! Here Sir! Goody Goody Goodson!'

Christine:

I'm not sure how – maybe I picked up on the initial movement of the moment he began to stumble – but I could sense Benjamin was about to fall. I looked across and saw that creepy, short-arse warlock behind us, bashing Benjamin on the back of the head with a paint pot.

Benjamin fell to the floor and I only made it a few steps further before the ominous shadow smoke from the road above spilled through my planned escape route and began to fill the underpass.

Benjamin Cooper:

Having my momentum halted by The Little Man with Paint in His Hand made my body stop and consider how eventful the evening had been. I wearily tried to shake away my disorientation and get back on to my feet. I could barely make it to my knees.

The underpass filled with darkness, followed by the sound of barking and sharp-soled boots punching the pavement towards us. Two growling hounds with piercing green eyes were led by a tall, poised figure. His sharp cheekboned face was cool white, bordering on the most delicate of pastel blues with a head of sharp, styled hair – dark black roots pushing frosted, platinum blonde tones to the edge of each exquisitely styled spike.

His unblinking yellow eyes were focused on the entire width and depth of the underpass. Initially staring not at me but deep into the background, before slowly tilting his head until his gaze found me. As our eyes clashed he let go of his hounds' leash and they raced towards me, yapping and barking before knocking me back to the ground. The foul beasts continued to snarl and bark but lingered on the spot as if held by an invisible lead, while the threat of their bite kept me rooted in my place.

The figure spoke; his voice was rich and deep, and reeked of aristocracy. 'I presume you're Benjamin Cooper - the young man I've heard oh so very much about. My name is Gideon Lachand and judging by the audacity of your actions over the past few weeks, I'm supposing you haven't heard of me at all.'

. . .

CHRISTINE:

I couldn't believe my eyes; he was back – my master, my tormentor, and the nightmare I thought I had woken from. The most sickening aspect was how healthy he looked. I had risked everything to bring about his downfall and yet he stood all these years later, unscarred and unaffected. I stumbled back a few steps until I froze on the spot, trembling and terrified as his glacial stare reasserted his dominance over me.

After he had introduced himself to Benjamin, he turned his attention towards me. 'Ah, Christine. My dear, errant Christine. It's such a delight to have found you again. Things at the printing plant just haven't been the same without your delicious desperation.' His gaggle of cronies entered the underpass as he spoke, cackling and ecstatic to see him hold court.

'But no matter,' Gideon declared, 'it is a situation soon to be rectified. Sheena, do you have the rope?'

'Oh, I certainly do, master,' Sheena Dafoe purred. She clicked her fingers and summoned two underling blood-drinkers who brought forth the last thing I wanted to see – a long piece of old decking rope that carried with it an unfathomable weight. It was covered with a slight-green tinge, an algae-like mist hinting that it was a device born from arcane methods.

'Do you remember this rope, Christine? Do you remember your bindings?' Gideon Lachand asked, trying to provoke a reaction from me.

Over the past few years I had often thought about what I would say to Gideon Lachand should I ever see him again, contemplating the words I'd use to scold him and throw back some of the pain he'd bestowed upon me. Instead, my mouth remained silent as the thick, coarse rope was slowly unrolled by his minions and wrapped around me.

Benjamin Cooper:

I watched powerless, surrendering to shock and apprehension as Christine whimpered, begged and shuddered as the rope bound her. Eventually, one of Lachand's larger and stronger followers strode forwards and carried her over his shoulder to the other side of the underpass and off to God knows where.

Nonchalantly, Gideon Lachand turned his attention towards me. 'And then there's you. What does one do with someone like you? I can't do much with a child *of lineage*. We are blood equals; I will gain nothing from you needing my salvation. Though, creating a little fear and respect might be fun, no?'

He paced towards me, clicking his fingers and sending his hounds away. Before I could get to my feet he pressed his index and middle fingers hard into my neck. I wasn't sure what he'd found beneath my skin, maybe some kind of nerve or pressure point, but his fingers pushing against it caused me to fall to my knees in front of him.

Moonlight played differently on his skin when he was close, illuminating the buried wrinkles and exposing traces of decay being held at bay by the consummation of blood. He twisted the pressure point on my neck in a steady, methodical motion and I began to feel my mouth widen as if there were a series of internal wires and jacks causing it to open against my will.

'Now then, young man, let's take a look at those fangs of yours. Visually quite impressive but how effective are they, truly?'

With his left hand continuing to firmly press against my neck he stepped in front of me and stretched out the fingers on his right hand before bringing them back together.

'Ultimately your bite is worthless. Let me demonstrate,' he slowly started to ease his flattened right hand into my mouth, pushing his long fingers beyond my teeth, edging towards the back of my tongue. 'I'd wager you'd love to bite my fingers off right now, wouldn't you?'

He was right but the pressure from whatever his left hand was doing made it impossible. He pushed further still until his fingertips were resting on the back of my tongue. I began to gag a little before starting to cough and gasp.

Sheena Dafoe squealed in delight and leapt forwards to crouch down beside me, stretching out the vowels of a hissed taunt sent directly into my ear, 'Bitch boy!'

Gideon smiled but was dismissive. 'No, no, Sheena – don't cheapen this. This is an important lesson for the boy.'

His hand went deeper still, causing me to make all kinds of desperate noises as I fought for breath.

'Oh I can feel the veins in my wrist brushing against your teeth. Imagine that, one bite, one vengeful pierce of the skin and you might have a shot at ending me and yet... you can't. How frustrating! Maybe if I can get my blood pumping it might make the vein swell?'

With his hand still sliding down towards my throat, Gideon began to tighten his hand into a fist, blocking my airway as

I whimpered and gasped, desperately hoping that my inhalations would be strong enough to draw oxygen over the gaps between his knuckles. He opened and closed his fist several times, shaking my head around like a ragdoll before removing his hand with a sudden, sharp force, causing me to fall back to the floor.

The calm of Gideon Lachand's voice had now been replaced with a strange kind of angry excitement. 'Your vulgar display outside the breaker's yard a few weeks ago cost me a lot of money and a lot of time. I do hope tonight's lesson has taught you to know your place. Your blood is strong but your will is weak. I trust you won't hinder my affairs ever again.'

Before I could regain my composure he crouched down beside me and once again placed his fingers against my neck, this time with a sudden twist that caused me to lose the ability to control nearly the whole of my body. The only movement occurring were spasms that seemed to jolt my body like dying fish having a futile flap in a fisherman's net.

With her long, dark hair flowing slightly in the night breeze, Sheena Dafoe draped herself over Gideon. She stared at his gaunt face with unbridled levels of admiration and lust, either unaware or unbothered that he was wiping his hand clean of the saliva, mucus and lord knows what else came out of my mouth onto her vintage velvet and lace dress.

As I lay prone on the floor awaiting my next involuntary spasm, I could hear a familiar sounding shuffle of feet and licking of lips approaching.

'Ah yes, Mr Goodson! Don't worry, I haven't forgotten about you,' Gideon assured, slowly unwrapping Sheena's arms from around him before ushering forward The Little Man with Paint in His Hand.

'You have been invaluable to my recovery over the past year and you deserve your reward!' Gideon swayed an open palm in my direction. 'He's all yours. Occasional spasms aside, your subject should be mostly still for another fifteen minutes or so, more than enough time for you to take what you need from him.'

With a cheery chuckle escaping through an exhalation of breath, Mr Goodson continued to shuffle forward and unfurled a brown, leather holdall beside me on the floor. I tried to turn my head towards it, only to find my body forced into another brief but strenuous spasm.

'Have fun,' Gideon called, as he turned on his heel and led his gaggle of followers out of the underpass, his two hounds racing past me to re-join their master.

Mr Goodson grunted and cooed his gratitude as he carefully removed several items from his holdall. From the corner of my eye I caught the glint of metal. He appeared to be holding a sort of scalpel, tipped with a thin, sharp blade. The middle section was curved, almost corkscrew-shaped and led down to a wooden handle, which Mr Goodson was attaching thin, rubber tubing to.

The taste of Gideon Lachand's foul hand continued to linger on my tongue, almost distracting me from Mr Goodson's antics beside me. After comparing various sizes of his strange scalpels, he reached for a pair of scissors and cut through my polo shirt, exposing my chest and arms.

Clasping his hands together, Mr Goodson wheezed in delight and began some strange explorations of my skin. He methodically walked his index and middle fingers like they were the legs of a tiny marching soldier across my body and down my arms, occasionally pausing over certain parts of my veins to give them a focused stroke followed by a sharp smack.

He then repeated this process, this time replacing the sharp smack with a quick slice with his scalpel. He'd pinch the skin a little after the nick and let my blood start trickling from the wound. I was soon bleeding from seven or eight incisions scattered around my arms and torso.

Mr Goodson took a moment to step back and admire his work. After taking a large inhalation of air, he held his scalpel high in the air and marched towards me, taking the instrument back to the initial incision but this time digging the blade deep within. Pushing the blade further and further into the wound until the twists and turns of the metallic corkscrew-shaped straw section of his instrument penetrated my skin. He then began to blow and suck on the length of rubber tubing attached to the handle, causing my blood to flow through it. Mr Goodson pinched the end of the tubing to keep the blood flow within and reached for a tartan flask to capture it. He repeated this process on four more of my wounds, leaving the others to continue to bleed without purpose while he tidied up his equipment. Maybe a flask full of my blood was all he needed. Before Mr Goodson shuffled off, he rubbed a small orange piece of sponge, which smelt of Listerine mouthwash and creosote over my wounds. I expected it to burn but oddly, I felt very little. Whether this was a result of whatever nerve trick Gideon Lachand had played on me or the fact I had just endured a level of unpleasantness that made the sting of a sponge on a cut seem redundant in comparison, I'll never know. However, whatever was on that sponge started to slow the bleeding from my wounds and, as I saw Mr Goodson's corduroy trouser legs take his squat little body up the steps and leave the underpass, I could feel the phantom-grip on my neck diminish and some small degree of control return to my body. A single tear began to roll from my eye but by the time it reached my cheeks I was curled up into a ball, sobbing my heart out.

I'm not sure how long I lay on that rotten floor, my face stained by tears, the tattered remains of my clothes stained with blood. I brought myself to my knees, nothing but a shell of humbled humiliation, afraid and unsure of how to bring what was left of me to the oncoming day.

Christine:

After being bound by that accursed rope, I was carried from the subway to the side of the road and dumped into the back of Banks and Long Tooth's hearse. They placed a tatty, fading Somerfield carrier bag over my head so I couldn't see where I was going but that was pointless – I knew exactly where we were headed. Gideon Lachand had essentially confirmed it to me when he'd mentioned the printing plant he used as a headquarters. The drive wasn't long and it wasn't a shock when the shopping bag was removed to find that we were deep within the Industrial Estate when the Hearse parked up.

I had been sat in the back of the hearse, dreading this destination. I had hoped that my presumptions were unfounded fears and that I wouldn't end up back in the hellhole I'd so desperately clawed and schemed to escape from.

Black smog filled the air and Gideon Lachand emerged through it, descending from the sky and landing a few feet in front of me. I wondered what had become of Benjamin and feared his fate. In this moment, my feelings revealed themselves to me. Gideon let out a slight yawn, exuding the nonchalant ease of someone who has just enjoyed a leisurely brunch.. One by one, all of his lackeys emerged from recently parked vehicles and surrounded him, looking very pleased with themselves. Sheena Dafoe shot me a smug smile before walking off toward the main building, affecting a strut that was a little awkward and not half as impressive as she thought it was.

Gideon Lachand shot me the briefest of glances before ordering his crew to take me inside. Turnstile facilitated his master's request by gesturing to a pair of muscular blood-drinkers–to carry out the task. They began to drag me off when a black dot caught my eye. It came closer and closer, growing larger and larger. As the black dot's true form was revealed to me I realised it was Igor. My loyal, brave Igor. A girl couldn't wish for a more wonderful familiar! Beating his little wings through the night, heading straight towards Gideon.

It wasn't a fight that my beloved, furry friend could possibly win but if he could just scratch Gideon Lachand's eyes or cause some sort of commotion, it might be enough to help escape this awful place.

Igor swooped down towards Gideon in one swift, graceful motion. I wished curses towards my master in venomous hushes under my breath. *Go on, Igor!* I whispered to myself. *Claw him! Bite him! Make him bleed!*

Yet all my hopes of salvation vanished as Gideon spun around and caught Igor in the palm of his right hand. With the casual indifference of someone discarding a Coke can, Gideon Lachand clenched his hand, squeezing Igor's body hard until the bones within it crunched, and tossed his crumpled remains into a skip as he walked past it.

I wanted to cry mournful tears. I wanted to feel seething, untamed anger. Instead, all I found was fear. Numbing, remorseful fear. Lost in my own despair, I found myself returned to the pit I had once freed myself from. The memories of my emancipation and escape felt devalued and insignificant, an act rendered not as a happy ending, but instead a brief futile gesture to be remembered as a mini-break from a life of servitude.

As I lay bound and helpless in the hollowed floor with a skylight window above me, memories of the long, fearful nights returned. How I did then and would now once more spend long hours of the night, terrified of the approaching sunrise. Staring up through the skylight watching the early hours pass and darkness begin to lift until the morning sun would begin to singe my skin. Gideon Lachand would feed and thrive from my need for his salvation. His face would be full of delight as I would cry, scream, howl and beg for him to drag me back into the shadows. As each night came I'd be dragged back and the cycle would repeat. Occasionally I'd try to call his bluff and refuse to cry out but he was more than happy to leave me with my skin beginning to burn, the more desperate my screams the more power he'd yield. It was a situation I was now stuck again in, I heard Long Tooth close the shutter door with a rattling slam and feared that this time there'd be no further escape.

CHAPTER 14
(UNTITLED)

Testimony: Gideon Lachand on his position leading up to and surrounding the events of the 1st July and his declaration for the future

Gideon Lachand:

Fuck the laws of the night, I owe you no testimony. Yet I will state my position, if only to clarify my intent.

I hold no compassion for compromise, as factors that attempt to hinder and divert glory are always persistent. Even as a swaddled babe, my needy, clinging mother would douse her nipples in her victim's blood before she fed me, slowing my physical progression and denying my body to age and grow. It was her loving way of keeping me close to her bosom for as long as she could get away with it. This was kept from my father, who surely must have wondered why his one-year-old son still looked like a newborn, but did nothing to aid me. My father (an upholder, appraiser, and undertaker by trade) was a spineless and spiritless creature who would second-guess himself out of any confrontation no matter what his lack of response may cost him.

Many decades later, long after I had been freed from the tit and allowed to grow, it was this same resistance to urgency that would lead to my father's downfall. By this stage, my mother had fallen in line with my father's diet of pig blood and secret feasting on corpses he'd been given to bury. This kept us alive but didn't keep us strong. When the vampire hunters finally found us, bringing their garlic, crucifixes and silver tipped weapons to our door, both he and my mother were murdered and our home burnt down. By the time they were staked and sent to the flames I had already left them to their fate and escaped through the deep, gnarled woods surrounding our abode. I had lost everything yet I felt no sorrow. I realised that the most valuable lesson had been bestowed upon me as if it were a gift – the understanding that it is in our nature as blood-drinkers to be the hunter and, should we deny that impulse, we become the prey. I had been set free from my parents' limited existence and intended to turn my blossoming dreams of conquest to reality.

Through the dark and delicious decades that followed, I methodically manipulated and murdered my way out of the wreckage of my family home in Brittany, across the English Channel and through the towns and cities of Kent. During the nineteenth century I mostly served under powerful, ancient blood-drinkers, experienced yet set far too firmly in their ways. Unwilling to see bigger pictures and adapt their approach. I saw them look down their noses at my bold visions. I saw them cast my counsel to the gutters and one by one, I saw each of them fall.

To be *of lineage* became a rarity and my status was something I soon decided to take advantage of. I went on a rampage. A crusade of consummation and conversion of such bloodthirsty breadth that even the laws of the night struggled to confine. I heard tales that certain powers feared that my work might expose our kind to the public but I think what they actually feared was the increasing scale of my operation. Certainly, increasing the numbers in my brood was beneficial, but sometimes the screams of my victims were my prize. Or perhaps just before that, the quieter moments when shock would give in to realisation and the bargaining would begin, that sweet, squeezing tension of a pleading pause.

I had an army at my command but I had always known that wouldn't be enough to chip away at the biggest glass ceiling in existence. I dared to dream; I learned how to navigate nightmares. I invested money, time and every ounce of my spirit into the realm of dark magik and progressive post-diabology study. I invited those to the table that my forefathers didn't trust. Why fear warlocks? They pose no threat. Warlocks don't seek power, they only crave achievement. I would need far more than fangs to achieve my ambitions. I didn't want to rule a coven; I wanted to rule the night itself.

But the frustrations always mount and the idle hands of others always create more of them. For every thief trying to steal your gold there's a hundred directionless men who'll rob you of your time. There's no moment of silence that they can't wait to fill with noise. Fussing, fighting and crying. Distractions. Pain. Making my head feel like it needs to bleed it all out. There's always something, like right now I can hear some fools kicking a ball against a skip or something outside. CLANG! CLANG! CLANG! Oh what price to finish just one fucking thought in my head?

There's always someone forcing me into their situation. For too many decades I served under and paid enforced-homage to Scratch. It was ridiculous that someone so powerful should linger in a small town like Sittingbourne and yet he remained. His machinations spread like weeds in an unkempt garden, causing drama and halting any chance of my own advancement in this world. Why should it be he who decides how my hours are spent? You have no idea how hungry I am to fill the silence with screams created from my own degeneracy, to drown out the gaudy populace of this town in a shadow cast cathartically from my own desire and then to finally have the quietened rabble in the palm of my hand; afraid, lost, scrambling and ripe for harvest.

Scratch, however, had his laws and his rules. Pseudo dogma that only truly served to keep him in power. Turnstile proved to be a loyal aide and together we plotted and planned and found a way to eliminate our savage master. When I was sure I had the manpower, the Goodson Family on-side and a plethora of pan-dimensional artefacts, I put a plan into action to rid this rotten little town and myself of dear old Scratch for good. My plan was impeccable but I hadn't counted on Christine's boldness.

My dear, difficult Christine. I presumed I had her well trained, broken, obedient. She'd spent so many long hours bound by accursed rope it's a miracle she had kept hold of her sanity to be honest. I was foolish to think her tears and whimpers were acceptance of her servitude. She slipped my leash and brought the beast to my door before I was ready to strike first. The vengeful lash of old Scratch burns and tears with depth and persistence. There could be no forgiveness for Christine. She did well to run and keep running.

And now she had the audacity to return and parade that frail trembling boy around as the successor to my throne. Admittedly, the blood that flows through his veins is rich and old, but he lacks experience or the fortitude to capitalise on it. I'd like to think the lesson I taught him in the subway would be enough to cause him to realise this and ensure he runs far, far away. I partially wish I had just ended him there and then in that dank tunnel but Turnstile's earlier counsel was wise, slaying one *of lineage* without Scratch's approval could cause complications.

Soon such worries will be behind me as it is I, Gideon Lachand, who owns the darkness of this town. It is I, who will rise in Scratch's absence. Soon this entire town will learn to serve me, their malevolent master and consequences or not, should that boy dare step up to me again I will gift his bones to the dust.

There isn't any competition left to halt my ascension; Scratch is far away, the boy is broken and afraid. I am no longer sat waiting, I am ready. This town is mine. Its people are mine. Their blood is mine. Let the harvest begin.

CHAPTER 15

ALL THESE THINGS INTO POSITION

TESTIMONY: BENJAMIN COOPER AND CHRISTINE ON LIFE AFTER the events of the 1st of July 1995

Benjamin Cooper:

The sky, once so full of stars, now sat empty. It had taken me many unsteady minutes to peel myself from the floor of the subway and push my trembling body past the exit, through to the pavement and open air on the other side. I remembered that first night being driven home in Christine's car and the way the stars had blossomed in the night's sky like a celestial garden. The stars had remained with us, watching down upon all of our misadventures over the past few weeks. But now they were gone, as if they had been taken from me along with Christine herself. My stomach churned as I considered the terrible fate she may have faced. It was a feeling of dread too hard to face and, to my shame, I found it easier to run from the guilt of abandoning her.

I had no idea what time it was by that stage; it could've been one in the morning, it could have been four, just some lost hour between midnight and dawn. I found myself glued to the railings, uncertain how to remove myself from them. The actuality and weight of my attack in the subway was starting to sink in.

I must have waited there for another hour at least before a patrolling cop car pulled up.

'You alright, son?' a big-boned copper in the passenger seat called out.

I failed to answer, my throat was still sore from Gideon's attack and the taste of his long bony fingers, like the clinging, sulphuric stench of a musty chemistry classroom, was still lingering in my saliva.

The Big-Boned Copper looked me up and down, squinting his eyes as they passed over my ripped t-shirt and the bloodstains that decorated it. 'What's happened to your clothes?'

I slipped into a slouch against the railings. 'I'm fine. I've just had a weird night...'

A thin cop who looked not unlike a ginger ferret was sitting in the driver's seat of the car. He gave his mate a nudge and a smile broke out across both of their faces. 'Been out clubbing, have you? Been down JJ's? Where are you off to now?'

I attempted to explain that I was looking for my friend but the taste in my mouth became too much. Leaning over the railed fence I spat out my discomfort while groaning out the second part of my sentence, '...I need to find her.'

'Bloody hell, youth eh? It's wasted on the young, innit?' The Big-Boned Cop chortled, fighting against the back of his chair and causing it to creak and rattle. 'If I found a bird willing to tear my clothes off and dig her nails in I wouldn't get hammered and go wandering off without her.'

'Blimey Gav, any bird who'd be willing to do that to you would have to be the hammered one,' PC Ginger Ferret quipped back with a pleased-as-punch look on his face, as though playing to an audience that wasn't there.

Gav the Big Boned Cop obligingly chuckled for the shortest clutch of seconds before turning his attention back to me. 'Seriously though son, you need to reassess things after tonight. Look at you, completely blotto with your missus Lord knows where. If you had been sensible with your drinking tonight you could be all cosy in bed with her - getting seconds.'

'Or thirds, at this time of night,' PC Ginger Ferret chipped in, once again trying to get the funniest line of the evening like his job depended on it. 'Where do you live, son? We'll drop you home.'

It suddenly occurred to me that I'd last left my home with both my father and Gary Thrill blowing bullet holes into vampires and several dead bodies laying around both inside and out. 'No no, it's fine, I just live down that way.'

'Alright then, get yourself home. If we see you about again tonight we'll have to take you in,' commanded PC Ginger Ferret in a tone that fluctuated between caring and patronising.

As he revved the engine to depart, Gav the Big Boned Cop hollered out the window, 'Good luck mate, I hope you find that girl you're looking for.'

For the past few hours I'd been hoping for a cop car to come out and rescue me but instead, all I got was some ribbing about a fictional sex life. I staggered away from the law, attempting to look as sturdy as possible but inside I was shivering, cold and hurt. A horrible, sinking feeling continued to wash over me that either Gideon or Goodson or that fucking hearse was going to pop out at any corner, so I took the backstreet of Shortlands Road rather than risk the possible exposure of walking alongside the A2.

The journey home was a slow trek with my brittle and shaken body carried wearily across cracked paving slabs by two tired, shuffling feet. On either side of me a vast expanse of cascading terrace houses stretched far beyond my sight; locked doors and drawn curtains shielding dozens of oblivious families from the horror and darkness in their town.

I soon found myself walking past the council flats leading down to my house and was struck by an avalanche of questions, doubts and worries. What if the police were still there? What if Gideon or his crew had travelled to my home to continue tormenting me? What if they'd done something to my dad and sister? And even if they hadn't, how could I go back to having a normal life with them after everything that's happened? All I knew is that I needed to get home. I needed to be back in my bedroom. I was always safe in my bedroom, always free from burdens. I arguably should never have left it in the first place.

When I got to my house it was oddly quiet and still. There wasn't any crime scene tape sealing it off; no bodies of cops or vampires. Most notably, my family wasn't there either. There was, however, a note. "Me & K are safe and well.

Gone to Auntie B. Call when you're back to let us know you're safe. Dad xx."

They'd legged it off to Hertfordshire to stay with my Aunt Becky. I tore up the note and threw it in the bin. With Gideon's taste lingering in my mouth, I wasn't in the mood to talk to anyone now. Maybe I'd call them tomorrow if the ringing and raging distress I felt flooding my body should ease. I was unable to make it up the stairs to my room and collapsed on the sofa, drifting off into confused pockets of sleep.

I found myself walking through the days that followed in a detached malaise; the space between minutes and hours were a strange blur. I lost hours staring into nothing, curled up in a foetal position on my bed, mostly lost to an over-riding sense of numbness, punctured occasionally by flashbacks, shudders and regrets. Occasionally, the faint scars caused by Mr Goodson's blades would sting and burn and I'd be reminded of his inane chattering and gurning face. Sometimes the opposite would be true – at night, my mind could be consumed by thoughts of him, reawakening the nagging soreness of his scalpel marks. Worse than any of that though were the stalking, invasive memories of my encounter with Gideon Lachand. They'd arrive whenever I was foolish enough to leave a space between my thoughts. His arrival through the smoke into the subway, his cold malicious voice, the bark of his hounds and then his hand deep in my mouth. I cleaned my teeth over and over again, blitzed through swig after swig of Listerine, trying to rid myself of the taste of his fingers, but it remained there in every bite, swallow and yawn.

After a day had been and gone, guilt arrived to join my trauma, with self-loathing tagging along as a plus one. My mind paraded all of my own murders and acts of cruelty that had occurred over the summer. Oh, how Christine and I had toyed with our prey and mocked them and laughed ourselves dizzy at their demise. I wondered if I had deserved to end up in that subway on that night, as if some kind of perverse karmic justice had been delivered. I'd make pledges to myself about returning to the unswerving normality of daytime living and never touching a drop of the red stuff again, but I knew I was lying. There was no going back. I had been corrupted and spoiled. I looked at the picture my father had given me of my birth mum holding me as a baby and wept. How the fuck had a moment of such purity and love descended into this?

The phone would continue to ring through the day; I was never in the right place mentally to answer it. I would curse the damn thing's persistent nagging call when it would spring to life and then curse myself for being too cowardly to answer it. It could have been my dad or Kelly, or the police, or one of Gideon Lachand's lot, but it didn't matter. Friend or foe, I was unable to talk to them. I eventually unplugged it just to stop from going crazy.

On the Thursday that followed, I eventually pushed myself out of the house and off to college. My heart never stopped racing as I glanced and double-checked every step of my route to ensure I was safe. The train ride there was an unwelcome reminder of how I felt earlier that year, as I anxiously shuffled down the aisle looking for a seat only to find local cliques of teens giggling and whispering hushed critiques in such a way that the contents were guarded from me but the intent was not. Becky Hollis tutted and muttered something possibly about me to her mates while Darren King hollered some kind of teasing banter in my direction followed up by a string of claims that he was, 'Just joking about.'

Eventually, the train arrived at Canterbury East and I departed, hoping to power through the day ahead and push some of my trauma away. However, as I worked my way through the platform full of students and commuters, I caught the eye of a middle-aged gentleman with greying, slicked-back hair, who was stood to the side of the ticket inspector. He slowly worked a slight smile out of the left-hand side of his mouth and gave me a nod. I recognised him immediately, he was one of Gideon Lachand's men, possibly called Turnstile. I panicked and my heart began to race again, thumping away like a kick drum as I tried to weave my way deep into a clutch of students heading through the ticket barrier on the other side from him. I pushed and scrambled through the backpacks and puffa jackets of my peers to a chorus of disapproval and complaint. I feared that Turnstile might just catch me outside the station but as I sprinted through the doors and up to the city wall, I looked back and thankfully he was nowhere to be seen.

I felt no relief from this. Why was Turnstile at the platform, conveniently just as my train arrived? Also, how could he survive in daylight? I presumed he was *of the night* rather than *of lineage*. Either way, he was almost certainly there to intimidate me. It was clear that Gideon Lachand still had designs on making my life a living nightmare. The day became tinged with a rattling, badgering unease where new worries washed over the previous ones, leaving me afraid and uncommunicative. At the end of a session at college, Mr

Claypole pulled me aside and began chatting away to me in an excited fashion. On and on he parped, pausing occasionally in case I wanted to interject. I think he was saying that my coursework was all up to date and of a good standard and that I wasn't going to get kicked off the Travel and Tourism course. I didn't know how to respond, my life had veered so far beyond passing a course about exchange rates and holiday brochures.

I dragged myself back home, keen to avoid any further entanglements. The house remained empty and the phone unplugged. I knew I really should plug it in and call my family but I couldn't face it tonight. I swore I'd do it tomorrow.

Christine:

At first I feigned defiance; laughing at my captors, kicking and spitting at their attempts to handle me, throwing threats and barbed insults at Gideon as he walked by.

'Break her and then build her,' was his only response. When I was his prisoner before, he delighted in being hands-on – controlling my every move, always with a watchful eye over every movement. This time, things were different. The location was the same – a grotty little unit in the industrial park that he'd use to run off brochures, leaflets and porn on a variety of printing press machines. I was still being left in a small pit underneath the unit's skylight during the twilight before dawn and only pulled away from the threat of incineration when I'd beg, cry and scream for my salvation. These days, however, I was under the supervision of two burly bastards being micromanaged by Sheena Dafoe. I was alarmed, in some ways, by this level of distance. During my previous incarceration, I was Gideon's prize asset and despite my fear of being fried occasionally overriding my critical faculties, it was generally clear that he mostly wanted me to survive. Sheena Dafoe, on the other hand, had always despised me and I could foresee an "accident" occurring where one of the burly bastards didn't pull me away from the sunlight quick enough. Back in the day, he would have fed Sheena to his hounds if she'd so much as suggested such a thing but, these days, he would barely respond to her requests to get rid of me. This was worrying.

Gideon Lachand was colder and, in turn, more frightening than the last time I'd seen him. There was now a steely detachment and determination to his manner, as if the final, fraying threads of connection to humanity had been severed following his punishment from Scratch. It made me question whether my involvement in thwarting his power play had been worth it. Blood-drinking seemed to be little more than a daily obligation these days, as he spent most of his time in lengthy counsel with Mr Goodson while titting about with a huge hourglass filled with green sand. Occasionally, Turnstile would turn up and join their pow-wows and, on one occasion, a name they mentioned made my ears prick up.

'And no news on the whereabouts of Mr Cooper?' Gideon asked, sending his most anticipated information request slithering into the conversation like a snake into long grass.

Turnstile's report was halted by the sound of metallic banging outside of the printing plant. It was a semi-regular racket, which I presumed must have been the sound of some of the newer members of the covenant playing football outside. It was odd, just how uncouth and yobbish Gideon's newest recruits were compared to the league of pseudo-dandies he used to knock about with, back in the '80s. I guess he was just making do with whatever he could get hold of these days in Kent.

Once the din from outside had subsided, Turnstile continued to talk. 'It appears his family has fled to Hertfordshire.'

Could that be right? Had Benjamin fled and just left me to rot here? I had hoped that he might be forming some sort of plan to rescue me. This was entirely my fault; I shouldn't have been so guarded with him. I should have trained him right. If I had, maybe he would have been able to put an end to Gideon's evil then and there in the subway. And I wouldn't be here, pleading for my life each day as the first rays of sun attempted to make prey out of the tips of my toes.

Benjamin Cooper:

I must have left the phone unplugged for another day or so before guilt took hold of me. I knew it was unfair on my dad and Kelly to leave them with escalating worries about my safety and whereabouts. Eventually, I plugged the phone back in and after searching for Aunty Becky's number in an old Garfield diary we kept by the phone, I nervously dialled the number and hoped it would go to the answerphone. My prayers were answered when I got to leave a mumbled message about being ok and finishing up college before making plans to visit them. I hung up swiftly and pulled the cord out of the wall again to avoid any return calls getting through.

I collapsed into the living room and dragged myself to the sofa. The room's once relaxing qualities had become a little tainted following the break-in and blood-drinker battle of the previous week. Memories of the dreadful evening kept hacking their way into my mind. It was the little details that lingered: the shock of crashing into the living room; the dead bodies in the street; Gideon Lachand staring into my helpless eyes as his slid his hand my mouth; Mr Goodson's fucking gurn. The trauma extended beyond my mind – I could still feel the sting of the wounds on my chest and the taste of Gideon's hand always returning to the back of my throat.

I knew I had to escape the house and the last few days of the college year were a good excuse, but the experience proved wretched. Increasingly, I found Darren King and Becky Hollis staring at me, giggling and whispering. It felt like they were relishing my downfall but I wondered how they could possibly know about it? My mind went on wild excursions; had someone told Darren King that I'd given him a can full of urine to drink and he'd decided to get revenge on me? Was Becky Hollis so embarrassed about me being a notch on her bedpost that she wanted to reduce me to the hollow shell I'd become? I wondered how they might be involved; they didn't seem to be the type that would be in league with Gideon Lachand, but who knows? Somebody must have tipped off Lachand's supporters about my whereabouts or my address. It surely had to have been them.

It played on my mind all day and the chattering between the pair and all their cliquey friends seemed to grow, with glances thrown in my direction followed by laughter. They all seemed so pleased with themselves. I sat there alone; cursing myself for the hubris and abandon I'd allowed myself to revel in over the last few weeks. For a few shining moments I thought I might actually be somebody of status, living a life of importance, but it was all a cruel trick, a trap waiting to be sprung. I had been humiliated, humbled and returned to the shit heap.

My heart felt wretched, my bones felt hollow and my face couldn't stop falling. On the train journey home, I felt someone take the seat beside me, which was odd as there were plenty of other seats available on the carriage.

A rich, smooth voice emerged. 'He wants the town, you know?'

'What?' I mumbled, looking to my side to find Turnstile in the seat next to me.

'Don't make a fuss,' he said coolly, 'I'm only here to talk and you're only required to listen.'

He waited until a couple of students passed before clearing his voice and speaking again. 'Gideon's grand plan is to rule Sittingbourne and frankly, your awakening is something of a spanner in the works.'

I was perplexed. 'What do you mean; he wants to "rule Sittingbourne"? Is he running for mayor or something? Why Sittingbourne anyway?'

'It's neatly stationed between the coast and the capital, and yet it's barely noticed or mentioned by anyone. An excellent place to build a town-sized coven and then expand into London and Europe,' Turnstile reasoned.

'Sittingbourne, full of vampires? I don't think the locals will be keen on that. I can tell you from experience they aren't too keen on goths.'

'Oh, dear boy, the locals will BE the loyal, devoted members of Gideon's coven. Men, women and oh yes, the children too. They will join us either by fancy or by force. Harvest is approaching.'

I went to stand up, enraged, but Turnstile pushed me back with a smile. 'Now, come, come, Young Benjamin, why would any of this matter to you? I thought you hated this town and the people in it. Why care for those who've never cared for you?'

'Why are you telling me this?' I asked, alarmed and afraid.

'Because Gideon wants to see you dead by the end of the day and I feel that a young man such as yourself deserves, at least, to be forewarned. So that they can make necessary arrangements and make peace with themselves for all the wrong choices they've made.'

'What if I leave town? I don't care about any of this.'

'It's too late for that. Gideon can't relax with you still in play. So, tonight it ends. We know everything about you and your family. If we have to chase you all the way to Hertfordshire and hunt you down at Rebecca's house, your kin will die too. You seem the type to avoid confrontation but things cannot be left as is.' Turnstile rose from the seat and adjusted his blazer. 'So, make peace with yourself.' And with that he slowly walked off down the aisle of the carriage without so much as a glance back.

A growing unease took hold of my nervous system as I glanced around the train, fearful that Gideon's disciples may be lying in wait, looking for the ideal opportunity to strike and trade my lifeless body for brownie points. As the train pulled into

Sittingbourne station, the dread grew further and I almost didn't get off. Masses of locals pushed and bustled past me and with every collision I flinched, expecting to feel the piercing tip or subtle slash of a blade. I was worried to stay out and about; I was worried to go home. I didn't know what to do with myself. I took myself into the high street and sought uncertain refuge in the most family-friendly shops. I started in WH Smiths before walking down to Woolies and then, in the late afternoon, pottering about in D&A and Blundell's toy shops. My hunters surely wouldn't strike with families around.

By the entrance to Roman Square, I passed the local legend known as the Whistling Postman collecting spare change for charity and I threw him a nod. I'm not sure why or what I was expecting – maybe I hoped he'd reveal himself to be some kind of vampire hunter, albeit one who knew I was one of the good ones and that he'd be able to help me. Sadly, despite a friendly nod in return, this didn't seem to be the case.

By the evening I found myself in the Ypres Tavern, sinking pints of Fosters with a lemonade top, with my back to the wall. Someone had queued up the vast majority of Radiohead's The Bends album on the jukebox, which soundtracked my predicament with a distressing sense of finality. Turnstile's advice to 'make peace with myself' kept resurfacing prominently within my thoughts, allying itself with my repeating trauma from the incident in the subway. It all began to make me long for the days when my mind wasn't continually fighting against these intrusions. I'd love nothing more than to make peace with myself but, what with all of that going on in my mind along with a foreboding anguish over the planned 'harvest' of the town, how could I? I thought about the true horror of what that harvest might look like; commuters being pulled into dark alleys on the way home, young lovers brutalised in bus stops and family homes having their doors kicked in and windows smashed as mothers, fathers and their screaming, terrified children were dragged off as if they were livestock.

The bell for closing time seemed to ring even earlier than usual that night and, with nowhere left to go, I slowly dragged my quivering, fretful body back across town towards my home in Woodberry Drive. Cars sped past me and I wondered if they were Banks and Longtooth's hearse. Local yobs would bellow at each other from further down the road and I wondered if they were blood-drinkers calling out my name. Streetlights cast the shadows of people passing and I'd wonder if this was the emergence of my assassin. I could feel it in the air, like the anxiety-accelerating moments of a bad dream peaking and erupting into a violent sleep-shattering conclusion. This, however, wasn't a nightmare, this was real. My death was scheduled and I had no option but to walk towards it. I thought of the stress I brought to my family. I thought about how I'd let down Christine. I even thought about Eliza and how I'd now never get the opportunity to take that encounter any further. I tied my mind in knots trying to convince myself that whoever my assassin was would have a code of ethics and make my death quick and painless. I knew in my heart of hearts that this was unlikely.

It had been a hot, sweaty evening but as I approached Snipes Hill, a light rain darted across the sky. Each drop I wiped from my eyes was mixed with tears as the enormity of my predicament took hold. As I approached my house, two great, beaming headlights shone directly at me. The light emerging from them was blinding and, even as I shielded my eyes from their glow, I couldn't make out the vehicle they were coming from. This was it; I could feel it deep with my stomach as it sank. Death: tonight's inescapable fate. I had nothing left to give, no fuel left to fight it. While walking in the road I fell to my knees in front of the blinding lights, sobbing and gasping. *Fuck it,* I thought to myself. Whichever or whoever of Gideon Lachand's coven had been sent to my home can just end it right here and right now. I was done with it all.

I heard the sound of the vehicle's door open and footsteps approaching me. I expected a heckle, a threat or some form of a declaration of my imminent demise. Instead I heard a familiar female voice. 'I'm sorry.'

I looked up through the rain and the beam of the vehicle lights. It was Louise D'Souza.

As she passed through the headlights of her dad's utility truck, I noticed a change to her usual perky demeanour. She looked distraught, terrified and as hopeless as I felt. She saw my shock and continued, 'I'm so very sorry. It was me. I'm to blame.'

'For what?' I asked, standing up and walking towards her.

Her hands were trembling and her voice was dry and shaky. 'I did it. I told them everything. Your name, your relationship with Christine and...'

'Go on' I urged, with a rising anger in my voice that was almost certain what the last confession would be.

She looked to the floor as her confession drifted into a mumble. 'And... well... I showed them where you live. I wasn't thinking straight. I'm so sorry.'

'I don't need sorry right now. I need to know why.'

'They promised they'd turn me into a blood-drinker.' She paused for a moment before firing out a flurry of words expanding on her betrayal. 'I mean, you wouldn't do it to me and then a blood-drinker called Turnstile found me. He made it all sound so easy and right, but now he and his gang are threatening to kill my family and me. They're talking about harvesting the town.'

I buried my face in the palm of my hand for a moment before raising my voice. 'Jesus Christ Louise, how could you be so fucking stupid?'

'You don't understand,' Louise's voice raised to meet mine and she started grabbing her own flesh. 'This skin, this blood running through my veins – it isn't me. I'm not who I should be. It's easy for you, born into that body, born into a form that fits...'

'Do you think I like looking like this? Going through life with people making comments about my pale skin and writing "Demon" on my picture in college. And then there's these fangs, the thirst and all the running around town doing horrible things.'

'I dunno, you seem to have been enjoying it lately.'

She wasn't wrong. It had been fun for a while but now I considered the carnage surrounding me.

I shook my head and tried to shake away her claim, 'You're looking at the wild nights rather than the morning after. You're talking about a handful of moments where I was out of my mind.'

'Shut up Benjamin, you know who you really are. When your walls come down and you embrace your spirit. You're a hunter; a rectifier of natural order. I'm begging you to drink me, feel me and free me.'

'You'd be *of the night.* You wouldn't be able to live a normal life. You've seen the sacrifices Christine has to make to survive. You'd have to drop out of college. Stay indoors all day. Running about all night trying to find blood to drink. For Christ's sake, Louise, what would your mother say?'

'Fuck her. I can't go on living like this. Even if you stop Turnstile and the harvest without my blood, my parents will push and push and push until I take some shitty job round here, marry some tosser and spend my days keeping up with the Joneses. A living death. I'll end up a fucking pill-popping zombie, stuck indoors all day anyway. Do it Benjamin, give yourself the power you deserve. Free me, rescue Christine, save Sittingbourne.'

I began to walk away, however my steps were hindered by Louise grabbing my arm while she hollered after me, 'Benjamin... Benjamin... Please, I'm begging you! Please! Please! I'm sorry!'

'Get off me,' I snapped, trying to shake her off my arm. 'You don't deserve a damn thing from me.'

Again she clutched on hysterically pleading, 'If it's so bad being a blood drinker then give it to me as punishment.'

'I'm not like that,' I shouted, 'I just want you gone.'

'Please, Benjamin! Take my blood! My loyalty! Remember what I discovered in that book I found, each person you convert gives you strength, it can give you powers. If not for yourself, do it for Christine! Do it for your sister! You're not strong enough to...'

Louise didn't get to finish the sentence – something snapped inside of me. I'm not sure what it was but it removed my composure and control. It could have been anger at her indirect involvement in the attack on my home, it could have been the sudden availability of blood after a period of withdrawal, it could have been the fear of losing people close to me to the harvest, or just sheer annoyance at Louise going on at me. Possibly a little bit of all of that. I spun on my heels, pushed Louise's body against the bonnet of her dad's utility truck and sank my teeth deep into her neck.

Her tanned, olive skin was smooth and inviting. My lips and teeth had little trouble navigating to her pulsating jugular and diving down to feast. My eyes met the eyes of my warped reflection in her windscreen as I began to drink her dry. My skin had never looked so pale and the blue-eyed soul of my young eyes had been replaced by a lightning bright shade of yellow. I looked distorted, damned and magnificent.

CHAPTER 16

RUNNING WITH THE SHADOWS OF THE NIGHT (PART. 1)

TESTIMONY: LOUISE D'SOUZA, BENJAMIN COOPER AND Christine, on the blood-soaked night of the 13th of July 1995

Louise D'Souza:

I've waited so long to be heard. At various points this year, I lost faith in the currency of my voice. My lips would reveal declarations, desires and demands and yet my words would seldom yield any results. My mother would talk over them, my father would ignore them and my peers would tolerate them while looking for jump-in points to continue their own narratives. It was disappointing but not unbearable. I resigned myself to live within the shadows of other people's all-consuming egos and prayed that the weight of their selfish indulgences didn't crush me. All of this changed when I met Benjamin, or at least when I started to spend time with him. The spaces he left within our conversations were refreshing; it not only meant that he was listening to me but also, I felt something else was happening. In the silence, my thoughts came to the forefront of my mind, as if I was suddenly the narrator of my life. I wondered for a while if there was some sort of telepathic link forming between us because I could sense a similar energy emanating from Benjamin. I had admired him from afar for a while – I was deeply jealous yet entranced by his ability to be as weird as he liked without fear of being ostracised, and I liked the way his bittersweet blue eyes conveyed a world that existed beyond college gossip and shitty nights out at meat-market nightclubs.

When I discovered that he and Christine were vampires my declarations, desires and demands increased. I wanted Benjamin to take me away from the compromise of each dreary day and gift me to the night, where lightning strikes at its brightest and the air is full of dreams. These thoughts increased over time, building and building until I was nearly driven to madness. All of it – everything I wanted the world to know about me, every plea to be understood, every desperate cry to be something more than the dreary girl my soul was trapped in. All of it encased and fighting for space in a bubble, which, as Benjamin's teeth pierced my skin, burst. So many years of pressure in my mind dissipated as all my aching words of longing became set free with each new thought trailing after them.

Benjamin Cooper:

Louise's blood was fresh and sweet; unlike any other I had tasted. I knew I had to stop feeding from her but it was hard to pull away. There was a relief that washed over me as I drank. A feeling of carefree abandon and the sense that her blood was washing away the putrid taste of Gideon Lachand from my mouth. I felt her arms reach out to my shoulders to push me off her but I desired more and more.

. . .

Louise D'Souza:

The rapturous feeling of emancipation when I felt Benjamin's fangs upon my neck caused me to gasp so sharply that I feared the sound may have split the night itself in two. Naturally the bite hurt but the sweet sensation of all my dreams coming true transcended the pain. I began to feel light-headed as my breaths became shorter. I realised that Benjamin was feeding too hard and I started to push him away. He was reluctant for a moment or two but eventually detached himself away from me. He looked different in that moment – colder and more animalistic. I had seen him in full vamp mode before so the change in his posture and eye colour wasn't shocking to me, but there was more intensity on this occasion. To my relief, his savage, yellow eyes faded back to their usual calm blue and he swiftly apologised.

I rested a little while, leaning my head on his shoulder before he walked me to my car. I had a long, black scarf in the back seat, which he tied around my neck to soak up the blood. It was a pleasant surprise to see the scarf work so well; I had coated it with a special formula made primarily from lobster, crab and shrimp shells. I'd found the instructions in the blood-drinker's lore book and had prepared it for this golden moment, should it arrive. I'd been carrying around a condom since my date with Benjamin on a similar just-in-case basis – it's crazy to think that the magic, bite-healing scarf is the item of the two that got used first. It's odd, I feel so much romantic potential when I'm alone with him but he's so awkward and distant when the opportunity arises. I mean, I've pretty much laid myself on the table for him and he's brushed me off. You'd at least think he'd take the opportunity to lose his virginity. My biggest fear is that I have this all wrong and Benjamin just doesn't like me at all, but then he reassures my doubts.

'We need to get you to a hospital,' he demands. There's sadness, care and empathy in his eyes as they scan my face. It's clear he feels something for me. Maybe he's just not ready to come to terms with it. Maybe it's too hard for him to define. I wish we could talk freely about it. Again, I feel like my thoughts are trying to form a connection with his, like a go-between to discuss the destination of all these unspecified emotions.

'It'll be fine. I haven't just wandered into this blind,' I reassured him. 'I've been reading up on blood lore in that Italian book I showed you. Apparently, it doesn't take that long for your DNA to be merged with mine. I should start to heal up soon enough.'

Benjamin still looked worried. 'Soon enough? What does that mean? Minutes? Hours? Weeks? Does it say how long it takes in that book of yours?'

'I think it's normally between an hour or two to heal up but you got greedy, so lord knows.'

Benjamin Cooper:

I was starting to regret my decision to turn Louise. I could already feel the avalanche of new complications begin to bear down on me. Although, I couldn't deny that consuming her blood had shaken me from the rut I'd been trapped in since my encounter with Gideon Lachand. Being a blood-drinker truly is a game of swings and roundabouts.

I had no further time to consider the pros and cons of having begun my own coven with Louise under my wing as a familiar-looking car pulled up beside us.

Gary Thrill stepped out of the vehicle and approached us in an understandably frantic manner. 'So, here you are! I've been looking for you. Are you going to tell me what the hell's going on around here?'

'I could ask you the same thing,' I answered. 'The last time we were both standing here on this road, it was decorated with crashed cars and dead bodies.'

Gary Thrill's demeanour changed to quiet discomfort. 'Things got weird. I helped your dad sort things out and then, when things were a little steadier, I tried to call the incident in but the signal kept cutting out. Then some short bloke in a parka turned up, lighting candles and sprinkling glitter about. A real creepy fellow, he kept murmuring on to himself in a weird voice.'

A shudder kicked its way down my spine. 'Eurgh, fucking Goodson.'

'Goodson? Is that his name?'

'Yeah it's his name. He's a warlock'

Gary stifled a laugh. 'For real? He can do magic and shit?'

'It seems that way. Or maybe he's just a sick freak who likes doing unnerving things.' I really wasn't sure what to believe anymore. Either way, he puts the hours into it. Thinking about it, he might have cast a spell to make people forget about the incident here. I remember my friend Christine telling me that a warlock once put a spell over the Ypres Tavern that yielded similar results.'

I'd barely finished talking before Gary Thrill jumped in. 'Wait! So that girl I saw you with WAS Christine? The local girl who went missing in the '80s?'

'One and the same.'

Gary Thrill's eyes were full of both wonder and trepidation. 'But she went missing a decade ago, how come she's still young?'

As Gary Thrill had already seen Goodson getting up to some bit of business or the other I figured I may as well fill him in on everything. 'Christine still looks young because she didn't go missing. Or at least, not in the way you'd presume. An evil bastard called Gideon Lachand turned her into a blood-drinker. She's now *of the night*, as they say.'

Gary raised a quizzical eyebrow, 'She's a vampire?'

'Basically, yeah. But don't let her catch you calling her that.'

'Lachand? I know that name. We had it connected to great swathes of crime in the area a few months back but we struggled to find proof the person even existed. We thought it must be a code name or a bizarre hoax... a myth.'

'Nah, he's real alright.' A distress of sorts fell over me as I remembered how easily he had dominated me in the subway, which then transformed into a sense of resolve and determination to stop him. 'That night you were here; he'd sent his minions as an attack on me and my family. I'm sure you've already worked this out but yes, I am a blood-drinker too but like Lachand himself, I am one *of lineage* – I was born this way. I can survive in sunlight and live a relatively normal life. I'm the only person in town who's a legitimate threat to him. He's taken Christine off to lord knows where and has a head full of horrific plans, the first of which is to make most people in this town part of his vampire army and then feed off the rest.'

I could see Gary Thrill weighing up a decision in his mind. 'And what about you? Do you want to turn people into vampires?'

'Nah I'm not into all that,' I attempted to assure him.

Gary Thrill seemed doubtful. 'Are you sure?'

'Yes. Positive.'

'So who's that pale girl in the car and why is the top of her neck covered in blood?'

'Oh, that's my college friend Louise D'Souza and she's bleeding because... erm, well yes, admittedly I have just turned her into a vampire.'

Gary Thrill arched his eyebrows. 'I thought you weren't into all that.'

Louise leant out of the utility truck to clarify. 'He's not. It's taken me weeks of nagging to get him to do it.'

'You actually wanted to be turned into a vampire?' Gary Thrill asked her, the pitch of his voice rising in exasperation.

'Oh yeah, more than anything,' Louise answered in a soft, cool tone that seemed to drift through the air on a dream.

Gary Thrill buried his face in his palm. 'Sweet Jesus! I really don't understand this town anymore.'

. . .

Christine:

Minutes and hours fell away from me in a haze. I felt ragged and exhausted, which made little sense as I'd largely been rooted to the same spot, bound by an accursed rope, for the past umpteen days. Between the threat of being murdered by Sheena Dafoe and the racket of the printing plant it was near impossible to get any rest. A bunch of coin-operated machines had been dumped at the furthest end of the main area of the plant and, for reasons I couldn't comprehend, were plugged in all day, every day. There were pinball machines, a jukebox, three vending machines and a whole bunch of fucking fruit machines, all chirping away. And then on top of all of that, there was still that infernal clanging noise outside.

One evening, I was awoken by an additional noise; Gideon was holding court ranting and raving about his harvest.

'Tomorrow we rise!' he bellowed. 'The harvest begins! The first step is more foot soldiers; so I need you to bring the victims to me, un-bled. I need them to be strong and athletic. Happy hunting! An endless night for all!'

Gideon's throng of supporters all repeated his new rallying cry of 'An endless night for all!' and cheered before most of them separated out across the plant, except for Sheena Dafoe who quickly stepped herself towards him. 'Excellent speech, my lord. I'm just wondering if you'd had any thoughts about what your plans for her are.' Sheena nodded her head in my direction with a disdainful look.

'Ah yes, Christine. I must admit, bringing her back here hasn't been as satisfying as I thought it'd be. Also, the gothic, punk rock look? So far from the zeitgeist! You can basically smell the '80s dripping from her. I'll make a deal with you, Sheena. Bring me in some of these modern indie girls to fill her previous role.'

'And then?' she asked, her eyes full of arousal and malice.

'And then, my dearest Sheena, they can watch as you set an example by dragging poor, used-up and useless Christine into the sunlight as she slowly yet satisfyingly burns away.'

My heart dropped to my stomach like a stone in a reservoir. I foolishly tried to wriggle out of the accursed rope as if I hadn't already spent day after day trying that. Sheena shot me a smug glance as she passed. In that moment it seemed certain that Sheena had defeated me once and for all but a moment doesn't always shape an outcome. I knew there had to be a way out of this. If Benjamin truly wasn't going to rescue me, I'd have to conceive another plan. I squinted my eyes and tried to whir my brain into action. I had plenty of chess pieces to play with but wasn't sure how to implement them. Every time it appeared that I had a tiny thought starting to morph into something decent, the clanging sound from outside would rear up again. CLANG! CLANG! CLANG! It went over and over again, before suddenly it eased and then vanished, the sound and its source drifting off to who knows where.

Benjamin Cooper:

I couldn't believe my own eyes when it happened. The three of us: Gary Thrill, Louise D'Souza and yours truly, were chatting about what should happen next. Both Gary and Louise were adamant that we should prioritise Christine's rescue but I was less certain.

Deep down, in my heart of hearts, I think I lacked confidence in my ability to take on Gideon Lachand and his horde, but to save face I spun it a different way. 'We will rescue Christine, but perhaps tomorrow. I mean, Louise has two holes in her neck for starters. I demand that she stays put and heals up. Plus, I think we need to learn a bit more about the world Gideon Lachand and Christine come from. I mean, apparently I can fly and Christine reckons she talks to bats and all kinds. Is that true or is it her bullshitting? Also, we have absolutely no idea where Lachand has taken her.'

And then, as if on cue, a dark shape swooped down from the sky above me and, with one wing stronger than the other, it hovered at eye level. It couldn't be, could it?

'Igor?' I asked the bat, flapping about in front of me.

The bat frantically chirped and clicked, occasionally nodding his head off to the right.

'Wait! Do you know where Christine is?'

Igor threw some energetic squawks in with his chirps and clicks before again nodding to the right.

'Now, what's all THIS about?' asked Gary Thrill, who had seen perhaps too much over the past week or so.

'It's Christine's familiar,' advised Louise, sliding back out of the truck and still clutching her scarf tightly to her neck.' He can lead us to wherever Gideon Lachand's lot has taken her.'

'Even so,' I answered, 'I can't go in single-handed and take the lot of them on.'

'I think you can,' Louise replied with a smile. 'I have a plan.'

Louise D'Souza:

'Do you still have that jacket?' I asked Benjamin. 'You know, the one with the mod target patch I sewed on.'

'It was in the boot of Christine's car, but who knows where that's been towed off to.'

'Well, I've got one less worry for you then,' Gary Thrill declared. 'It's in your dad's garage. I tracked it down while you were missing and brought it back here.'

'Why would you do that?' Benjamin appeared to be suspicious and nervous.

Gary sighed, 'because this entire situation is way too wild to bring into the station. Until I can get a grip on what's happening with you and all your Munster mates I want everything involved with that night contained in one area.'

Benjamin still seemed confused by Gary Thrill's decision but his next question was for me. 'Ok, but what's my jacket gonna do?'

'Do you remember when I told you about what I'd read in that Italian book I have, you know about flight and other powers for those *of lineage*? If I've understood it correctly all abilities are garnered from the currency of devotion felt by those they've turned. Well, Lachand mostly gains his power from fear, which is a forced manufacturing of devotion. It's strong, but not as strong as true devotion.'

'What do you mean?' Benjamin looked uneasy.

I decided to lay it out straight to him. 'Well, when I sewed that patch onto your jacket, it was an act of love.'

'Oh I mean, well...' Benjamin spluttered. He had already brushed me off once and I could tell he wasn't keen to do it a second time.

'Bloody hell Benjamin; stop being so awkward about everything. There's more to love than romance and sex. There's family love, friendship love... just feeling love for the fire within someone to such a degree that you want to help it keep burning.' In that moment I knew I held love for him but it was still processing and I began to question the form it would ultimately take.

Benjamin Cooper:

If I understood things correctly, with both her blood inside of me and the power of the patch on my jacket I would be carrying the power of the devotion she felt for me as I went to battle a bunch of vampires. I must declare it all felt a little too sudden for me, as if, without consent, I'd become both married and a goth in one fell swoop.

Either way, I couldn't deny the new swell of untamed energy pumping through my veins since I turned Louise into a blood-drinker. As she healed from my bite, I could feel my blood surge and take hold of my thoughts and heartbeat. Emotionally, it was a one-way transaction – I felt little other than a light gratitude for her service to me. It seemed that some form of guilt should arrive soon as a penance for my selfish act, but I was surprised to discover that nothing came to challenge my morals. I could see why the likes of Gideon Lachand would become addicted to making others *of the night* and, for the first time, truly felt the crushing weight of the implications of his planned harvest. No one should be allowed to have that much power. What if he can't control it or, more worryingly, what if he can? I had to stop this; I wouldn't be able to rest until I did. Where there was once fear now ran fury, my blood exploding through veins like a howling scream.

Louise D'Souza:

It was incredible to see the fire ignite inside of Benjamin after he put his jacket on. He looked eager; ravenous. He thumped his fists hard on the bonnet of Christine's car, steadying his hungry panting into a series of sharp inhalations. He then got into the car and started feverishly tearing through the glove compartment until he found a vial of blood. I'd read warnings about the effects of mixing blood types during my studies and urged him against drinking it, with no success. He knocked it back, ran his tongue over his fangs and I watched in astonishment as the irises in his eyes distorted and changed from blue to yellow.

Benjamin marched towards Igor who was perched on a fence across the road. 'Right, you – bat. Show me the way to Christine.'

With an unsteady wing, Igor flew overhead and passed the roof of Benjamin's house.

Gary gestured towards his car. 'Get in - I'll drive.'

'No,' declared Benjamin, gently pushing Gary Thrill aside, 'I'm going to fly there!'

'You're going to fly?' Gary asked, shocked.

'I can fly. Ask her,' he threw a pointed finger towards me.

'I mean, perhaps. But I think you'd need to study and practise and...'

'And NOTHING!' he blustered. 'I've had your blood; some random blood and I've got a jacket with a RAF mod target-thing patch on. I'm beyond being ready to fly and if that doesn't work? Gary, I'm drinking your blood next.'

'What?' Gary exclaimed.

Benjamin flashed him a smile. 'Psych! Just kidding.'

And with that, he took a run up and sort of glided through the air for a moment or two before clipping a wheelie bin with his foot and tumbling to the floor.

'It's fine! It's fine! I've got it now,' he said, dusting himself off and taking another run up. To our amazement, he did indeed have it. He went drifting off into the night with his unbuttoned jacket flapping in the breeze.

CHAPTER 17
RUNNING WITH THE SHADOWS OF THE NIGHT (PART. 2)

TESTIMONY: LOUISE D'SOUZA, BENJAMIN COOPER AND Christine on the blood-soaked night of the 13th of July 1995

Christine:

The evening had brought an unsavoury hint of malice in the air, as Gideon had instructed all of his family (as he was now calling his followers) to come to the printing plant for a full debrief before he began the harvest the next day. They loitered and cackled as he walked amongst them, delighting in his role of patriarch and idol. The news that I was no longer of interest to Gideon as an asset was a worry, and the sight of Sheena Dafoe constantly whispering in his ear while throwing poisonous glances my way did little to alleviate my concern. After one lengthy hate pitch, I saw Gideon nod approvingly and a smile break out on her face.

I watched closely as Gideon stepped up onto his makeshift podium. 'Very well, very well,' he said, silencing an over-eager Sheena before addressing the room. 'If I could have everyone's attention. Tomorrow will see us begin our harvest of the town but before we all go off and fulfil our roles; may I suggest a little blood ritual for luck? We shall take it in turns to cut at Christine's skin. I don't want to see anyone getting crazy with it. Just one, small nip with the scalpel and then pass it on. Before we start, it would be great if a couple of you could drag her under the skylight so the sad, old moon hanging over us can shine a little sorrow upon her.'

Two weasel-looking fucks grabbed me underneath my arms and dragged me into the moonlight beaming through the glass of the skylight above.

Once I was in position Gideon gave the next order. 'Remove the accursed rope but keep her pinned down.'

They heaved the rope off and pinned me down. I tried to wriggle and fight back but the days and nights without blood consumption had left me weak and unsteady.

'And finally,' said Gideon, laying his scalpel in Sheena's open hand, 'Ms Dafoe, would you like the honour of taking the first slit?'

Sheena smirked and flicked her long, dark hair back over her shoulders. 'Oh, it would be my pleasure.'

She began to stride towards me when, all of the sudden, every light in the printing plant went out.

You wouldn't think that blood-drinkers would be afraid of the dark but a striking unease took hold of every last one of them.

'A blown fuse, perhaps?' offered Turnstile, stepping forward to stand beside his master.

'No, stay vigilant,' Gideon Lachand ordered.

From deep within the gloom, a bright light emerged. It was only small but it shone with a stark contrast to the darkness around us. I realised that it must have been one of the coin-operated machines. A glowing arc of light joined it, illuminating the whole jukebox just as the sound of Pat Benatar's multi-tracked voice boomed from the speakers positioned around the printing plant. There was only one person I knew who was likely to pop on some Pat Benatar at a time like this and I prayed that it was him.

Something that looked like a gloopy, red basketball came whizzing like a comet down the centre of the printing plant and smashed into Gideon Lachand's chest and arms, causing his face to fall. In his hands lay the severed head and pained final expression of Mr Goodson, drenched in lashings of dripping, crimson blood.

Benjamin:

Following Igor, I had made my way to the printing plant. The building was full of noise and light. Luckily, Gideon Lachand was holding court, which was distracting his followers and making it easy to slide on in via a fire escape. At first, I was a little perplexed about why it had been left open, but, as I approached, I understood that it was to enable the escape of a dreadful stench my nostrils were picking up. The source of the smell became visible as I snuck into a small area behind various pipes, generators and meters, where I witnessed Mr Goodson up to something unsavoury. He was burbling away to himself, pouring vials of blood and other fluids into a huge vat while cheerily stirring his concoction with a large wooden spoon. The sight of him enraged me, causing memories of what he did to me to churn in my guts. I found myself marching up to him and then rabbit-punching him hard in the back of the head, causing him to collapse headfirst into his crimson cocktail. I immediately grabbed him by his thinning greasy hair and pushed his head deep into the vat. I could feel him gurgling, squirming and wriggling – desperate for air – but I pushed down harder and further until all life left his body. I yanked his torso away from the vat and stuck my hand into his mouth's blood-filled, pleading, final grimace. With an untamed hunger for vengeance hurtling through my veins I pulled back with my hand, tearing Mr Goodson's head from his neck and shoulders.

Peering around the corner I could see a long gangway straight down the middle of the plant and, at the end of it, stood Lachand. My fear of him had evolved into something more visceral; a burning, pulsing need to hurt him, to destroy him. I hit the fuses to plunge the building into darkness; there were a lot of Lachand loyalists in the building that night and I needed the element of surprise and confusion to get through them all. A backup generator sparked up the jukebox, which was unintended, but I figured a little fight music might provide the inspiration I'd need. With two fingers up Goodson's nostrils and my thumb in his mouth I held his dripping head like a bowling ball and aimed it straight at Gideon.

Christine:

A handful of emergency lights flickered on but ample pockets of darkness still dominated the room. Gideon dropped Mr Goodson's head without sentiment and angrily ordered six of his goons to walk down the aisle and check out what was happening. One by one, they were pulled out of the light by a figure in the darkness sound tracked by a scream, a crunch and finally silence. The mysterious assailant strode into the light and, to my deepest joy, my prayers had been answered as Benjamin Cooper stood, looking prouder and more powerful than I'd ever seen him. Benjamin and Gideon's yellow eyes locked and, to my surprise, Gideon blinked first. He hollered for more men to take Benjamin down, only for my rescuer to take three skips forward, rise into the air and begin gliding towards us.

Shanks, Long Tooth and a handful of other blood-drinkers ran to block Benjamin's path. As Benjamin descended upon them, Gideon barked an order at Sheena. 'Don't let him get what he's come here for! Take Christine and dispose of her.'

'My pleasure,' Sheena purred, as she pulled me by my hair, up towards the largest printing press machine in the building.

I tried to fight her off but I was too blood-starved. 'I'm going to enjoy doing this. The last sound you're going to hear is my glee as I crush your ugly, queer face.'

She propped me up against the huge metal rollers of the machine and looked around for the controls. I closed my eyes and gritted my teeth, feeling an immense frustration that Sheena Dafoe would seal my fate. Benjamin was occupied with Gideon's followers, he couldn't see me let alone save me and I had no fight left in my body to fend for myself. It appeared that there would be no salvation but then a huge crashing noise emerged from the large double doors located on the side of the building. A familiar-looking utility truck had come crashing through. With the last ounce of strength I had, I dived off to the side just as the truck slammed straight into Sheena, pinning her against the machine. I glanced up to see who was driving and amazed to see my very own midnight angel, Louise, at the wheel. Admittedly she had looked better. Don't get me wrong she was still gorgeous but she didn't look very well at all.

Louise D'Souza:

Before taking off into the night, Benjamin had instructed me to wait back at my house and heal up. He had a point I suppose, I had just had a whole lot of blood sucked out of my neck and my genetic structure was in the process of transforming into a vampire, but the sheer excitement of finally being able to live my dream took over and I decided to follow him in my dad's truck. By the time I had arrived at the industrial park I had begun to feel a little woozy and, after witnessing Benjamin land by the old printing press, I think I sort of passed out. I was sharply shaken back to consciousness when I crashed through two huge double doors with my foot pushing down hard on the accelerator. I could see Christine looking fragile and weak, being manhandled by the smug goth cow I'd seen hanging around during my misguided association with Turnstile. I immediately slammed on the brake, easing off just enough to ram Sheena against some big printing press machine. It was ridiculously big; lord knows what they printed here. When I was at school the rumour that went around was that it was porn but there are not enough wanks in the world to justify a jazz mag machine of that size.

Christine:

'Jump in the back, I'm getting you out of here!' Louise hollered at me out of her rolled-down window. She was pale-faced and groggy but still had the voice of Venus.

I took a moment to chortle at the sight of Sheena Dafoe rammed up against the printing press, but my laughter was cut short when she suddenly snapped back to life and began hissing at us.

'Shit!' screamed Louise.

'Shit!" I screamed back.

Sheena started clawing viciously at the truck's bonnet with the pupils in her yellow eyes narrowing to become almost snake-like. She must have taken some dark magik potion that evening to heighten her enjoyment of my planned demise. If Louise reversed, it would have freed Sheena who, being all juiced up on voodoo, could have been capable of anything. A plan quickly formed in my head.

'Ram her again!' I yelled to Louise who reversed slightly before slamming her vehicle back into Sheena. The impact caused Sheena's head to crash back against the metal rollers of the printing press, at which point I dived for the start switch on the machine's control panel. I staggered away as quickly as I could and jumped up onto the back of the truck.

'Ok, get us out of here,' I yelled, giving the back window a couple knocks.

Louise reversed back hard, sending us back through the smashed-open double doors. Sheena attempted to pursue us but found herself, at first halted and then, dragged backwards. She discovered, to her dismay, that the ends of her luscious, long, dark hair had been resting on the rollers when I started the machine and her locks were now caught and being spun into its inner gears, belts and motors.

We heard her frantic cries for help escalate into blood curdling screams as we escaped the building. We didn't stick around to witness her fate but it can't have been pretty.

Benjamin Cooper:

Having flung a plethora of known associates and newer recruits from Gideon Lachand's coven aside, I paced after their master while they nursed their bruises. Lachand had retreated up a flight of dark, iron stairs to his office, over-looking the printing plant floor. While climbing the stairs I heard the crash of the double doors being bashed in and saw Louise rescuing Christine. I felt a certain frustration that Louise hadn't followed my instructions to stay behind and rest but was glad that Christine was safe. I could fully focus on tearing down Lachand and his planned harvest.

Lachand's retreat had been tactical rather than an act of cowardice and I felt the swift strike of an iron cane crash against my head as I reached the top of the staircase. Lachand followed this up with some hard kicks to my head as I collapsed to the floor. On the fourth or fifth kick I managed to catch his foot and flip him onto his back. I scrambled back to my feet and pursued him into his office. Turnstile was there already and threw his master a wooden stake. In one fluid motion Lachand spun and attempted to stake me through the heart but, more by luck than skill, I blocked it with my right forearm. With my left hand, I began to punch him repeatedly in the head and pushed him towards the centre of his office. As the pair of us slumped over his desk the stake fell out of Lachand's hand. Despite being disarmed, Lachand continued to attack me, clawing at my face and jabbing me in the side of my head. While I was distracted by the strikes, Lachand gave me a swift kick in the balls, causing me to stumble backwards.

He turned towards Turnstile who had picked up a huge wooden hourglass filled with strange, emerald-coloured sand that somehow appeared both gloomy and luminous at the same time. 'Get that thing out of here. NOW!' Lachand barked.

Feeling fired-up and spiky following the kick to the balls, I pushed Turnstile aside and grabbed the hourglass as he stumbled. In one strike, I smashed it across Gideon Lachand's stupid, foppish face. Splinters from the wooden frame shot out across the office, chased by the piercing shards of glass from its twin domes. The sand exploded around us before quickly settling into a lingering drift, covering our faces and infiltrating our eyes, nostrils and mouths.

I rubbed my face, ready for Lachand's next move but he just stood static, looking at me with a sense of exasperation and fear. 'WHY? WHY WOULD YOU DO THAT? ARE YOU MAD? DO YOU KNOW WHAT YOU'VE DONE?' His face was one of startled disdain, white eyeballs and fangs poking out of a mask of green dust and small streams of crimson.

Lachand attempted to throw a punch but I caught it in the palm of my hand and pushed him to the floor. Something had happened, something that had made him noticeably weaker. I picked up the stake lying on his office floor and walked towards him, ready to end his malevolent rule over this town. He looked towards Turnstile for help, only to find his once-loyal servant turn his gaze to me and bend the knee, apparently switching allegiance.

'Turnstile! You bastard! You idiot! After what's just happened? Do you think this milquetoast child can save you from *him*?' Lachand sounded desperate and full of panic. His words stumbled out of a breathless mouth, struggling for space as he continued to cough out the green sand from the hourglass. With one great push, Lachand made his way towards the window and flung himself out, flying off into the night.

I turned back to Turnstile who was still bowing to me. He could see my perplexed expression. 'It's like I told you,' Turnstile said humbly, 'tonight it ends. Now go and secure some inner-peace, you'll never be free if Gideon survives.'

I looked over Turnstile's shoulders, across the staircase and out over the floor of the plant, and saw Lachand's entire coven following his lead and bending the knee towards me. Admittedly there seemed a lot of reluctance and hatred in their faces but I was glad they had surrendered. Now there was just one last loose end to tie up.

Christine:

While driving away from the printing plant, I saw Gideon flying away followed by an also-airborne Benjamin in hot pursuit. I was amazed to see him like this; I wondered what had happened during my time bound by that accursed rope. Looking at the state of Louise, I presumed that he'd turned her and was feeding off of her love for him. I didn't know he had it in him, the dirty dog! My jealous heart made me paranoid that he'd also fucked her in my absence but I knew it wasn't the time for petty internal drama. Louise seemed to have clocked Benjamin on the chase and hollered something about needing to go and help him out.

Eventually Gideon seemed to falter and slowly descend from the sky. He seemed weakened and frail but still burned with enough fire to continue his escape on foot. We chased him through the Murston district and into the cabbage fields that lay between the town and the village of Bapchild. I had no idea where Gideon was running to – possibly to escape the border of Sittingbourne and any magik boundaries that existed there, but more likely it was an act of desperation. He eventually ran out of breath and came to a pause with Benjamin descending eight feet or so behind him.

Young Mr Cooper looked wild that night, his eyes staring soullessly ahead and his body poised and angular. Clutching a stake in his hand, he made his way towards Gideon who held out his hand as if he was a traffic cop.

'Wait!' my former master declared, 'I don't know what you've consumed tonight or what kind of deal you've made to increase your power but let me tell you that this ends with me walking off to the A2 and you fucking off back to Sittingbourne. I'll give you your due, you've had one hell of a night and I underestimated you, but at the end of the day you're still just that good little boy from Woodbury Drive. Throw that stake away boy and stop posing like you're the dark of the night, something we both know that you aren't.'

A tangled frustration washed over Benjamin's face and while his posture kept its poised malice, a tear escaped his eye as the stake dropped from his hand. Gideon scoffed and turned to walk away. However instead of finding the path to freedom he walked straight into the flapping wings and screeching vocalisations of Igor. As he swatted away at the most excellent bat in the universe Gideon spun back around only to find Benjamin spring up beside him and sink two vengeful fangs straight into his neck.

I stood amazed. Holy shit – there's some things blood-drinkers just don't do, things that there are unwritten rules about and one of those things is that those *of lineage* don't feed off of those *of lineage*. I shudder to think what Scratch would make of such antics.

It was incredible to see Benjamin feast on Gideon Lachand so ravenously though. I wondered what the outcome of this might be; powerful blood mixed with powerful blood, centuries of lineage colliding. My wonder turned to fear. What if Benjamin bled him dry? What kind of person would sweet little Benjamin become after digesting ten pints worth of blood from the most despicable person I've ever known? The more Benjamin fed, the bluer his skin went and the more his pupils faded amongst the distant yellow of his irises. I was sure I had lost him, just as many others *of lineage* had been corrupted by consumption fuelled by greed but then, something unexpected happened. Benjamin looked up, made eye contact with me and with a beckoning nod, urged me to come forward and feed.

Benjamin:

Most of the evening had been a strange blur but something inside suddenly woke me when I fed on Gideon. I could feel power swelling in my veins: new strengths; so many opportunities; the destruction of my weaknesses; future threats being eliminated by the fear of me alone. It felt amazing, like an ego erection. Christine had once explained that blood-drinkers' eyes turn yellow because they're in a state of rapture and excitement about taking someone's life-force and swamping it with their own, so I bet in that moment mine were Day-Glo. So much power and all mine, I could now do whatever I wanted. I had hundreds of years worth of blood power waiting for me to digest. I was near immortal. I had an army of vampires who now had to obey my command. I could destroy the likes of Darren King in an instant, should he so much as chortle in my direction. I could rob every bank in town, piss all over the statue of the Bargeman in the high street and I could march up to Eliza and make her mine. But, I realised I didn't want any of that. All of the vampires in that printing plant hated me, so even if I did control them I knew in my heart of hearts that they'd never be truly loyal. Darren King may be a tosser, but he doesn't deserve to be murdered. I could rob the banks but I don't need the drama, likewise I could piss all over the Bargeman statue but there's a perfectly serviceable (if a little grim) public toilet a minute up the road, near the library. And then there's Eliza. Should a crush on a brief acquaintance hold so much emotional currency? Perhaps she's the love of my life or maybe it was just a giddy encounter, full of possibility, during an eventful evening. Either way, should we ever be brought together again, and should she express an interest – I'll earn her love with the light within that longs to shine rather than the darkness that seeks to dim it.

The question then presented itself – what on Earth should I do with all this powerful, dark magik blood pouring out of this arsehole's neck? I mean, something good had to come out of this violent summer. And it hit me; what could blood *of lineage* do to those born *of the night* if a large enough quantity was drunk? Maybe Christine wouldn't have to be so afraid of sunlight. Maybe I hadn't totally ruined Louise's normal life and we'd be able to get away without her Mum finding out I'd turned her daughter into a vampire. It had to be worth a try, right?

Christine:

I swaggered towards the fallen remains of the once-almighty Gideon Lachand with my wicked mouth flicking out a switchblade smile. He was clinging on to his existence and appeared stunned at the audacity of my fearless approach. If he was taken aback by my lack of worry I can only imagine what went through his head when Benjamin pulled his mouth away from the shooting jet of blood and I tagged in. While I fed from him, Gideon made one last sour groan before his head slumped forward.

Benjamin found a half-full bottle of red wine in the utility truck and made his way back to Gideon's corpse/blood dispensary. He emptied the remains of the bottle as he walked back towards me, leaving a trailing stain of scarlet vino in his wake. With a sly smile on his face, he lifted Gideon's arm and gnawed his hand off. More blood exploded out of the arteries, which Benjamin soon decanted into the empty wine bottle.

The flow of blood eased to mere clots and trickles as Gideon's body began to feel stiff and heavy. I felt full and Benjamin gave me a nod to indicate he too was satisfied.

'We need to give this to Louise,' Benjamin said, holding up the bottle of blood while wiping his mouth on the sleeve of his jacket. 'We owe her.'

A wave of realisation and excitement crashed against the shore of my heart. Louise and I would be sharing blood *of lineage*. I didn't know exactly what this might achieve but I'd witnessed enough blood play between warlocks and high-ranking night folk to know it wasn't nothing. I buried my smile and kept my hopes and wishes to myself, lest Benjamin have doubts and change his mind.

As we turned back to the car, the corpse of Gideon Lachand lurched towards us, with his one un-severed hand reaching towards us. Through a desperate gasp of breath, a startling scream left his wide, fang-bearing mouth. I don't know how he'd popped back to life. Maybe we hadn't drained him enough or he may have had some sort of dark magik still cruising through his veins. Judging by the way his eyes rolled back in his head as a startling mixture of green and red goo streamed out of the corners of their lids like ugly, drunk tears, I presumed the latter.

Somehow, he launched himself towards us and was about to strike when Igor swooped in, clamped his tiny bat jaws around Lachand's jugular and chewed until the veins and sinew were threadbare, causing his head to flop over to the side. Igor must have drunk some of the sweet stuff too; his broken wing had healed and his eyes shone like diamond white fog lights. Igor hovered in the air and gave out a high-pitched shriek.

A couple of hundred rats heard the signal and came scuttling out from the deep, dark trees at the edge of the field, into the long grass. They darted between the cabbages, heeding Igor's call. They swarmed over Gideon's fallen body, chewed the head away from its neck and scurried off; carrying the decimated remains of the decapitated body beyond the cabbages, into the long grass and back into the deep, dark trees. The rodents of Bapchild ate well that night.

. . .

Louise D'Souza:

As I came round, I could feel a glass bottle being gently pushed against my lips and a warm, rich liquid washing over my tongue. Things felt foggy but I could hear Benjamin and Christine's voices reassuring me that everything was ok. There was a weird smell in the air like the stench of fire, farts and a lost pet rotting under the floorboards.

Benjamin noticed me recoiling from the odour and gave a nod to a pile of cabbages on fire with something spherical burning on top of it. 'It's Gideon's head. We're getting rid of it.'

'He won't be coming back from this,' Christine smirked.

We sat together until the fire died out. I felt like a thousand conversations hung in the air but Christine and Benjamin seemed comfortable to sit in silence and I didn't want to disrupt that. I noticed that the sun was starting to rise and it dawned on me that I was in danger. Christine noticed my alarm and took my hand. 'It's ok; we fed you Gideon's blood. He was *of lineage*. Dawn and dusk can't hurt us now.'

We smiled as the sun rose, though Christine qualified with a shrug, 'Midday's still a no-no, so kiss goodbye to your lunchtimes.'

Christine:

To see the sun and feel it gently warm my skin after all these years of fleeing from it was an incredible experience. Impulsively I had taken Louise by the hand to reassure her and, while it was the most fleeting of moments, my heart dined out for days on our brief physical interaction.

I threw my arms up in the air like a victory sign. 'So, that's the end of Gideon Lachand. He can't hurt us anymore.'

Benjamin poked the dying embers of the fire and grumbled, 'Speak for yourself. He kicked me hard in the balls and they're still aching.'

'Well, at least you've now met Igor and know I'm not full of shit. I'll receive your apology when you're ready to give it.'

'What apology?' Benjamin protested.

'An apology for all the times you called me a liar or pulled faces when I said Igor could talk.'

Benjamin wasn't having it. 'Now, wait a minute! I'll admit that I met a bat that it appears you've trained like a circus animal or something, but I didn't hear a single human word come from his furry lips.'

Tsk! Such closed-minded nonsense, of course Igor can talk.

CHAPTER 18

REMEMBER WHEN THE CLOCK STRIKES TWELVE... (THE LOSERS ALWAYS WIN)

Testimony: Igor the Bat, Benjamin Cooper, Louise D'Souza and Christine on life following the events of the 13th of July 1995

Igor the Bat:

Well, of course Christine can communicate with me. Just as I can communicate with her. The great misconception that the likes of Benjamin Cooper have is that I'm pushing human dialogue out of my furry little mouth and that isn't the case at all. Oh no, no, no. It's more a case of her reading my thoughts and likewise, me reading hers. Admittedly, we occasionally vocalise to add a little sauce to it, which is akin to the way you humans flap your hands about and pull ridiculous faces while talking. It's a garnish to the conversation's main meal. So how do Christine and I read each other's internal dialogue? Is it telepathy or some kind of finely tuned empathy? Nobody knows for sure. I mean, why do we automatically generate these testimonies? How do you receive them? Are they requested? Are they an intrusion? And, when they've been experienced, where do they go? Do they fade back into obscurity or are they stored and savored for all time?

Maybe the bigger question is whether we can, and indeed should, trust testimony. As much as I love Christine, I've never found her testimony to be the whole truth. She likes to take charge of the narrative, even if that means lying to herself. She has a clear picture of who Christine is, was and will be, and woe betide any inconvenient truths that attempt to get in the way of that. I'm not being a two-faced bitch by telling you this. I've said it to her face a hundred times or more. In fact, I was joking with her about it earlier that day.

I caught a glimpse of her at the edge of town, painting the phrase, 'Christine the Vampire eats here!' in gaudy hot pink nail varnish on the WELCOME TO SITTINGBOURNE sign.

'Keeping yourself busy, I see!' I said to her, as I swooped down.

'Just marking my territory,' she replied with a smile. 'Y'know, what with my Benjamin being the all-new, all-powerful king of the night. I can really strut around town as free as I like now. Everything has come up roses.'

'Indeed,' I said to her. 'Your evil, previous master has been drained, devoured and destroyed. Your naive, new master is too nice by half and wouldn't even consider keeping you on a leash. The girl you fancy is a newly turned blood-drinker who's going to need a shoulder to cry on when the harsh reality of her new life comes crashing down on her. I'm not saying that you got yourself kidnapped by Gideon Lachand on purpose or led Benjamin into that subway to provoke change but things really couldn't have gone better for you if you'd planned it all yourself, could they?'

It was a cheeky accusation made purely out of jest, though Christine gave a slight smile that made me wonder. Still, it was reassuring to see that she had found a group of humanoid friends. Benjamin had declared, via Turnstile, that all of Gideon Lachand's former followers were free to live their lives in town but were only allowed to drink from blood donations. They were, at least for now, complying with this new rule but dissent and dissatisfaction were sure to grow. So I'm glad that the three of them now had each other for support and it made me feel a little more assured of Christine's well-being when I would clock off duty and return to the belfry to be with my bat lady friend.

Benjamin Cooper:

A few days after we took down Gideon Lachand, my dad and Kelly came home. It was a very awkward reunion and I had to give a bunch of apologies. Gary Thrill had become something of a go-between for my family and I. He and my father had concocted a bizarre and convoluted story to tell Kelly about me getting involved with drugs, and dealers being responsible for the attack on our home. I had no input in any of this or even knowledge that they were doing it and was now stuck living a lie when I'd rather have just told her the truth about all my blood-drinking and what not.

Gary's increased presence in our life was a bit annoying but it paid dividends to have a copper on my side. In fact, after I left to rescue Christie and confront Gideon, he'd called in a suspected drug deal on the opposite end of town to divert police resources from the drama at the industrial estate.

Most amusingly, this had led to the fortuitous arrest of The Grunge Tosser himself, Aiden Actually, who was caught with a frankly pathetic amount of pot on him. He got off with a caution but it'd left him as something of a laughing stock. Rumours spread around Kent about how he'd begged the cops to let him go as he was an 'aspiring musician' and wouldn't be able to tour internationally if he got a criminal record. Kelly told me all about it and how she'd kicked him thoroughly to the kerb, though quite worryingly this did encourage an increasingly apparent interest in Gary Thrill, who she lit up around despite him being twelve years older than her. Old enough to be her father biologically, if not legally.

Still, it was useful keeping Gary Thrill around. Christine, Louise and I had unintentionally entered into a business relationship of sorts with him, where he'd highlight wrong 'uns for us to feed on and then blame the death on drugs or joyriding, or somesuch. We'd get a decent feed, he'd get a case closed and Sittingbourne would be that little bit safer. It was an arrangement he referenced when he caught me staring at the Batman Forever quad poster outside the cinema.

'Batman, eh? That's kinda like us, right?' he cheerily propositioned, sidling up beside me, sticking his hands casually into the pockets of his cream-coloured chinos.

He'd taken me by surprise and I didn't catch his drift. 'Eh?'

'I'm like Commissioner Gordon getting the scoops from the inside and you're like Batman, the dark mysterious outsider getting shit done and standing about on rooftops.'

'Commissioner Gordon and Batman? Steady on, we're barely Chief O'Hara and Robin. Anyhow, how can I help you? Have you got someone you want us to eat?'

'Not right now, but I'm working on it. Nah, what I was actually wondering is if your sister Kelly was around this weekend. I've made her a tape of Prince bootleg stuff she was asking me about.'

Kelly was indeed around but there's no way I was letting that fully-grown, 28-year-old man give my little sister Prince bootleg tapes. 'No, she's visiting her boyfriend.' I replied, inventing a future brother-in-law and coating my increasingly complicated life in another lie.

'No worries, mate,' said Gary, looking a little dejected. So, what are you doing loitering outside the cinema on your lonesome? I reckon you've missed the last screening of the night by a good hour or so.'

I brushed him off with a 'Nah' and felt a slight blush of my cheek as I truly examined the reasons that had led me to standing forlornly outside of Sittingbourne's Cannon cinema on a sun kissed Thursday evening. Despite defeating Gideon Lachand and enjoying a safe reunion with my family, there was still one element of the summer left unfulfilled – the slight sketch of a date, half-arranged between Eliza and I weeks ago. It was silly to consider it anything more than beer chat or a throwaway suggestion and yet, there I was, staring at a movie poster like it might turn into a magic mirror, offering me news and counsel about her thoughts, feelings and whereabouts. Not only had I missed the last screening of the night, but it was also sure to be the last screening of the movie at the cinema. The dream was over.

'Fair enough,' replied Gary Thrill thankfully defusing the awkward pause. 'So, is Christine going to be in town tonight?'

'I'm not sure, but if I see her I'll let her know that you asked after her.'

This wasn't the first time he'd indicated that he'd like to chat to Christine, which was understandable. His interest made total sense, after all she'd been a school friend of his and he was a detective being tantalized with the answer to an unsolved local mystery. Christine, however, wasn't keen at all to meet up with him and the one time she saw him approaching she fled into the night. Despite everything we'd been through that summer, I still felt like I didn't really know the real Christine. On a surface level she could be incredibly candid and yet, when it came to deeper revelations, she was extremely guarded.

Christine:

I had made it to the rooftop of Iceland before Benjamin and Louise that night. The evening air had been blessed with that certain summer smell; sun-baked asphalt and a town full of gardens peaking in the heat. I'd seen Gary lurking around the High Street, styling and profiling in his chinos and Ben Sherman shirt with the sleeves rolled up, so I'd kept a low profile. The shady 'vampire vigilante' operation he was allowing us to operate was a perk but I wasn't happy about someone from my past being involved. Other than that, the summer of '95 had blossomed into a rather wonderful period. Gideon Lachand was gone, I felt free and safe as I walked through the night, and in Benjamin and Louise, I had found some excellent blood-buddies. Benjamin and I were very different in so many ways and yet being around him always felt really easy and enjoyable. He was an oxymoron in the most endearing sense, like a mild mannered wild card. I never quite knew what conversational or emotional tangents he might go off on but I knew I was safe and the randomness of his ways humoured me. And then there was Louise. My attraction to her showed no signs of fading but I was able to keep it hidden as a secret bonus emotion. It was enough of a treat to spend time with her as friends; she was true to her own heart and her conversation was smart and sweet. She also had a way cooler taste in music than Benjamin did and was keen to school me on newer bands like Type O Negative and Inkubus Sukkubus. She gladly referred to herself as a vampire and I'd found myself doing the same. I was free of so many shackles. Being around her made me feel as young as I looked.

Louise D'Souza:

It had been a strange couple of weeks since the night we took down Gideon Lachand and I'd been turned into a blood-drinker. Despite the extra protection from the sun that drinking Gideon Lachand's blood had given us, Christine was correct about the danger of being exposed to direct sunlight. I was mostly fine in mornings and evenings but now it appeared being outdoors during lunch times and afternoons was a strict no-no. I made the mistake of casually stepping out of college one lunchtime and nearly had my arm scorched off. I also had to be mindful of the two telltale fang marks on my neck. It seems I'm condemned to a life of scarfs, chokers and polo neck sweaters, which I'm ok with to be honest. The biggest challenge I've faced so far was the day following Benjamin's bite, when I fell ill and felt truly terrible. My body and spirit were exhausted and achy for a long clutch of days. I wisely took myself off to bed and hid from the world, telling my mum and dad that I had some kind of 'flu. My mum bizarrely got in a complete flap over it, desperately trying to get me to go to the doctors. At first I thought she was keen to get some antibiotics into me, but on the second day the truth came rumbling out – she'd somehow got it into her head that I'd lost my virginity to that 'dreadful boy' (I'm presuming she meant Benjamin) and that it was of grave importance that I get a morning-after pill in case I was pregnant. I ended up selling her a story that Benjamin was gay and not interested in me in that way, which is why we'd had a falling out that time he'd come to study. It got her out of my hair but I did worry about how I'd get around this fabrication should Benjamin and I ever become an official item. Although with both of us now being forever young blood-drinkers, we had decades - maybe centuries rather than months left of care-free adolescence; we could easily wait out the last twenty or thirty years of my mum's life before being fully free to spend our lives together. That being said, with Benjamin being as he is, it could take him a hundred years to realise how good we could be together. I found the idea of a slowly unfolding love affair between Benjamin and myself incredibly sexy, though to be fair, since being turned into a blood-drinker I found myself feeling sexy about an unexpected plethora of things.

There was one night a couple of days ago where after drinking blood from a local wife beater, I went back to Christine's flat and the three of us blissed out on a blood buzz while listening to her random selection of weird old rock albums, and for reasons I can't explain, I got so incredibly turned on I had to excuse myself and went back home where I had the most satisfying masturbatory experience of my life. I got so lost in the moment I have no idea how much noise I made but realistically there must have been quite a bit. I pray to god that my parents were asleep.

Still, my increased feelings of foxiness had unlocked all kinds of benefits in the day-to-day world. I found myself being more flirtatious and had an almost sociopathic urge to use my new sensuality against weak-willed men to get what I wanted at their expense. From quivering boys giving up their seats on crowded trains to receiving free drinks from paunchy middle-aged barmen experiencing their first full-blooded hard-on in years, it seemed that my ship had come in. It was also quite a laugh to unlock a little bi-curiosity in some of the repressed women around town. I'd see them wash their glances over me and then turn away either shaken awake or out of shame. The biggest perk of all of this was that I had secured the longing of a timid, lonely man called Barry who worked at the nearby ambulance station. He was more than happy to gift me blood bags in exchange for a little light flirting and some reassurance that, despite the world acting otherwise, he was indeed a powerful and attractive man. I know what you're thinking and you're probably right; all this tarting around will probably end in tears, but after years of being ignored it feels otherworldly to be seen and adored while, in the case of Ambulance Barry, I desperately needed the blood-bags. Not just to feed on but to also try and win a little favour with Benjamin and Christine. They were kind to me and very nurturing but I don't think they thought of me as a true, fully grown, blood-drinker yet. For example, they wouldn't let me be part of any kills. Every time they received a mission from Gary they'd just-so-happen to carry it out before I came to meet them and I'd get given the remains from Christine's flask. I'd question them on it and push for a more active role but they'd just say "maybe in a month or so." It seemed unfair and made me occasionally a little paranoid, but tonight Barry had secured me some of the rare B-negative stuff and I hoped it might win me some brownie points with them.

Benjamin Cooper:

I made my way up to the rooftop and was greeted by Christine pulling a disgruntled face.

'What's up?' I asked, fearing the kind of news that Christine liked to drop on me when she hasn't got a smirk on her face. 'Is there someone else from your shady past that's arrived back in town to make my life a living nightmare for a week or two?'

'No. Fucking modern pop music,' she moaned giving a sharp, jagged nod over the edge of the roof towards the sound of 'Crazy For You' by Let Loose blaring out of a car's speakers.

Christine squinted her eyes and realised that it was the tune I had been humming along to as I had hoisted myself up to join her. 'Wait! Do you actually like this shit?'

'A bit,' I said, playing it cool. The truth was I had bought a copy of Smash Hits once, mostly because it had a free cover-mounted cassette with the track on it, but I wasn't prepared to fight for the song's honour.

Christine shook her head despairingly and mumbled, 'For fuck's sake.'

Luckily my pride was saved when Louise showed up, skipping across the rooftop, singing the chorus ironically and gently waving a clutch of rare B-negative blood bags.

I thanked Louise for the feed and peered over the edge to check out who was playing the track. Amusingly, it was coming from Darren King's new car. It was parked up beside the Blockbuster video shop and he was there snogging the face off of Becky Hollis. They had rather swiftly become an official couple in the last few weeks of college and had even announced their engagement on the last day of term. They'd promised everyone in the class that they'd be invited to the wedding, which was apparently happening next spring. I doubt they truly meant absolutely everyone including the likes of me. I mean, after everything that had happened this summer, even if they did invite me I couldn't possibly go. Though with my piss flowing around in him and my cum flowing around in her, it's like I've already got them a His & Hers Invasive Bodily Fluid kit as a wedding present.

Christine downed the contents of her blood-bag in one and staggered forwards to see what I was looking at.

'Is that the wanker who called me Shakespears Sister?' she asked, remembering the one time she'd encountered the sparkling wit of Darren King during that fateful night at the Ypres Tavern.

'Yep, the one and only Darren King,' I answered, taking a casual sip of the red stuff.

'Good,' she smirked as she raised her mostly-empty blood bag up in the air as if she was about to throw it at him. I quickly jumped up and grabbed her arm before she could let it fly.

'For god's sake, Christine, don't let people know we come up here to drink blood! This is a good hang out spot, we can't afford to lose it.' While I was slightly concerned about that, the real truth was that I didn't want to provoke a situation where Becky Hollis would get involved and our regrettable fuck was somehow exposed.

'Yeah I suppose you're right Benji,' Christine beamed through her blood buzz while flinging her arm around my shoulders, 'we've got a good thing going on, ain't we? You, me and Louise – the creatures of the night, together again and running this town.'

It was nice to finally have friends, and with Gideon Lachand gone, all my college work up to date and the poptastic sound of Let Loose filling the street, things realistically couldn't be better. Technically, it was an evening that should have felt like a happy ending, yet it didn't. It didn't feel like anything. I missed the wonder of those warm June nights when spring bled into summer. I remembered seeing the stars illuminate a trail across the sky that first night Christine drove me home. Where had they gone? The sky had seemed cold and empty for weeks, ever since that night Gideon brought me to my knees. I wondered if that was the true cost of his assault. Had he taken the sheer essence of joy away from me for good, or was it something worse? Had he actually forced me to confront a more frightening truth? Could it be that flickers of hope and freshly-stuck flames of excitement only burn for the briefest of time before they have to surrender to the inevitable crush of darkness as the night's story fades away into the vacuum of a new dreadful day?

The sound of footsteps and chatter emerged from the east and I watched dozens of people, mostly groups of teens, leaving the cinema's final screening of Batman Forever. My heart sank further, and in that moment a sickening realisation presented itself to me; the words Eliza and I shared that evening had been little more than that. It was a brief memory; one that I'd placed too much stock in and built up way too high. I would have to let it go; find a new source of yearning. Wait for the night to offer up new characters and serendipitous encounters.

And then.

Another pair of footsteps made their way from the west of the High Street. To my surprise and relief I saw her - Eliza, making her way towards the departing crowd, craning her neck to find someone. She began to fidget with a strand of her golden hair as it refused to remain tucked behind her ear, reminding me of the first time I saw her standing at the bar at the Ypres Tavern. Several sunrises might have occurred since that moment but that night had endured.

After the last of the crowd had passed her by, she bit her bottom lip and looked deep into the summer night's sky. She then began to turn her head towards the rooftop. Had she seen me in the corner of her eye, or somehow sensed me? I couldn't be reacquainted with her like this, on a blood-binge with my vampire friends and in the midst of an existential crisis. I swung back into the shadows against the wall of the neighbouring building. I almost immediately cursed myself for acting defensively, and when I took the plunge to look back towards the street, Eliza was no longer there. Still, despite her absence, something else had returned – a sweet, burning reassurance that our brief encounter had resonated with her just as it had with me. With that feeling came a renewed faith for the future and a fresh desire to tackle the good and bad that it might bring.

And then the sky remembered its stars. They returned, blinking back, almost one at a time, nestling against a deep-seated moon that shone brightly in the civil twilight. A lived life is often hindered by horror, despair and darkness but as that one young, summer rooftop moment washed over me, everything for once felt alright.

Also by
Phoenix Phil Morley

Available now: SURVIVE THE UNIVERSE (Parts 1 & 2)

FINISH WORK. GET CHANGED. SURVIVE THE UNIVERSE

When Ryan Tyler leaves his mundane day job to join the Royal Guard in the Kingdom of Vastrid, he finds himself flung into battle on day two, alongside a cosmically-powered warrior, a thief and a hybrid cat-monkey.

Meanwhile, fellow Royal Guard Callie Haywood yearns for adventure and the chance to use her squandered talents as a pilot.

As the malevolent Shadox Corporation unleash their sinister attack on Vastrid, Ryan and Callie must face threats forged from the far reaches of space and master the strange, repeating visions which plague their minds and hint at a fate that is both frightening and fascinating.

SURVIVE THE UNIVERSE is a fast paced, fun to read futuristic fairy-tale space opera filled with humour, horror and heart. The novel contains the first two parts of SURVIVE THE UNIVERSE saga and tells the story of a wild galactic adventure that mixes snappy, humorous dialogue, intense action and tense, edge-of-your-seat horror.

AVAILABLE NOW FROM ALL GOOD BOOKSTORES

PRAISE FOR SURVIVE THE UNIVERSE:

"Four chapters in and I'm HOOKED!" - Steve McLean (comedian, writer, Action Figure Archive)

"5 Stars. This one goes at 100 mph. There are some big characters leaping off the pages here that'll spark your fantasy casting off strongly" - 5 star Amazon review

"A massive space opera that sort of takes all the cool bits of Star Wars and splices them to all the cool bits of Blake's 7. And it's got this hungry cat thing in it too that I loved" - Peter Richard Adams (writer, Pod To Pluto podcast)

"Bought on a whim mainly because I liked the front cover and really enjoyed it. There are some clever touches and good characters, I would recommend it" - 5 star Amazon review

"I had so much fun reading this book and will miss spending time with the characters. I look forward to catching up with them in the proposed sequel" - 5 star Goodreads review

"I dug this book a lot. The characters are well considered, the writing is tight and smooth, but it's really the story and the world (or should that be universe?) building which will leave you needing to know what happens to our protagonists. A compelling Sci fi yarn and a great Young Adult/Bratpack type romance story, but doesn't scrimp on either genre. Keen to see what this guy puts out next." - 5 star Amazon review

"A ripping story, full of well thought out and nicely rounded characters. Someone else (amazon reviewer) referenced Blake's 7 and the Breakfast Club, and I was surprised to find that I totally saw the reference. Really good fun, and well worth a read!Go for it!" - Mike Hibbert (author)

"Enjoyed books 1 & 2. Now waiting to read books 3 & 4." - 5 star Goodreads revi

'A fun sci-fi romp. Reminds me of the Red Dwarf novels meets Star Wars. Set in a sprawling outer space Universe, a lot of the worlds in Survive The Universe kinda conjure up the futuristic island of City of Bohane by Kevin Barry.' - Frankie Moloney (DJ, The Bugle podcast, The Face Radio)

MUSICAL INSPIRATIONS

Listen to the BITE BACK! Playlist on Spotify:

1. Gimme! Gimme! Gimme! (A Man After Midnight) - ABBA

2. Self Control - LAURA BRANIGAN

3. We Are The Pigs - SUEDE

4. Lenny - SUPERGRASS

5. Drink The Elixir - SALAD

6. Fixing A Hole - THE BEATLES

7. She's In Parties - BAUHAUS

8. Wow And Flutter - STEREOLAB

9. Stargazer - SIOUXSIE AND THE BANSHEES

10. Tell Me When - THE HUMAN LEAGUE

11. Rock Lobster - THE B52's

12. Eloise - THE DAMNED

13. Disorder - JOY DIVISION

14. Wake up Boo! -THE BOO RADLEYS

15. Loose - THERAPY?

16. Now They'll Sleep - BELLY

17. Cannibal Surf Babe - MARILLION

18. Digging The Grave - FAITH NO MORE

19. 2:1 - ELASTICA

20. When Do I Get To Sing "My Way" - SPARKS

21.Can I Run - L7

22. Street Spirit (Fade Out) - RADIOHEAD

23. Shadows Of The Night - PAT BENATAR

24. Crazy For You - LET LOOSE

25. Creatures Of The Night - KISS

Yeah I know that I've picked all this 90's music for a book based on vampires while leaving Oasis' aptly titled Live Forever on the shelf. I tried to find a space for it in the story but it just didn't gel. I'm sure Liam and Noel won't mind, their contributions to the Summer of Britpop are recognised elsewhere. Speaking of which…

Back in June 1995, Benjamin Cooper's little sister Kelly made him a cassette compilation of 'britpop music'. Not all of it is strictly Britpop (or even British) but it paints a picture of that time and place.

Listen to her compilation on Spotify:

BRITPOPPIN' (Kelly's Britpop C90)

Side 1.

1. Lenny - SUPERGRASS

2. Some Might Say - OASIS

3. My Dark Star - SUEDE

4. Seems Hard - THE CARDIGANS

5. Vegas (single version) - SLEEPER

6. Are You Blue Or Are You Blind - THE BLUETONES

7. Day Of The Triffids - ASH

8. Jamie - WEEZER

9. Fine Time - CAST

10. Where Have you Been Tonight - SHED 7

11. Loose - THERAPY?

12. I Wanna Go Where The People Go - THE WiLDHEARTS

Side 2.

1. Waking Up - ELASTICA

2. Badhead - BLUR

3. Just Looking' - THE CHARLATANS

4. Love In June - THE WANNADIES

5. I'll Manage Somehow - MENSWE@R

6. Discolite - TEENAGE FANCLUB

7. Bones - RADIOHEAD

8. You're Always Right - THESE ANIMAL MEN

9. Haunted By You - GENE

10. Yes - MCALMONT and BUTLER

11. Underwear - PULP

12. Find The Answer Within - THE BOO RADLEYS

Christine prefers albums though...

CHRISTINE'S TOP TEN ALBUMS

1. The Head On The Door - THE CURE

2. Scary Monsters & Super Creeps - DAVID BOWIE

3. Misplaced Childhood - MARILLION

4. Creatures Of The Night - KISS

5. Hyaena - SIOUXSIE AND THE BANSHEES

6. Raw Power - IGGY AND THE STOOGES

7. Killer - ALICE COOPER

8. Generation Terrorists - MANIC STREET PREACHERS

9. Easter - PATTI SMITH

10. Ocean Rain - ECHO & THE BUNNYMEN

BENJAMIN'S TOP TEN SONGS

1. Somewhere In My Heart - AZTEC CAMERA

2. The Sun Always Shines On TV - A-HA

3. Tonight Is What It Means To Be Young - FIRE INC.

4. Got To Be Certain - KYLIE MINOGUE

5. Absolute Beginners - DAVID BOWIE

6.Randy Scouse Git -THE MONKEES

7. S.O.S - ABBA

8. Always On My Mind - PET SHOP BOYS

9. Borderline - MADONNA

10. All Summer Long - THE BEACH BOYS

SECOND EDIT SCRAPBOOK

Too much information?

SECOND EDIT SCRAPBOOK

Birth Mum: To be fair to my biological dad it's not been easy for him. I'm not sure what the deal is with my birth mother. I was always told that she died just after I was born but I've never known what of and I've never been told of a gravestone let alone visited it. I've seen a couple of photographs and know her name (Victoria) but other than that she's a complete mystery to me. I've been privy to a few slips of tongues and a couple of overheard whispered conversations that seem to indicate that she went missing and was never found but she was long gone before I was old enough to understand much of anything and then my step-mum was in my dad's life soon after. **Stickers:** 'Cool,' she replied calmly, 'I tell you what. I'll make you a tape as a starting point.' 'Awesome. Just one thing though...' 'Yeah yeah I know. I'll leave the stickers.' She knows me so well. Bloody love putting the stickers on cassettes. Even the fiddly little rectangle ones with numbers on them; I'll find any excuse to give a tape a Volume number. **Travel and Tourism:** Within forty minutes of leaving the house I was sat on a train heading towards Canterbury. I had somehow found myself almost halfway through a two-year course studying Travel and Tourism. It wasn't going well but if I could get myself together, decode what the hell my tutors were expecting with my work and actually start getting the marks I needed I could end up with GNVQ Advanced diploma. This would ultimately, I guess, help secure me a job in a hotel or a branch of Thomas Cook or something, I dunno. I harbour absolute zero ambitions to work in a hotel or Thomas Cook but here I am. I don't know *what* I'm doing on this course but I know *how* I ended up here. My big meeting with the Careers Guidance Bloke occurred a few weeks after my step-mum died and I really wasn't up for the appointment. He wasn't overweight but his clammy, boiled bacon invoking bright pink flushed faced and blazer button challenging paunch indicated a penchant for liquid lunches and the chippy. Nothing wrong with that but he took one look at me and made all sorts of presumptions about my character so fairs fair, right? Apparently I wasn't strong enough for manual work, I wasn't assertive enough for sales. Not that I wanted any of these jobs but I figure if he's going to be a judgy motherfucker about me I'm entitled to my perceptions about him. Anyhow, he was a complete dickhead who appeared to delight in quashing every tiny suggestion of where and how I might find my future source of income. Though maybe he had a point, I went to St. Johns High School Boys; apparently the third worst school in the county at the time and my vague ambitions were admittedly a little lofty. It was a school that had become such a lost cause it was currently being closed down, mixed with girl's school next door and rebranded. Its reputation was such that even the shops in the high street wouldn't employ pupils from the school for even the most mundane jobs. Christ, if Sainsbury's wouldn't employ someone from St. Johns to stack shelves what chance would I have becoming a researcher at the BBC or some shit? After twenty odd minutes of enduring a tedious guessing game of 'What job do you want? No, not that!' and the spiteful character assassinations that followed, the Complete Dickhead Careers Guidance Bloke gave a lamentable sigh and presented me with three options. He seemed keen to get it wrapped up, probably didn't want to miss pub lunchtime opening hours, the sweaty fuck. The three options were (drumroll please); work at the paper mill (no thanks), fruit picking and packing (fuck off) or do a B-Tec First in Business Studies at some undetermined college (yes if only to end this god-awful car crash meeting). The best thing about the Business Studies course was that I only needed ONE GCSE graded C or above and I already had that as (for whatever weird reason) English that year was based purely on course work so I was already as good as in. Of course, nothing in my life is ever as easy as that, is it? I turned up on the sign up day thing only to find that I hadn't been put down for Business but Travel and Tourism and despite a brief attempt to rectify this I eventually just lost my nerve, got lazy and ended up in a classroom learning about travel agents and exchange rates. The plan was to switch to Business Studies for the B-Tec National two year follow up course after I had completed the Travel and Tourism course but then they switched from B-Tec to GNVQ and apparently I couldn't do that anymore. I tried to argue my case but some little, bouncy guy with a thin beard who looked like Mr. Claypole from Rentaghost but he just kept talking over me and once again I lost my nerve. Maybe the Complete

Dickhead Sweaty Fuck Career Guidance Bloke did actually have the measure of me after all, maybe popping apples into boxes and erm, paper mill-ing (lord knows what they do in there) *is* all I'm good for. Either way, I have once again found myself stuck in a classroom learning about travel agents and exchange rates. I'm one year in, with a supposed another year to go though if my grades don't improve I have a feeling that I will be 'asked to leave'. This will not go down well with Biological Dad who seems to harbour the expectation that after three years of post-secondary school education I'll waltz into some kind of high ranking civil servant role or something (no, I haven't told him I fucked up getting enrolled on the Business and Finance course. I'll cross that bridge when I come to it.) **Darren King's Lack of Love Life (uncut):** The parade of young ladies made their way down the aisle, perhaps being drawn to his throat-scraping, phlegm-harvesting noises like they were animalistic mating calls. Although saying that, despite his magnetic appeal to members of the opposite sex, it never appeared to go anywhere beyond them following him around. Likewise, he in turn never seemed that interested in taking it anywhere beyond using weak innuendo and roistering to secure their chirping approval. Though there was a wild week of giggles and incessant chatter a few months ago when he went on a date with someone from his platonic harem, one of the quieter girls called Louise D'Souza. The morning after however found the excitement of the date reduced to strangely reverent and earnest conversations about how the pair of them were going to remain just friends. It was a result that the clique all accepted but I could tell the anti-climax had caused an unspoken but noticeable discontent amongst his flock. I found it all very odd but having never gone on a date I have zero frame of reference for such trivialities so that's to be expected. **Benjamin on Kelly (Chapter 4):** She seemed a lot happier than the last time I'd seen her, though with the last of her GCSE exams out of the way she'd been left to enjoy the solitude of an empty house, far from the inevitable ever-growing rumour mill worm feeding off giggles throughout the garden of England. I feared what might unfold in the coming days and weeks as gossip has a terrible habit of returning to its primary subject mutated into a grossly exaggerated form. **Scratch:** There was of course Scratch, he was still a consideration. I'd never met him but I'd heard of him, even before I was *of the night.* A shadowy figure in town, heir to small crime empire said to go back generations. That's how most teenagers initially hear about him, after you become part of the dark magik scene the stories grow wilder and more frightening. Luckily those *of lineage* knew to respect his rank and would never look to get on the wrong side of him. It appeared that drugs, prostitution and lord knows what else can only take a final boss bastard so far and Scratch was looking to go legit to break through his own coke stained glass ceiling. As such, a lot of the big players in the blood-drinking game had fled to pastures less governed, leaving the rest at the mercy of the hunters and the nutters in the (self named) Crucifix Crew. My one little kill wouldn't be enough to get Scratch narked, if anything I'd heard he had a certain sympathy for my kind and his ire was directed as those that had caused it but I wondered if word might reach ears less favourable. I could feel a certain heavy tension in the air. Even with Scratch running a tight ship at the moment I didn't feel like I had enough contingencies in place. I really needed to secure the inherited talents of that young man in the window from the night before. **SU Café:** There were two hours to squander before I had be back in class, so I headed through the doors at the rear of the college man block and hit the Student Union café. It was a bit of a grubby affair there but they had a jukebox and they sold Unigate chocolate milkshakes at a very reasonable price. Most of the right side of the café was infested by the double denim rockers and the metalheads, I'm not sure if this had been a thing from before my time here but certainly on my first day at the college I saw all of the kids of a certain ilk, whether they knew each other or not, float towards each other and into that corner of the café like iron fillings being drawn to a magnet. And ever since that moment they had established that area as their homeland, from opening to closing there'd be at least one of them there to hold the space while the others went off to their classes. They didn't seem to like me very much, which is odd because you'd think they'd jump at the chance of having someone who apparently looks like a demon amongst their party. What with all the Iron Maiden patches on their jackets and the D&D manuals and White Dwarf magazines they gather round I should really be their ideal companion but apparently not. It does make me laugh, how the Metalheads bang on about being outsiders and individuals when they hang out in large groups and all wear the standard uniform of denim, leather and band t-shirt. To be honest, I am a little jealous of the conformity and convenience of being in that crowd. I never know how I'm supposed to dress as an ABBA and Beach Boys fan or indeed what my cultural tribe even is. I suppose there was now Britpop in my life, I wondered if indie bands did patches you can sew on to jeans and such like. So with 'Lenny' by Supergrass kicking off Kelly's Britpoppping tape, the sound filling my ears and amplifying my heightening smugness over the vengeance of the fizzy piss, I quickly picked up a chocolate milk, threw an ironic yet celebratory devil horn hand gesture at the Metalheads and made my way out of the campus and towards the Indoor Market. **Christine in the cubicle:** Lord knows what he was doing in there, it sounded like he was peeing on metal or something. Maybe into a can. Very odd but intriguing. **THE PATCH AND THE JACKET (UNCUT):** The walk back to college felt longer than usual with my every step weighed down by the conversational expectations of having Louise walking beside me. We eventually made our way into the grounds of the campus and I began to put my patch into the front pouch of my backpack. 'So where you going to stitch that patch?' Louise asked. Several students from our class were eyeballing the situation. I wanted out of the moment as soon as possible and in my haste, answered without thought, 'I dunno, I can't sew. On the arm of my jacket I guess.' 'I can stitch it on for you, if you want,' she verbally presented her help as a vague offer but her grabbing hands towards my patch felt more like a demand. My mind raced to find a way out of this loose proposal but I felt all eyes upon us and the considerations conspired against my usual talents of social avoidance. She gestured at the denim jacket I was wearing and an excuse found it's way to my lips, 'Oh hang on I'll need this for the way home. What if it rains or if I need to keep the wind off me.' Typically the sun came out, brighter than it had all week and Louise started banging on about a heatwave approaching. Again I was dragged down into a battle between resisting the unwanted help and an urge to speed up the transaction and escape the glances of everyone around. In the end I had to concede and hand over the jacket, it was quicker, cleaner and easier that way around, at least I wouldn't have to carry it home from the station if it did get as beastly hot as everyone seem to think it was going to get. I hoped that would satisfy her need to intrude into my life but still she continued, 'So if you give me your number I can call you when it's done.' Oh hell no, I don't hand anyone my telephone number; lord only knows what people might do with that sort of information. I couldn't even begin to imagine the horror of sitting in my house night after night chained to the terror that phone on the table in the corner of the living room might suddenly break the healing silence of my home with it's nervy bleat of a ring. I mumbled an excuse about our phone line being down. She then offered to just 'drop it round' on Sunday – I wasn't having that either. I've got enough uninvited guest trouble what with old yellow eyes lurking about every evening so I suggested we meet up. She asked where and when and I figured a busy spot on a Saturday night might be best as I could grab my jacket and then, as politely as possible, kinda lose her in the crowd and get back home to my bedroom. I suggested we meet the following evening around 9.30 at The Ypres Tavern in Sittingbourne, as I knew it's a bit of a popular place for the Westlands lot. While I was clearing all that up I saw Kelly stood by the grit bins near the block's second entrance. It was a bit of unexpected appearance and it distracted me as I was waving off Louise who seemed confused about the arrangement and asked what date it'd be so I clarified, 'Yeah. Tomorrow night: 10th of June. 9:30. Don't be late.'**Benjamin on Louise's looks:**Everyone bangs on about how pretty Louise is but I've never got the appeal. She's a bit generic looking really, all in all. I could imagine her modeling for C&A or something, I suppose. I think everyone rates her looks because she's got a tan, a little perky nose and smiles a lot to show off her white, straight teeth. I think she looks a bit like a dolphin from some angles, maybe that's the appeal but it's not really my kind of thing. **Phil Oakey:**Between songs I discovered they knew the band from Worcester but were merely acquaintances and had only come to Canterbury because their friend wanted to come to track an ex-boyfriend who'd moved here. After Slimfit had finished, the three of us found ourselves nodding along to some Stereolab song or other and talk turned to music. They explained they liked indie music but didn't know much about it. The shorter of the two girls explained she mainly liked the 80's music her Mum listened to like the Human League, which sounded ideal to me. I thought about bringing up how much I love the album Phil Oakey and Giorgio Moroder made after Together In Electric Dreams was a hit but by her own admission she was more of 'greatest hits kinda girl' so I thought better of it lest I scare her off. Like a two-way relay they took it on turns to head to the bar offering to buy me drinks each time. Soon I was returning the favour and found myself six or seven pints deep quickly, with important concerns such as making it back to the station for the final train home or saving my sister from Grunge Tosser lost to the fog of festivities surrounding me. **Van Gough Sky Buttercream:**The night's sky cradled the road ahead of us, and the storm within it began to transform. Shrugging itself away looking like layers of rich violet buttercream icing texturing the skies in twisting, tumbling Van Goughian swirls; feeling like a birthday and Christmas coming at me all at once. **Palm Reading :** This means your thoughts, your mind aren't focused on logical intelligence. You operate on an instinct and a connection to existence beyond time, place, life and death.' **Christine on Kate:**Her protective friend Kate would be there, keeping an eye on his suitability with the same compliant fervour she had harnessed for that evening's time keeping. **Boo Reference:** I think maybe if things were a bit quieter everyone would have the space and clarity to find the answer within (Boo Radleys reference on this occasion was not intended but is welcome). **Titbits:** That being said, there were two large piles of old magazines from the 60's and 70's called Titbits. By the title you'd probably presume they were porn but, aside from the odd picture of Joan Collins and her contemporaries in their skimps, it was mostly full of the most random articles. For example, one issue from 1973 had Kate O'Mara on the cover with some emphasis on her cleavage, though next to her they promoted a lead story about stately homes. I have no idea who the target audience was but my Dad was apparently a subscriber, which possibly says a lot about a lot. While these dusty magazines had piqued my interest, I was more interested in the large wooden box that lay beneath them. **Jacket On:** I dozed off later that evening with the radio on and found myself opening my eyes on a pretty breezy Wednesday. I wondered where summer had gone and feared the wind whipping my body on the way to college but remembered I had my denim jacket back, now with a mod target patch, still sat in the River Island shopping bag that I'd dumped on the floor in my room after crashing back home sometime early last Sunday. **V-Plates:** Becky drew her knickers towards her using her foot and rolled them back on. 'Bloody hell, that felt good. But it was a no-strings, one-off, right? Don't tell a soul. I'm sure you want to let everyone know you're not a virgin anymore but be a gentleman and keep it a secret, alright?' The thing about this is that I had actually lost my virginity a couple of years ago. It was during a family trip to the South of France with a really attractive girl who had one of those European variations on the name Matilda. I'm not sure if she was French or Spanish or a bit of both. Either way after a couple of la bière blonde grandes it just sort of happened. Much like the encounter with Becky but way more enjoyable. I've never told anyone about this because being known as a virgin is frankly way less embarrassing than telling people 'Actually I HAVE had sex. It was with a girl I met on holiday who I don't have a photograph of and I'm not sure of her name.' It feels like a lie just thinking about it. **Shag Regrets:** I'd given away a lot of myself by indulging in something that wasn't on my wish list. I'm not sure what she wanted to get out of it but she seemed neither thrilled nor disgusted about our liaison. Had I been fucked and dumped? Did I even care? **Benjamin seeking Eliza:** I'd find myself squinting at pictures of the singer of the Cardigans or models in the clothes catalogues stored under my bed trying to imagine it was Eliza just to satisfy my need to see her face again. **Misplaced Childhood:** I was a little disheartened when Benjamin threw haughty heckles and derision at my love of Marillion. The Misplaced Childhood album is possibly the last profound moment I had as a human. I always think back fondly to that album coming out in the summer of 1985, kicking back on my bed and getting lost in the sonic fever dream spilling from my stereo's speakers. Still, Benjamin was more obliging when it came to listening to their latest album than he was to a lot of my classic goth stuff so maybe I'll get him on board in the future. **Postponed Introductions:** They could make life difficult for us though, which was something we'd need to consider but I was worried about losing Benjamin and I knew it was news that wouldn't land comfortably so I decided to cross that bridge when we came to it. **Way-hey:** 'Oh yes,' Louise beamed, 'I've told her so much about you. Like how funny you are and how you're good at listening to me when I'm having a mope. Of course, I haven't told her *everything* we get up to.''Wayhey!' hollered an on-cue Darren King, walking through the carriage picking up on Louise's previous sentence. She shot him a disdainful glance before continuing; 'Anyhow she's looking forward to getting to know you better during dinner.' **Sheena or Eliza:** And I did want her. In the most superficial way possible, I mean she was undeniably attractive. She was an inch or two taller than I was, probably five foot eleven possibly pushing six foot, with an hourglass figure wrapped in velvet and lace dress. Her eyes were a piercing flash of sapphire and her high-cheekboned face was framed by long, jet-black hair, perfectly straight until the ends, which curled around in front of her breasts as if the strands were trying to guess where the centre of her nipples might be. My interest in her was a shallow pool and I resented my thoughts for paddling in it. I preferred submerging into the deep ocean my crush on Eliza created and the hope for something 'pure and good and right' (to quote Meatloaf) these feelings generated instead. All of that was washed away when I realised I was objectifying both them, one in a Page Three pose and the other on a pedestal. My shame pushing through both options like a Wild West sheriff bursting through two saloon doors and shooting down any chance of arousal before it blossomed fully.**The Knowledge:**With the cop car hot on our heels, Christine sped past the houses of varied size and appearance that graced each side of Vincent Road and gathered a huge amount of accelarion as we sped down the sloping gradient of Keswick Avenue. My home was in sight, there at the bottom of a T-junction that separated Keswick and Woodbury – just one right turn and I'd be there.**TUNE IN AND RIP THE KNOB OFF:** She had the album on vinyl and it was hardly the sort of thing my Dad's favourite Invicta FM would play.**Gideon**

(We don't need you whole lifestory, mate):However cruel and inhumane you may consider my actions it must be considered that I've never lived a human's life. My parents, as weak and unambitious as they may have been, lived the lives of blood drinkers. I would later discover via diaries, regression spells and explorations of past testimonies that even as a swaddled babe, my needy, clinging mother would douse her nipples in blood before she fed me to slow my aging and keep me close to her bosom for as log as she could get away for. This would naturally be kept from my father who would ponder why his one-year-old son still looked like a new born. My mother would fret and worry about this being discovered and would try to tapper off this peculiar practice but her distress at growth spurts and independence would reawaken her compulsion. She needn't have worried as my Father was a spineless and spiritless creature who would second guess himself out of any confrontation no matter what his lack of action may cost him. He had grown up with his own struggles admittedly, smuggled out of Scotland to France at some point during the Eighteenth century by my unmarried blood-drinking Grandmother to escape some form of drama or other. Escaping into the deep trees of the Paimpont Forest in Brittany, the lived in a makeshift shack for many months until a local warlock made a marriage match between my Grandmother and local blood drinker who moved his new wife and step son into his home - the luxurious Manoir du Lis. The marriage wasn't a happy one. My father was denied his step father's surname but not his wrath and spent many evenings feeling the brunt of the Lord's frustration being transferred through a leather strap. Eventually my father was spared as a rival blood drinker looked to take over the Manoir du Lis and engaged the Lord of the Manoir du Lis in battle, this however spilled out of the forest and towards a nearby village where angry, frightened villagers burned and brutalised them and left them weakened in the woods where daylight soon arrived to finish both of them off. The Rival left little as a legacy except a daughter – my mother, a child taken in and groomed by my Grandmother to be her son's bride. A year or so after my birth Grandmother was slain by the wolves, leaving only my father and mother to govern the Manoir du Lis lost in a state of passive ennui and malaise. Existing with a lack of urgency that would see them both murdered and our home burnt down when the vampire hunters finally found us bringing their garlic, crucifixes and silver tipped weapons to our door. I left them to their fate and escaped through the woods. I had lost everything but I felt no sorrow, I realised that the most valuable lesson had been bestowed upon me as if it were a gift, that it is our nature is to be the hunter and should we deny that impulse we become the prey. I had been set free from my parents limited existence and I intended to take my blossoming dreams of conquest to the highest degree. **RWTSOTN:** He went drifting off into the night with his unbuttoned jacket flapping in the breeze. I couldn't help but worry about his state though. I had pushed and pushed for him to go and rescue Christine but the change in his manner after all the power-ups was slightly unnerving, in that moment I FELT maybe we should have taken our time and come up with an actual plan. **CALL BACK 'HOME SHOPPING CATALOGUE-IS-A-JAZZ-MAG-IS-A-SHOP-PING CATALOGUE!?!' JOKE THAT DIDN'T SEEM TO WORK ALAS** She discovered, to her dismay, that the ends of her luscious, long, dark hair had been resting on the rollers when I started the machine and her locks were now caught and being spun into its inner gears, belts and motors. It was a ridiculously big machine, lord knows what they print here these days, back in the '80s I think they printed those great big home-shopping catalogues. **FIN**